Rowan
Revived

A NOVEL

TAYLOR DANAE COLBERT

ROWAN REVIVED ADVANCED

Copyright © 2019 Taylor Danae Colbert

Published: Taylor Danae Colbert 2019

www.taylordanaecolbert.com

Editing: Lizzy McLellan Ravitch

Cover Design: Taylor Danae Colbert

ISBN: 9781691537945

To my babies. You are my reasons.

PROLOGUE

Mrs. Rowan smiles as the young reporter gets out of her silver Nissan. Her too-high pumps crunch in the gravel as she approaches the porch steps.

"Beverly," Mrs. Rowan says, pushing herself up from the white wooden rocking chair she had sat in every morning for the last thirty years. She noticed, these days, that it was a little more difficult for her to stand up from it. But if she used the momentum from a rock forward, she could get up on her feet just fine.

"Hello, Mrs. Rowan, thank you so much for making time for me this morning," Beverly says. She's tall and thin, with auburn hair and big, blue eyes. She's probably no older than twenty-two or twenty-three. She's fresh out of college, and the world is still so vast and exciting for her. Except, her world was limited to the shores of the Chesapeake, and anywhere within a fifty-mile radius of the *Chesapeake Times'* readership.

"It's my pleasure. I made some lemonade, and I thought we could go out back and sit by the water."

"That sounds lovely," Beverly says, clutching on to her laptop and two or three notebooks. Mrs. Rowan leads her through the vast foyer, framed by the grand staircase that splits at the top, cascading down on either side of it. She watches as Beverly followed her, jaw dropped, eyes all over the impressive entryway. Mrs. Rowan smiles. She still felt a bolt of pride each time someone fell in love with this place.

They walk through the foyer, passing a spacious sitting room with big couches and floor-to-ceiling bookshelves, and into the parlor.

"Wow," Beverly whispers, staring out of the huge parlor windows at the Bay. "This is really, *really* beautiful. What a view."

"Yeah," Mrs. Rowan says, nodding out at the bay. "Still takes my breath away, every morning. Shall we?" she asks, holding open the door to the patio.

As they take their seats on two of the Adirondack chairs that are perched at the edge of the patio, a warm, familiar, bay breeze blows through stems of the weeping willows that lounge on the lawn before them.

"Okay, Mrs. Rowan," Beverly says, pulling out a small recorder and a pen from her briefcase. "Do you mind if I record this?"

"No problem," Mrs. Rowan nods, taking a sip of her lemonade and leaning back in her chair.

"Great. So," Beverly goes on, clicking the on button, "first things first, what brought you to the Chesapeake?"

Mrs. Rowan smiles.

"Look around you," she says, holding her hands out. "I like to think that I didn't find the Bay, but that it found me. It's a love affair, really, and once I found it, I knew I could never leave." Beverly smiles, her eyes wide with wonder.

"So you ran the Rowan Inn for..."

"Thirty years," Mrs. Rowan says.

"Wow. Thirty years. What an accomplishment. And now your son runs it, correct?"

Mrs. Rowan smiles.

"Yep. It's all in the family. I still help out, inside, particularly, but he really took the reins. I'm really proud of him."

"That is beautiful," Beverly says, typing a few notes. "So, you originally ran the inn with your husband, right?"

Mrs. Rowan's eyes flash to Beverly, then she looks down at the opal ring on her finger, wiggling it in the sunlight. She sighs, her eyes moving out to the blue line where the water meets the sky. She remembers the first time she laid eyes on him, and smiles to herself. She hadn't realized it then, but he had her then, hook, link, and sinker.

1

LENA

I knew it was going to be a bad night the second I walked down the hallway to Millie's apartment door. There was only dead silence on the other side of the door—a tell-tale sign that Tiger went off on one of his outbursts again. No sounds of Caleb's little feet running, no television in the background, no toys crashing all over the place. Just silence.

I'm out of breath from running the twelve blocks between our two apartment buildings, then up three flights of stairs to their walk-up. I bang on the door, but there's no answer. I bang on it again.

"Mill, it's me, can you come to the door?" I ask. But again, nothing. I reach into my coat pocket with a shaky hand, and pull out my keychain, fiddling with the key to their apartment.

I finally shove it in the lock, and the second I open the door, I want to throw up.

The kitchen table is on its side, and the remnants of a spaghetti dinner lie scattered on the floor. My heart is beating in my throat as I start searching everywhere for my sister and nephew.

"Mill? Mill!" I call, but there's still no answer. "Caleb? Cay, where ya at, buddy?"

I make my way down the hall to my sister's room. A chair is knocked over in the corner of the room, a picture frame broken, hanging crooked on the wall. Clothes are strewn everywhere. This is definitely the worst I've seen the apartment look. I run back down the hall to Caleb's room, but before I push the door open, I take a long breath, steadying myself for what I might see.

When I open it, I almost drop to my knees.

My sister is lying on the floor, her eyes closed, blood trickling from a deep gash on the side of her head. There's blood pooling on the ground beneath her, and onto my four-year-old nephew's pants. He's lifted her head onto his lap. With one hand, he's stroking her blood-soaked hair. With the other, he's clutching his teddy bear to his chest. His teddy bear that is now also covered in blood. Caleb's eyes are glassy, glazed over. He looks up at me, but I'm not confident that he actually *sees* me. I'm not sure he can see much of anything, except for the memory of what his father just did to his mother, playing over and over again in his mind.

"Jesus Christ, Millie!" I scream. But then I remember Caleb. I've startled him now, and he's slid himself across the floor, still clutching his gory bear.

"Hey, Cay, hey buddy, it's okay, everything's gonna be okay, you hear me?" I ask him, fighting like hell to swallow back my tears. He can't see me cry. He nods slowly, and I see the tears welling in his eyes. The shock has passed, and the horror of what he's just seen—for probably the hundredth time in his short life—is starting to creep in.

"Okay, Cay. Remember where the towels are?" I ask

him, calmly checking my sister's wrist for a pulse. There is one. Thank God.

He nods.

"Okay, good boy, Cay. Can you go ahead and grab a few towels for me, buddy? And when you're done, I want you to go to the living room and turn on some T.V., okay?" I ask. He nods again, scurrying out of the room. He's back in a flash with a small hand towel. I survey the amount of blood on the ground, and I know this won't do the job. But hey, he's four. He shouldn't have to be cleaning up his mother's blood. Especially when that blood came from the hands of his father.

He also shouldn't have to know to call his auntie whenever his daddy gets angry. Yet here I am.

"Good job, buddy. Okay, now, go watch some TV while I help Mommy, okay?" I ask. As soon as he's out of sight, I have my phone to my ear, dialing 911. As they answer, Millie's eyes open, slowly at first, then they flutter wildly.

"Mill..." I say, knowing that she will panic as soon as she comes to. "Mill, it's okay, I'm here. I've got you—hi, yes, my sister has been attacked and we need—" I start to answer the operator, but Millie's flailing hands knock the phone from my ear.

"Don't, Lena," she manages to get out. I almost snort in laughter. We've been through this a million times. She never wants me to call 911 because she's afraid it will make him more mad. A few threatening sentences on a restraining order aren't exactly strong enough to hold back Tiger Bentley. We know that. But it feels so irresponsible, so ignorant, not to do *anything*. In the grand scheme of things, she's probably right. The cops will come, they'll take her to the hospital, they'll get Tiger's information. They'll look for him, they won't find him, and they will give her another restraining order—which, as we know from experience, won't make a difference. She will likely give in and let him back in before he gives up and moves on.

It's not because my sister is weak. She's not. She's actually really fucking strong. But she still has it in her head—the one that son of a bitch has beat on too many times—that she loves him. She still believes that if he didn't love her, he wouldn't get so mad. That he loses it sometimes only because he cares *so* much. That he's her only way to survive. That staying with him is the only way to keep a roof over her son's head. Her brain is wired to see what Tiger wants her to see.

And I know that I can't make her see what I see. I know that I can't force her to see it until she's ready. I know this from a childhood's worth of experience, watching our mother. And that's why this kills me so much, each time it happens.

"Ma'am? Ma'am?" I hear the 911 operator calling at me from my phone on the floor. My eyes meet Millie's, soft and green, and right now, surrounded by blood and purple skin. My beautiful sister, reduced to a bloody pulp. Again.

God, I want to kill him.

I take a breath, reach down and grab my phone.

"I'm sorry, it was a mistake," I say into the phone. "No need to send anyone. We're okay here," I say. I click the end button, my stomach filling with a swirling mix of nerves and anger. I reach down, dabbing her open wound with the hand towel.

"Can you sit up?" I ask her. She nods, her eyebrows knitting together in pain. I help her up slowly, leaning her against Caleb's bed. I grab another towel from the hall closet for the blood on the floor, and a third for her head. I swipe the first aid kit from the bottom shelf, all too familiar with where it's kept. After I survey the cut, clean it with peroxide, and cover it with gauze, I sit back against the bed, pulling her into me close. My beautiful, brave, battered big sister. I need to cry so badly right now. But I can't. Not now. We sit in silence for a few minutes.

"Is Caleb okay?" she asks.

"Yeah, he's watching TV," I say. Then I look around the room. All the late-night calls I've gotten, all the times I've come to the rescue, my sister has always been in her own room—when she knows Tiger's growing angry, she leads him to their bedroom, away from Caleb. But tonight, she's in her son's room.

"Mill...why are you in here?" I ask. I swallow, not knowing if I want the answer.

All the times Tiger's raised a hand to my sister, he hasn't laid a finger on Caleb. Yet.

She swallows, reaching a hand up to the gash. She squints her eyes. Then she looks at me. I stare back at her, wide-eyed.

"Millie...did he touch him? Did anything happen to Caleb?" I ask. My voice is shaking now, and there's not a damn thing I can do to stop it. I scoot back, prompting her to give me an answer. She shakes her head slowly as tears start to roll down her face.

"He didn't," she says, and I let out a long breath. "But I think he was going to."

She looks up at me, and there's something different in my sister's eyes tonight. Usually, after these nights, she's tired, broken. She is again tonight, but she's also got a fire in her eyes. I take her hand.

"Mill," I say. She looks up at me. "We have to go."

I've said this to her before. I've tried to convince her and Caleb to move in with me. It would be cramped in my tiny little apartment across town, and Lord knows that Beth, my high-maintenance roommate, would have nothing good to say about a four-year-old joining us. But we would make it work until we could afford something bigger. And then we'd go, and be far, far away from Tiger.

Tiger Bentley. The name alone makes me dry heave. I had a feeling about him, the moment Millie introduced him to me. Something about a guy who goes by "Tiger," sort of sets you off. But she was in love, and it was fast. My sister was always dating, our whole adolescence. Constantly searching for the love we never got as kids. The Winter house was a cold one to grow up in, figuratively speaking. I, on the other hand, took the opposite route. I'd rather be alone than risk loving someone who masked their anger, their demons, as love. Someone like my father.

But try as I had, I could never convince her. She was in love. And Tiger is Caleb's father. He needs his dad, she'd say. But we both know that it's not true. We both know she just needed to find a little bit of strength.

And tonight, I think my sister has found just that.

"Yeah," she whispers. "We need to go."

That's all I need—just a quick confirmation and I burst into action before she can second-guess herself. I spring up, reaching for Caleb's small backpack underneath his bed, looping it around my arm. If we were going to move, we needed to go fast. After a boxing match with my sister's face, Tiger usually hits a few bars and strip clubs to cool off. Then, he'd come back at God knows what hour, drunk, apologetic, dripping with sweat and booze and self-hatred for what he'd done.

I help my sister to her feet, and tell her to go sit with Caleb. I'll take care of everything. And I do.

I throw every article of clothing I can find into any type

of bag I can find. I grab a few pairs of Caleb's shoes, and a few pairs of my sister's. I grab toothbrushes, hair brushes, coats, a few of Caleb's toys. I pack a few snacks in a baggie. I help Caleb scrub the blood off his hands and change his clothes. As I walk down the hallway, I pause at the door of my sister and Tiger's bedroom. I go back to Caleb's room, grab his miniature, blood-soaked pants and lay them ever-so carefully on Tiger's pillow. Just a sweet little reminder of what he'd made his little boy witness tonight. I scan the apartment for anything I might have missed.

"Okay, guys," I say, "let's get going."

"Where are we going?" Caleb asks, looking up from the couch. I see tears forming in Millie's eyes again. I swallow back my own.

"We're going to go on a little trip, buddy," I tell him. "You, me and Mommy."

"Where are we going?" he asks again. I look at Millie. I don't quite know the answer to that yet. "Are we spending the night at your house, Aunt Lee?"

"No buddy, not tonight. It's a surprise," I tell him. "But we do need to stop at my apartment so that I can pack a few things, okay?"

He nods and stands slowly from the couch. He turns back to Millie and patiently waits for her to stand.

"Is your head okay, mommy?" he asks. She smiles and kneels down to kiss his head. My sister really is an amazing mother.

"Yes, baby. I'm okay," she says. Then Caleb looks back to me.

"Is daddy coming with us?" he asks. Millie swallows so loud, it sounds like a cartoon.

"Not this time, buddy," I answer, reaching out a hand to him. He thinks about it for a moment, and I wonder what thoughts are flying around in that little head of his. I run my fingers through his curly brown hair—inherited from my sister. He smiles shyly and takes my hand, wrapping his palm around my fingers. Millie kneels down to pick up some of the bags, but I stop her. The gash has stopped bleeding, but I need to get ice on it. The swelling is bad. I fetch a bag of frozen broccoli from the freezer and press it to her head. Once she's holding onto it, I grab every bag except for Caleb's, which he has strapped to his back like a big boy, and we walk out the front door. As we reach the top of the steps, I hear someone calling out to us.

It's Mrs. Hinders, Millie's sweet-as-pie, ancient-as-dirt next door neighbor.

"Is everything okay with you kids?" she asks. "There was so much commotion tonight." Then she catches a glimpse of Millie's face, and she gasps. "Oh, Millie," she whispers, covering her mouth.

Millie's eyes drop to the floor in shame.

"We're okay, Mrs. Hinders," I say, shuffling Caleb and Millie along.

"Are you leaving for good?" she asks quietly, and I detect a hint of hope in her voice. You don't live next door to tables flipping and not know what's going on. I look up at her.

"I think so," I say softly. She nods her head, then waves me over. I motion for Millie and Caleb to keep walking, and I turn back to Mrs. Hinders.

"You're a guardian angel for those two," she whispers, her voice trembling. She reaches into her pocket and pulls out a change purse.

"Oh, no, Mrs. Hinders, we can't—" I say, but she holds her hand up.

She pulls out a wad of bills, and tucks them into my

hand. Damn. There's a *lot* of money here. Mrs. Hinders don't play.

"Now, get somewhere far," she says, wrapping me in a long hug. "And take care of them." I nod, then scurry off.

We're already exhausted by the time we reach my apartment, but I know we have to keep moving. Once we get inside, Millie takes a much-needed shower, and I help Caleb change into some pajamas. I don't know where we will end up tonight, but I know he won't be awake to find out.

I pack a bunch of my own stuff into the only suitcase I own, and I realize how much I'll have to leave behind.

And yet, none of it seems to matter.

I grab my phone off the nightstand and text my manager.

Hi, Don. I'm sorry to do this, but I won't be in tomorrow for my shift. Actually, I won't be in for a while.

What? He writes back. I feel a twinge of guilt. He's not the most understanding man, but Don gave me a waitressing job six years ago, and he's been loyal. He gives me the best shifts, the best sections in the restaurant, and usually gives me one weekend night off a week. This is going to crush him.

I write Beth a note, leave a check on the table to cover the next month's rent—thank God our lease is almost up.

And then I panic. I have no idea how I'm going to survive. How *we're* going to survive. I know for a fact Millie has nothing saved. Tiger made all the money—though we're not exactly sure what he did. She was totally dependent on him. I swallow. Not anymore. We will make this work. We have to. For Caleb.

"Okay, gang," I say, "let's hit the road."

As we walk to the door, Millie touches my hand.

"Lena, are you sure you want to leave all this behind?" she asks. I look around. My apartment isn't much to look at. I mean, I'm proud of it. I'm proud of the little life I've built here, surviving without help, at the ripe age of twenty-four. But now, it's time to live for my family. They need me. And we're going to make this work. I smile and nod.

"It's just an apartment," I say. "Who knows. Maybe we will be back someday."

As we make our way down to where my car is parked on the street. I look around. Millie and I have lived in Boston our entire lives. And yet, as we're about to pull away, I don't feel anything holding me back. Nothing except for bad memories, no room to move, no room to breathe. We stayed because it was what we knew. We stayed because it was familiar. But now, none of that is enough reason to stay.

Caleb settles into the backseat, his blue knit blanket tucked around him, his eyes already heavy. I look at my sister, and she takes my hand, giving it a little squeeze.

"Let's do this," I say, putting the car in drive, and driving away from the only home I've ever known.

2

LENA

We've been driving for about nine hours now, and Caleb and Millie have both been sleeping for almost the entire ride. I stopped once to pee and get some hot fries, but I can feel myself fading. We're headed south, and I still have no idea where we are going. We've gone down much of the east coast, and last I checked, we were somewhere in Maryland. I drive for a few more minutes, and then pull off in front of a strip mall that's right off the highway. I put the car in park, take a deep breath, and lean my seat back.

I'm not quite sure how much time has passed, but I wake to something poking my cheek.

"Aunt Lee, why are we sleeping in the car?" Caleb asks me, continuously poking me with his toy dinosaur. I blink a few times, pull my seat back up, and resituate myself. The sun is shining through the windows now, and the clock in my car says it's seven in the morning. Millie is still sound asleep in the passenger seat, and I know she needs it. The purple on her forehead has now turned into a deep bluish-black, and I know she's going to be hurting when she wakes up. The convenience store in the strip mall is open. I smile at Caleb through the rearview mirror.

"Want some breakfast?" I ask. He smiles and jumps out of the car.

We go inside, and I give him a ten-dollar budget. It may as well have been a million. He chooses a red Gatorade, a glazed donut, some chips for later, and a small bouncy ball from the front counter. I grab some protein bars and coffee for Millie and me, and a small bottle of ibuprofen. She's going to need it.

"Okay, buddy. Let's head to the car. We're going to eat on the drive," I tell him, taking his hand.

"Where we going, Aunt Lee?" he asks, for the third time since we decided to leave. And yet, I still don't have an answer for him. I pull back onto the highway.

"Buddy, get ready to look out the window in a few seconds," I tell him, as I see signs for the Chesapeake Bay Bridge ahead.

"Why?"

"Because in a few seconds, we're going to be as high as the clouds." I can hear him shuffling in his seat to look out the window. And as we cross the bridge, climbing a little bit higher, I hear him gasp, his big eyes wide as he practically presses his nose to the window. I smile.

"WHOAAA!" he cries, and Millie jumps.

"How long have I been sleeping?" she asks. Then, she's very aware of her surroundings. "Jesus Christ!"

Oops. My sister might be afraid of heights. She sinks back into her seat, shielding her eyes from the view.

"Mommy, look! We're as high as the birds!" Caleb cries.

I laugh and hand her the coffee.

"Drink this, and take those," I say, pointing to the medicine. She does what I tell her, squinting her eyes so that they are just barely open.

"Where are we going?" she asks me. I sigh.

We're finally to the other side of the bridge, and I see a highway sign. There's about a hundred miles to some place called Ocean City. I can't bear the thought of driving another hundred miles. We pass a few other signs, until one catches my eye.

It's not a normal highway sign—it's sort of a shit-brown color, with faded, cracked white letters. But I can just make it out: ROWAN INN, 35 MILES.

I smile.

"There," I say, happy to have an answer.

"The Rowan Inn?" Millie asks. "What's that?" I shrug and smile.

"I don't know. But it's not Boston," I say. She smiles and grabs her phone.

"Wow, this place looks really nice," she says, showing me a few photos. "'A secret gem on Maryland's eastern shore, the Rowan Inn is a beautiful bed and breakfast tucked away on the shores of the Chesapeake,'" she reads from the website. "'Owned and operated by Jack and Scarlett Rowan since 1975, the Rowan Inn has won awards for its standards in hospitality for over a decade straight. Enjoy bay views from our beautiful guest rooms, have breakfast in our gourmet kitchen, and savor lunch or dinner at our four-star restaurant right here on the property.'"

"Wow," I say.

"'Fish off the pier, or take one of our kayaks out for a day on the bay,'" she goes on. "Jeez, Lena, can we afford this?" I swallow. I emptied my bank account, and I have the money from Mrs. Hinders. But I have no idea how long we will be without income.

"Fishin'!" Caleb says. "I wanna go fishin'!" I smile and look back to Millie.

"We will make it work," I tell her, patting her knee. We will make it all work, for as long as we have to. She smiles and leans back in her chair. And for the first time in a while, I watch my sister take in a long breath, and let it out nice and slow.

Yeah, we will make this work.

But, as quickly as the moment of peace hits her, it disappears with a single vibration of her phone.

She looks down, eyes wide.

Tiger. Seems about time, he probably just awoke from a drunken sleep.

"What does it say?" I ask. She swallows.

"He wants to know where we are," she whispers. I peek in the rearview mirror. Caleb's in the backseat, still playing with his toys.

"Don't answer," I say. She rolls her eyes.

"Obviously," she says. "But he's going to keep trying."

"And we're going to keep ignoring it. In fact, we're going to drop our phones the first chance we get. Get new numbers, everything," I say.

She nods. After a few minutes, the phone starts going haywire. Calls, texts. Each time, she swallows and clicks it off. My heart breaks for her, because I can see the torment inside of her.

She knows what she has to do, but she also knows that the man she thinks she loves is back in Boston, panicking over where his woman and child are. He's alone, and I know there's a piece of her that feels for him. That wants to be there for him.

I have to be stronger than that piece. I reach my hand over, and gently take the phone from her hand. I wait for her to snatch it back, but she doesn't. I hold down the power button, and let it shut off. Then, I do the same to my own.

Not today, Tiger.

Soon, we come up on another sign for the inn. Five miles away. Five miles from a little bit of freedom. Five miles from a comfy bed, some beautiful bay views, and a happy little nephew. Five miles from a rested, healing sister. Five little miles.

I take exit seven like the last highway sign said, and we pull off onto a flat, straight road. We're surrounded by corn-fields on either side. We come to a stop sign. There's a wooden sign ahead of us that reads, ROWAN INN, with an arrow to the right.

"Guess we're going right," Millie says. But just as I'm about to turn, I hear a blaring horn coming from the left. A bright red pickup truck flies past us, honking away at me as I enter the intersection.

"Hey, motherfucker!" I yell out the window, "Ever heard of a fucking stop sign?"

I turn back to my sister and Caleb, who are both staring at me wide-eyed. Luckily, we've been training Caleb since birth not to repeat curse words. Unfortunately, there's just no such thing as censoring a Winter sister's mouth.

"Jesus, what an asshole," Millie says.

We drive a little ways, and we realize that we're the only ones on the road.

We come to a short cement bridge, and Caleb is infatu-ated by the water.

"Look, Mommy! Look at the water! Are there fishes in there?" he asks.

"Yeah, baby, I'm sure there are," she says. Then I can feel her looking in my direction. "Is it just me, or is this the longest five miles ever?" I nod. With every inch we crawl further onto the marshy peninsula, I should probably be a little freaked out. This could be the perfect setting for a murder movie. But I'm not. Because every inch is another inch further, and safer, from Tiger.

At the end of the bridge, the road turns to dirt. We follow along for about another mile, before we come to one more wooden sign. It's hanging by a rusted metal chain that's broken on one side, but when we turn our heads, we can read "Welcome to the Rowan Inn." The paint is chipping off the sign, and there's ivy overgrown up the post. I pause before I turn. Suddenly, I don't have such a good feeling about this. I take a breath. This kid is getting his damn fish. I turn down the gravel driveway that's clouded by overgrown trees and shrubs. But when we finally reach a clearing, I see it for the first time.

The Rowan Inn.

It doesn't quite look like it looked on the website.

It's a huge colonial style house, white with green shutters—although, most of them appear to be hanging on by a thread. It has a massive porch, but the steps are warped and caving in. There's a large gravel parking lot to the side, but it's empty. A red barn stands off to the other side of the house, with a sign above the doors that says, "Restaurant," but the doors are closed.

But despite the disappointing first impression, the inn takes my breath away. It's still beautiful. It's still not Boston. It's still far, far away from Tiger Bentley.

I can tell Millie is less than confident that we've found our retreat. The inn looks old, rundown, and pretty damn vacant. But Caleb can hear the gentle waves hitting the shore on the other side of the house. He's kicking his little feet with excitement.

"We're here! Can we go fishin' now?" he asks. I look at Millie and smile.

We need this place to work. We will make it work.

We hop out of the car, and it feels *so* damn good to stretch my legs. I can't wait to pee, change, and sleep. After we fish, of course.

We walk up the front porch steps—carefully—and I try to turn the knob. Only, it doesn't turn. Because it's locked.

Shit.

I turn to Millie and Caleb. Millie's eyes are filled with uncertainty, and Caleb's are filled with nothing but excitement. We're staying at this goddamn inn.

"I wonder if we have to go in on the the other side," I say. I make my way back down the front porch steps, just as a rumble comes from the top of the long driveway.

Just then, a bright red pickup truck—the same one that sent me into a cursing frenzy just moments before—comes to a screeching halt, sending dirt and dust swirling into the sky. As the dust clears, I lay eyes on him.

He's tall—really tall—and broad. His face is covered in stubble, and his sandy blond hair is shaggy and unkempt. But as he takes a few steps closer, his eyes are the bluest I've ever seen, and for a half-a-second, my breath catches in my throat. I'm peering at him through the dust, and I can feel him doing the same to me. He's wearing a plaid button up, and the sleeves are rolled to his elbows, unveiling some extra-toned forearms. His ratty jeans are paired with brown work boots, and he's got a baseball hat on backwards. Despite his ensemble, he's actually kind of breath-taking—sort of like the inn. But he also almost just killed us, so I overlook that. I unconsciously cross my arms.

"Can I help you?" he asks. As he's sizing me up and down, I suddenly hear barking in the distance. It grows louder and louder, and I see a giant brown dog bounding across the huge yard toward the man.

When he reaches the man, he jumps on him, wagging his tail.

"Okay, okay, boy, okay," he says. "Shh, Coby, calm down."

"A dog!" Caleb says, taking off down the porch steps.

"Caleb!" Millie and I both call in unison, but we're too late.

Caleb reaches the dog who is more than happy to return the favor. Before the three of us know it, the two are rolling around in the grass and dirt, Caleb letting out a shriek of laughter as the dog licks his face to no end.

"Well, I guess that's one way to get him to bathe," Millie laughs nervously. "Come on, Cay," she calls.

After the man gets the dog to calm down and sit at his feet, he looks up at us again.

"Can I help you?" he asks again.

"No, thanks. We're just waiting for the owners. We need a room," I say. Before he says anything, I glare at him. "You know, you almost killed us back there."

He looks at me with a tilted head.

"You were in the middle of the damn intersection," he says, nonchalantly, as he makes his way around to the cab of his truck. He pulls out a long piece of wood, and carries it toward the front porch.

"You had a stop sign," I say.

"It's a stop sign," he says. "Not a stop-and-wait-for-an-hour sign."

I roll my eyes.

"We have a kid, asshole," I say. My language catches him off guard, and he looks at me through a side-eye.

"I see that. So you should probably drive more carefully," he says, walking back toward the truck to grab another piece of lumber.

I hear Millie snort from behind me, and I glare at her.

"Whatever. We will just wait around back for them to get back," I say, ushering Caleb and Millie along.

"That's fine, but the owner is already here," he calls from the cab of the truck. I freeze.

"They are? Where?" I ask. A sly smirk tugs at his lips.

"You're lookin' at him. Mr. Asshole, at your service," he says, tipping his hat, then pulling it back on his head tightly.

"What?" I ask. He doesn't reply, he just walks past me with another piece of wood.

"The website said that a couple owned it, Mr. and Mrs. Rowan?" Millie asks.

His attitude changes a bit as he prepares to respond to Millie. He stands a little straighter, looks her in the eye a little longer. I see him studying the black-and-blue on her face, but then he looks away quickly.

"They're dead," he says, walking back to the truck. "I own this shithole now."

I look up at house. I remember the photos on the website—clean, stunning, so well-kept. And now, here it is, in shambles, like a tarnishing piece of silver.

"Who are you?" I ask. He turns to me, wiping a bead of sweat onto his sleeve.

"Jesse Rowan," he says.

"Rowan?" I ask.

"Rowan. Like the sign!" Caleb says. Jesse looks down at Caleb, who's back to stroking the dog. That smile tugs at his lips again.

"Like the sign," he says with a smile.

"Were they your parents?" Millie asks. Jesse nods.

"Yep."

"When did they…" she asks. I look at her.

"Last year. Car accident," he says, so nonchalantly, you would never know he was talking about his own parents.

"I'm so sorry," Millie says. He nods, and walks by again. How much freakin' wood does he need?

But as the porch steps shift under Millie's feet, I realize he probably needs a lot.

No. This can't be happening. Our perfect little sanctuary on the water cannot be owned—or, more appropriately, destroyed—by Mr. Asshole Red Truck. It can't be. I sigh. I don't like this guy. But right now, I need him to not be an asshole. I need him to just be Mr. Red Truck.

"Yes, we're so sorry to hear that," I say, trying to change my tone a bit. "Look, we've come a really long way, and my nephew was really excited to go fishing. Can we still get a room?" Jesse stands up straight, looking from me, to Millie, to Caleb. He sighs.

"Inn's closed, sorry," he says, walking up the front porch and unlocking the door. The screen door slams behind him, and I feel my heart crumbling in my chest. I look at Millie, and Caleb, who's now paying much more attention to us than he is to the dog.

No.

We will make this work.

I stomp up the steps and pound on the door. But there's no answer. I rap at it again, but nothing.

"Hello?" I call through the screen. There's a long pause.

"Inn's closed," he calls back.

Not today, asshole.

I open the screen door and let myself inside.

"Lena!" Millie calls, but I don't look back.

When I get inside, I forget about my mission for a second. I'm taken back by the sight of the inside of the house. While it could definitely use some TLC, it's stunning. There's a big staircase leading down to the foyer, and light streaming in from windows everywhere. To my left is a large sitting room, with couches and chairs enough for thirty people. To my right is another sitting room, with a piano, and bookshelves that take up the entire back wall. I walk through the foyer, and my jaw drops. At the back of the house is a massive parlor, with floor-to-ceiling windows. A row of armchairs is pointed toward them, looking out over the deep blue bay. The bay outside the huge windows looks like a painting, but it's brought to life by the cattails blowing in the breeze on the shore, as if gesturing toward the long wooden pier to the left. It's absolutely breathtaking, even with the "do not enter," sign that's blocking the dock.

"Jesus, what are you doing in here?" I hear Jesse ask, and I jump. Ah, yes, back to the mission.

"Look, we've been driving for a while. We've gone through a lot the last twenty-four hours, and we really just need a place to crash. My nephew has been dying to fish. Please, just let us have a room for a few nights, and I will figure out another place to go," I plead. Ugh. I hate begging, particularly when it's to some tall, handsomely gruff, smug ass. But I really need this room. *We* really need this room. Any other inn or motel just wouldn't do. Because getting back in that car, and backtracking toward the highway could be fatal. The only way to ensure Millie wouldn't back down was to keep moving forward.

He gives me a look, raising one of his thick eyebrows and tilting his head slightly to the side.

"No," he says, moving past me and walking into the kitchen. "The inn is closed. Now if you'll kindly—"

"I'll pay you double the normal room fee," I say. This makes him stop in his tracks. He turns slowly to me. He looks me up and down, slowly, and I feel myself squirming a bit. I don't look my best; my face is worn down from hours of driving, and sleeplessly reliving the experience of finding my bloody sister on the floor. I haven't showered in twenty-four hours, and my dark hair is in more of a rat's nest than a bun. But I'm not here to seduce the innkeeper. I'm here to get some damn rest.

Then, he breaks into that half, broken smile.

"Shit," he says, filling up a glass with water from the big white ceramic sink. "Anyone willing to pay double to stay in this shithole is fine by me." He nods toward the staircase. "Have at it."

I feel my shoulders drop involuntarily as I close my eyes for a brief moment. Finally. A freakin' win.

I follow him out of the kitchen, through the foyer and toward the front door. He grabs his keys off the small entryway table, and pushes the screen door open. He turns back to me, and when our eyes meet, I feel this little flip in my stomach. It's annoying, because he's still an ass.

"Ah, pick any room you want. Keys are behind the front desk there," he says, pointing to a desk at the front of the foyer. "There might be pillows up there somewhere. I don't really know. We don't have a chef anymore, so there won't be dinner or breakfast, but there's a Stop 'n' Shop a few miles up the road if you need something. Coby will just be running around, so don't mind him."

I look out at the dog, running in circles around the property. He brings a sort of innocent, comic relief to everything, and I think I love him. Then Jesse heads out the door, hops down the steps and gets back in his stupid red truck. As he pulls away, I look to my left. Millie and Caleb are sitting on two old rocking chairs on the porch, swaying back and forth, flipping through the pages of one of Caleb's books. Millie looks at me, fear and hope in her eyes. I smile.

"Let's go pick a room," I say.

"Yayyy!" Caleb says, hopping off of her lap and running through the front door. "Whoaaa!" I hear him call again, as he takes in his surroundings. I laugh as Millie wraps me in a tight hug.

"I don't know how you do this, but I'm just...I can't even..." she says, and I hear her voice cracking. I squeeze her tight.

"Stop, Mill. Just breathe. We're gonna be okay," I tell her, kissing her cheek.

She might be three years older, but the truth is, I've been taking care of her for a long, long time. I wouldn't have it any other way.

She follows Caleb inside, and as I move to follow, I turn my head and look down the long driveway, a trail of dust from his truck still settling to the ground. As much as I hate to admit it, Mr. Rowan sort of saved the day.

3

JESSE

I'm flying back down the dirt road and over the bridge, the inn shrinking in my rearview mirror. I have nowhere I need to be right now, and yet, here I am, driving away. But if I stayed around the bossy brunette much longer, my head might explode.

I had exactly two things planned for today: relax all day, work all night.

I wasn't expecting to turn the inn into some sort of shelter for wandering women and children. Although, I have to admit, the kid's kind of fun. And he will keep Coby busy, which is nice. His mom seems nice enough. She's quiet, but I can see that he's her whole world.

The sister, though.

If I can't get rid of her soon enough, she might make me lose it. I can already tell.

She's kind of short—her sister's definitely got a few inches on her—but she's tough. I can tell she's scrappy. She's probably used to getting whatever she wants as soon as she crosses those olive arms and sticks out that bottom lip. And here I am, just one more sucker who gave in.

But she's not staying for free. I was getting so used to talking to myself around the inn; it's been a long time since another person—or three—have actually *stayed* there.

I can't figure this crew out. They're definitely running from something, or someone, but it's none of my damn business. If they're desperate enough to pay double the nightly rate to stay in a non-operational inn, who am I to refuse their money? That would just be bad business.

I pull into Billy's—the only gas station in Baycrest—and hop out to fill up. I never go without at least a half a tank, but it seems like the right time to fill 'er up. As I'm leaning against the bed of my truck while it pumps, I hear a familiar voice.

"Mr. Rowan," Trace Wilder says as he holds his hand out to me. "Haven't seen you in a while."

"Hey, Trace," I say. "Good to see you, man. Still not used to you being back in town." He smiles as he unlocks his truck.

"Funny. The moment I stepped foot back in this town, I wanted to kick myself for ever leaving," he says. "I'm telling you, man. There's nothing like this place."

I smile and nod, but I'm not buying it. "Well, man, I'm glad things worked out with you and Em. We all knew you two were meant for each other. We just had to wait for you to figure it out," I say with a smile. He laughs, but his mood changes quickly.

"Hey, listen, man, I wanted to say I'm sorry again about your parents. I know I wasn't here when everything happened, so I wanted to give my condolences again. I've been meaning to come by the inn but I just..." his voice trails off for a minute. Then he starts again. "The whole town has been feeling their absence this past year, but I can't imagine what it's like for you." I nod as I screw my gas cap back on.

"Thanks, man. Means a lot." I shake his hand and hop back in my truck.

Trace is a few years older than me, but everyone from Baycrest knows everyone else. Half of the people that grew up here couldn't wait to get out. They left for college, and never came back. The other half of us, we're still here. Running our families' businesses—or, in my case, running it into the ground—starting our own families, settling down just like our parents did before us.

Trace, on the other hand, is one of the few who tried both. He went to college out in California. He graduated and got some big-time job out there, but he hated it. He hated every second. We were all shocked when he came back, but we knew exactly why he did: Emily Barnes. His high school sweetheart. She was a lifer, like me. Stayed back in Baycrest to help her mom, Edith, run the diner, and never wanted anything more. When Trace left, everyone was shocked. It took him a few years, but he got smart and came back. Of course, Emily wasn't the type of girl to stay single for long—hell, I even made a move or two on her at the Broken Shell from time to time, but we all knew she'd never look at any of us the way she looked at Trace. It took almost no time for the two of them to mend their past, kiss, make up, and get married.

Mom was always trying to match me up with her friends' daughters. I had a few girlfriends in high school that turned into weekend hookups after we graduated. But none of them really stuck. Everyone in Baycrest sort of cycles through each other, until we figure out who works together, and who doesn't.

I'm a Baycrest lifer—or, at least, I thought I would be

until my parents died. Now, I have no idea where I'm going to live out the rest of my life. I used to love the feeling this town gave me—the way I knew it all like the back of my hand. Now, it's just a reminder that it will never be the same. There's nothing left here for me.

And as I pull back down the gravel driveway and see the inn, I realize I couldn't be more right. Sometimes, I feel so shitty that I let things get this bad. I mean, things around the place were always falling apart. It was built in the 1920s. But after I lost them, I lost everything. I don't know how to do this without them. I don't want to. I loved this place. It was a huge part of me. But that part of me is buried right along with mom and dad.

Now, all that's left to do is to sell it and cut my losses. High-tail it out of Baycrest, and find somewhere to start over, doing whatever the fuck I want, without the reminder that I let them down, again.

When I finally put the truck in park and hop out, I almost stumble and fall when I see her again. The one that talks a lot. The pushy one. Jesus, I forgot they were here for a second.

The kid's still running around the yard, his mom following close behind him.

But the sister, she's walking slowly around the house, staring up at it like it's some sort of gigantic diamond. She's running her fingers along the wood, trailing them around in a wispy line as she walks. The breeze rolls off the bay and through her long, coal-colored hair—no longer in a bun— and for a minute, I forget that she's a bit of a pain in the ass. But as quickly as her eyes find me, my eyes drop to the ground.

She looks up at me as I walk toward the barn.

"Hey," she says. I clear my throat, but I feel all weird.

Not nervous, but kind of...I don't know, jittery. I'm not sure why. She *really* is a pain. But the few times I've seen her crack a smile at the kid, or the dog, I just...I don't know.

So I don't say anything. I just nod.

I walk into the barn and shut the doors behind me, then scoot over to the window. She goes back to looking up at the house. She's looking at it like it's not falling apart at the seams. She's looking at it the way...the way my mom used to look at it. Shit. The way *I* used to look at it before it started crumbling down.

She lifts her long hair off the back of her neck, pulling it back up into a ponytail, and exposing her bare shoulders. I feel this slight twitch in other regions, and I want to kick myself.

Get it together, Jess. She's a paying customer, and you're outta here as soon as you can find someone dumb enough to buy this place.

She looks up quickly, just as a frisbee comes flying through the air, landing right at her feet. She laughs and bends over slowly, slowly, her tiny little jean shorts riding up...*buzz*. I jump as my phone goes off in my back pocket. I snatch it out, frustrated both at the fact that I had to stop looking, and at the fact that I *wanted* to look so bad.

As soon as I see who's calling, I wish I hadn't even looked.

"Yeah?" I say. She scoffs on the other end.

"Nice. That's the way you're gonna answer?" she asks. I can practically *hear* her crossing her arms through the phone.

"What can I do for you today?"

"I wanted to give you a heads-up that I'm coming home," she says. I roll my eyes and slide my hand down my face. There are a few people left in this world that give me a little bit of peace and solitude ever since my parents died.

My sister is not usually one of them.

"For what?" I ask.

"Jesse, if you ever want to sell this place, you're going to have to actually do something about it. The house is a fucking disaster. It's never going to sell if we leave it like this," Josie says. I roll my eyes again, but I know she's right. There's a lot of frustrating things about my sister, but probably the worst is that most of the time, she truly *is* right.

"Great. Looking forward to it," I say, sarcasm oozing from my voice.

"Don't sound so excited, you ass," she says. "See you tomorrow."

4

LENA

I wake up when I feel a tiny foot gently kicking me in the gut. We let Caleb pick the room, and he chose one of the smaller ones because it had a view of the water. The rooms were all charming, each with an old, cherry wood four-post beds, a small bathroom, and a rocking chair in the corner. Our room also has a window seat, where I spent much of last night sitting and staring out. The moon shone so bright over the bay, I couldn't sleep.

I heard Jesse get back around one in the morning. Coby's collar jingling at the front door woke me. I heard him put his keys down, go to the fridge, and crack open what I could only assume was a beer—since the only thing in the fridge when I opened it earlier in the day was a six-pack and a half-eaten sandwich that was starting to smell.

I heard the back door open, and I climbed onto the window seat. I watched him take a swig of the beer, then chuck the can across the lawn. He walked down to the shore, his silhouette all I could make out in the moonlight. I watched as he sat down in the grass, looking out over the bay. He leaned his head back, letting the breeze blow through his hair. After a few minutes, he stood back up, turning toward the house. And that's when he caught me, spying on him through a window in his own house. I sprung from the seat and climbed into bed. Moments later, I heard the big barn doors sliding open out front. I snuck out the into the hallway and to the big window at the end. I watched him lift the latch and disappear inside the barn. Then the doors slid—and slammed—shut.

We found two pillows in a linen closet in the hallway last night, but no sheets or bedding. The three of us squeezed together underneath Caleb's child-size blanket, but somehow, by morning, Caleb had both pillows and the entire blanket to himself. I was too tired to care, though. I can't remember the last time I slept so hard.

I slide stealthily off the bed and over to my suitcase on the ground. I find a white tank top, and pull on the same ratty jean shorts I wore yesterday. I brush my hair out and twist it into a braid. As I reach for the door, I hear him.

"Can we go fishin' *now?*" Caleb asks. I smile and put a finger to my lips, motioning to a very-much sleeping Millie. I wave him toward me, and he springs off the bed. I help him get dressed, and we quietly sneak out of the door to let my sister catch up on the sleep she hasn't gotten in years.

As we make our way down the big staircase, Caleb is practically bouncing off each step.

"I'm gonna catch a blue one, and a green one. Oh, and a shark! A big *huge* shark. But I'm gonna let him go free after I catch him," he says. I smile. "Oh! I forgot my dinosaur." He turns to run back up the steps.

"Okay, buddy," I say. "But keep quiet so you don't wake your mama." I get to the bottom of the steps, and I stop when I hear high heels clicking across the wood floors.

"How could you let it get *this* bad?" I hear a woman's

voice ask. She appears in the curved doorway of the parlor, and freezes when she sees me. "Oh," she says, startled.

Jesse appears close behind her, looking up at me. I see a bit of surprise in his eyes, too, and I wonder if he forgot we were even here.

"Hello," the woman says to me. "You have...a guest?"

Jesse doesn't say anything—he just nods. A sly smile forms on her face, and I realize she thinks I'm here for him. Like, a lady friend. A lady friend that spent the night *with* him. Gross.

The woman is tall and slim, with a cream blouse tucked into a skin-tight black pencil skirt. Her hair and makeup are impeccable, and she's got the same striking bluish-green eyes as Jesse.

"H-hi, I'm Lena," I say, to her, and I catch Jesse's eye on me. I realize this is the first time he's actually heard my name, because he was too careless to ask for it. Suddenly, I hear the pattering of little feet flying down the stairs behind me.

"And I'm Caleb!"

Her eyes grow wide, and then she smiles at us.

"Hi, Caleb," she says warmly. His little cheeks flush pink as he tucks himself behind me on the bottom step.

"Are you all...staying here?" the woman asks. Caleb nods. She turns to Jesse again.

"They are paying guests," he says, clearly worried that the woman is making the same assumption that I think she is.

"Paying?" she says, turning to face him completely. She takes a few steps closer to him, her voice going quieter. "Please tell me you, like, made the beds at least?"

Jesse doesn't answer.

"Pillows?" she asks. He shrugs. She leans into one hip

and crosses her arms over her chest. "Did you at least dust the fucking furniture?"

Then she remembers Caleb.

"Oh," she says, covering her mouth, "sorry, sweetie."

"It's okay," Caleb says. "I know I'm not supposed to say the fuck-word."

My jaw drops as Caleb hops off the bottom step, making his dinosaurs fly through the air as he does.

"I'm so sorry for my mouth," the woman says to me, putting a hand to her chest. I smile and wave it off.

"I told them they could stay as-is. The inn is technically closed," Jesse says. I can't figure out who this woman is, but I sort of like the way she looks him directly in the eye. The way she owns the room. The way she makes him back into a corner a bit, gruffness and all.

"Yeah. We're paying double," Caleb says, his eyes still on his dinosaur. I swallow. This kid catches way too much.

Now, the woman's eyes are squinty and pointed directly at Jesse, fire burning behind them.

"My word," she whispers, taking a breath. She turns to us quickly. "I'm so sorry. My brother has never been the best at the hospitality business." Then, she saunters over to him. She takes her big-ass Coach bag off of her shoulder, and swings it at him as hard as she can. She pulls it back, and swings again.

"Are you friggin' kidding me? You're charging them *double* to sleep on a bed with no pillows, a bathroom with no towels, and no goddamn breakfast?" He's shielding himself from the blows, and I am trying desperately not to laugh. Caleb's eyes are wide with excitement.

The woman collects herself and walks toward us again.

"I am so, so sorry. I'm Josie Rowan, Jesse's older, and *much* wiser sister," she says, sticking out a perfectly-manicured hand to me. "You're not paying double—the nighty cost will be just fine, and your first night will be completely free seeing as you would have been better off sleeping in the barn with the other *animal* that lives out there. My brother here will have breakfast ready for you in a jiff—"

"Oh, no, really. We were just about to go grab some food, and—"

"No, no. Please, the cost of breakfast is in the nightly fee. I'll have the beds made up this morning, too, and your rooms will be cleaned by lunch. Again, so sorry. If my parents could see how this place looked while you were staying here, they'd be jumping off the dock. So sorry, again. If there's anything you need, please, let us know."

Then, she turns to Jesse and nods to the front door. He sighs, grabs his keys off the table, and trudges out the door like a sad puppy.

I sneak over to one of the huge windows in the front room, and see Josie reaching into her wallet. She pulls out a credit card and shoves it in Jesse's direction. Then she points to his truck as if he's a child. He stomps over to it and drives off, full temper-tantrum mode. I chuckle to myself. I am a *big* fan of Josie Rowan.

She pulls her cell phone out of her bag as he speeds off, with the ease of a woman whose purse is perfectly organized, and I hear her requesting a cleaning service for the afternoon. She marches back up the porch steps, her heels clicking across the wood. She steps inside and sighs.

"I am just...I'm so sorry about all this. I promise this is not how things normally are here."

"Oh, it's fine, really," I say, waving her off. "We're just happy to be here."

"Where are ya'll traveling from?" she asks, her long, straight blonde hair falling perfectly on her shoulders.

"Boston," I say. She nods.

"That's a long ways away. Just a weekend trip?" she asks.

"We might not go back to see my daddy," Caleb says, just before he runs out the front door to catch up with Coby in the grass. Josie looks toward me.

I swallow nervously.

"I don't need to know," she says, holding up her hands. "But just know that you are welcome to a room here as long as you need it. Lord knows, we could use the business."

"I'm so sorry to hear about your parents. It looked like they really did a lot with this place," I say. She smiles and nods, walking toward the parlor. I follow her, and she motions to a wicker chair.

"They did. This place was the gem of the Chesapeake for over forty years," she says, a sadness creeping into her voice. She sits down in the chair next to me and crosses one of her long legs over the other.

"When we lost them, my brother sort of lost himself," she says. I nod. I get that, way more than most people would.

"So, your parents left the inn to you two?" I asked.

"Yes," she says, "but I'm just out of law school—change of careers, for me—and fresh at a firm in D.C." Ah, that explains all the designer stuff and the impeccable taste in shoes. "So I'm afraid I'm not much help. It was all sort of left to Jess, and as you can see, it was a bit much for him. He's hoping to fix it up enough to sell it, which will tear us both apart. But I'm not sure what other options we have... I can only make it out here once or twice a month." Her blue eyes trail to windows, staring out over the bay.

"Growing up here must have been amazing," I say,

following her gaze. I can't imagine having a place like this to myself, and then having to let it go.

"It was," she says, smiling. "It was a complete dream."

A little while later, I hear the rumbling of Jesse's truck pull up. He trudges back up the porch steps, Caleb and Coby following close behind him.

He walks past us and into the kitchen, dropping a ton of grocery bags on the big wooden table in the center.

Josie and I start to help him unpack the groceries, and Caleb parks himself at the table.

Jesse grabs a small brown bag from the corner of the table and walks over to Caleb.

"Special delivery," he says, plopping it down in front of him. Caleb rustles through the bag and pulls out a giant chocolate donut.

"Yum!" he says, biting into it like he's never eaten a day in his life.

"Thank you," I say to Jesse. He nods, walking by me like I barely exist. I don't know why, seeing as he has been nothing but an ass since I got here, but I *want* to exist to him.

"So, what do you two have planned today?" Josie asks, pulling up a chair at the table next to Caleb.

"Fishin'!" Caleb says, licking the chocolate from his fingers.

"Oh, well, uh, the dock's got a few missing planks. It's closed," Jesse says. Josie glares at him, and he just scratches his head and walks toward the door. He turns slowly to Caleb. "Sorry, kid."

Jesse exits the kitchen slowly, and we hear him go out the front door and down the porch steps.

"Aunt Lee, I wanted to fish," Caleb says, and my heart is breaking from the sadness in his eyes.

"I'm sorry, sweetie," Josie says. "Do you like swings?" Caleb perks up a little, nodding his little head. "We have an awesome tire swing out back. After you finish your donut, I can show you?"

"Okay," he mutters.

"So, you're his aunt?" Josie asks, turning to me.

"Oh, yes," I say. "My sister is asleep upstairs."

She nods.

"Ah, wonderful. Well tonight, I have one of our old chefs coming to make dinner," Josie says. Wow, this place really was full-service. "You two enjoy your morning. I'm gonna go see what I can help my crazy brother with around here."

"Thanks, Josie," I say.

As soon as Caleb is done with his final bite, he hops up from the table.

"Can we swing now?" he asks. I smile and nod, dragging him to the sink to clean him up. We step outside, and I'm instantly calmed by the combination of the shining sun and the sound of the soft bay waves lapping against the dock.

Caleb pulls me toward the huge oak tree that sits a few yards back from the water where the giant tire swing sits. He climbs on.

"Push me, Aunt Lee!" he shouts. I do, back and forth, closing my eyes to soak in the sun.

"For fuck's sake, Jesse," I hear Josie saying from way across the yard. "I have a feeling they've been through some shit. Can't you just fix the goddamn dock for the kid?"

"Jesus Christ, Josie," he says. "If all you're gonna do is bitch at me while you're here, you might as well take your ass back to D.C. We've been through some shit, too. I have an inn to sell. I don't have time for this," he says, storming into the big red barn and slamming the doors shut behind him. That seems to be his signature move.

For lunch, Caleb, Millie and I drive over the bridge into town. There's a small sandwich shop on the water that Josie told us about called Leaman's. Out back is a big playground, and Caleb is loving life.

"So, what's the sister like?" Millie asks, clapping the crumbs off of her hands.

"She's great," I say. "Nothing like Jesse. She's got her shit together. Super sweet," I say.

"Yeah, well. Let's not be too quick to judge. I don't exactly have my shit together," Millie says with a sad smile. I take her hand.

"Hey," I say. She looks up at me. "We're gonna get our shit together. Without him."

She nods, resting her head on my shoulder.

DINNER THAT NIGHT IS AMAZING. The chef made a huge pot of Maryland crab soup, a gigantic Caesar salad, and Chicken Chesapeake as the main course. For dessert, he brings out a rich cheesecake, and before we know it, Caleb is rubbing his eyes.

"Okay, little man," Millie says, scooping him up from the table. "You've had an adventurous day. I think it's time for some bed." Normally, Caleb avoids bedtime like the plague. But I think a few days on the bay have done him good and zapped a lot of his pent-up energy. He raises his arms for Millie, and they say goodnight.

"I hope we can fish soon, mama," we hear him say as they make their way out of the room.

My eyes flash to Jesse from across the table.

"Well, I'm going to get some shut-eye myself," Josie says,

standing from the table. "I have a long drive back to the city tomorrow. Goodnight, all."

"Goodnight, Josie," I say. "Thank you again. Dinner was amazing." She pats my shoulder before she makes her way upstairs. And before I know it, it's just Jesse and I.

He stands up from the table, and turns awkwardly. I think if it were socially acceptable, and if he wasn't so afraid his sister might see, he would have actually run away from me. He pauses and scratches the back of his head.

"Well, uh, I'm gonna head out, so uh, night," he says, starting to make his way to the backdoor.

"I heard you're trying to sell the place," I say. I'm not ready for him to leave yet for some inexplicable reason. He pauses at the back door.

"Yeah," he says.

"I'm sorry about how everything went down after your parents passed," I say, Millie's warning against being too quick to judge ringing in my ear. Maybe if I just show him a little compassion, he'll show me another side to him. "Josie says this all sort of fell on you."

He turns to me slightly.

"Did she tell you how I let it all go to shit?" he asks with a scoff.

"No," I say. "She said it was a big burden to bear, though. It must be hard to let it all go." He scoffs again.

"It's easier than you think," he says. "I can't wait to be done with this place."

Then he turns, and storms out the back door.

Okay, I was wrong.

This guy doesn't have another side.

5

JESSE

I wake up to the sun beating down on my face and a pain in my back, and I realize I fell asleep on the dock again. I pull myself up and walk back off the water to go change. As I'm making my way around the house, I freeze when I see her on the patio.

She's got her nose in another book—I'm pretty sure this is not the same one she was reading yesterday, or the day before that. Not that I'm paying that much attention.

As I walk hesitantly toward her, she lifts her eyes to me. I freeze.

"I made sure you were breathing," she says. I nod and scratch the back of my neck. It's this habit I have when I get uncomfortable or...jittery.

"Uh, thanks," I say. I feel like I need to explain it to her. Tell her that sometimes I have trouble sleeping in the barn, or the house, or anywhere, really, where I have any sort of memory of them. But I don't. And what's even more interesting, is she doesn't ask.

"Maybe you should leave a pillow or a blanket out here, if you're gonna keep having slumber parties under the stars," she says, closing the book and hopping up from the chair. She disappears through the back door, and although my eyes are basically glued to her ass, my fists are clenched in annoyance. Man, she's a pain.

And after all that shit my sister made me do for them while she was here...ugh. Not exactly how I was intending on spending my weekend—catering to a kid and two women, one of whom has the ability to piss me off from a mile away. But Josie was right: they are paying customers. I can practically feel my mom's knowing glare and hear her toe tapping.

Damn, what I wouldn't give to see her standing like that in the kitchen again, telling me to "remember to tend to the guests."

Pops with a hand on her shoulder.

"Listen to your mama, Jess," I can hear him say. A flash of a sad smile washes over my lips as I walk back into the barn. Sometimes when I'm here, it's like they are right here with me. But when I remember they're not, it feels like this place is crushing me.

I walk up the steps to my room and nudge the door open, taking off my shirt as I walk. This barn is my space. My parents let me move out here when I graduated from high school, and to be fair, it was a sweet little bachelor pad. It was easy as hell, sneaking girls in here when I was younger. It's my sanctuary, this barn. My parents added working plumbing, insulated my room, and gave me the freedom I wanted. After they died last year, I couldn't bring myself to move back into the house. That was their space. This is mine.

I walk into my bathroom and turn the shower on, unbuttoning my jeans as I move. I spin around, and just as I'm about to pull on the waistband of my boxers, I freeze.

45

Because she's here, standing in the doorway of my bedroom, staring at me while I'm practically naked.

"What the fuck!" I call out, stepping backward into the bathroom and slamming the door. I grab the towel off the rack and wrap it around my waist before I open it back up, completely fuming.

But when I open the door, she's gone. I sprint out of my bedroom and look down the stairs. She's running down them and jolting across the barn floor.

"Hey!" I call again. She freezes at the barn doors. I march down the steps, growling under my breath. "What the hell were you doing?" She turns to me slowly, her big blue eyes wide as she stares up at me.

I watch as they scan my body, and I get that twitch in my crotch again. I inhale sharply and shake it off. I lean on one of my hips and cross my arms over my chest. I raise an eyebrow, waiting for an answer.

"Caleb took off after Coby. I thought they might have come in here," she says. I take a step closer to her, breathing her in as I do. We're a few inches apart now, and I'm glaring down at her. Her face is inches from my bare chest. And though I'm trying to be tough, intimidating, keeping up that "leave me alone" attitude, the flowery smell of her hair is driving me a little nuts. So much so that I take a step back. I exhale and clear my throat.

"They're not in here," I say. She nods. "But I am. This is my room. I'd appreciate a knock now and then. Or better yet, just no visitors at all."

Now, she crosses her arms over her chest and shoots me a look.

"You're such a welcoming host," she says. I shrug my shoulders.

"That's why I'm sellin' the place. Not so good at the

family business," I tell her. She rolls her eyes, then they catch mine. Slowly, but surely, they drop to my jawline, to my chest, and down to my stomach. I watch as her eyebrow twitches ever so lightly, then she turns on her heel and leaves the barn. I'd be lying if I said I didn't watch her, with every damn step she took away from me.

LATER THAT NIGHT, I'm back at the Broken Shell. It's right before the busy hour, and I'm drying off some glasses behind the bar, staring blankly ahead at a painting of the bay that sits crooked on the wall.

"What's eatin' you?" Berta asks, carrying over another crate of glasses from the dishwasher.

I let out a long sigh and shrug my shoulders.

"Nothin'," I say, but she rolls her eyes, and honestly, I should know better. Aside from my parents and my sister, no one really knows me like Berta. "I had a busy weekend. We have some guests at the inn, and—"

"Whoa, whoa...guests?" she asks. I nod.

"They rolled in last week," I say. Berta shifts her head back.

"They?"

"Yeah. This woman, her kid, and her *sister*," I say, with a bitter snip on my tongue as I mention her. Berta looks at me for a minute, then a sly smile crosses over her lips.

"So the sister's cute, huh?" she asks, leaning up against the bar.

"Actually, she's a giant pain in my ass," I say, lifting up one of the crates to stack it on another. Berta lets out a snort.

"That don't mean she's not cute," she says. I give her a playful look and keep stacking. I will not confirm or deny. "Well, look. It can't hurt to have the business, Josie's right.

And besides, it's also not a bad thing for you to have some damn human interaction for a change. I worry about you, Jess."

She throws a towel up over her shoulder and puts her hands on her hips as she gives me those sad eyes.

"I know you do," I say, lifting the last crate of glasses up under the counter, getting ready for the rush. "But you don't need to. Soon enough, I'll get that place sold, and I'll be somewhere, sipping some fruity-ass drink on a beach without a care in the world."

That's my plan, or lack thereof. Take what's left of my inheritance, the money I save from working here, and whatever I can get from the inn, and take off. Somewhere blue and sandy and warm, with no memories of my parents to haunt me. No reminders of what I couldn't do for them. I flash Berta a smile, but she doesn't return it. Her eyes drop, and I can see the sadness in them instantly.

"We will miss you around here, Jess. This whole town will," she says. Just then, like clockwork, the stampede of locals storms through the doors. And I'm glad, because I don't really want to keep having this conversation. The truth is, I don't know what I'll do when I leave. I don't know who I am without Baycrest. But one thing I do know is that I don't like who I've become. It's time to go.

I'm back behind the bar, pouring drinks, listening to Rob's crummy band playing the same shit he's been playing here for fifteen years. But the people of Baycrest are loyal. They keep comin' back.

I turn around to make a couple of tequila shots, when I hear her.

"How about one of those for me, handsome?" she asks. Normally, I'd be spinning around so quickly, I'd almost break the rest of the glasses on the counter. I'd let Berta know I needed five, I'd wipe off my hands, scoot out the side of the bar, take her hand, and follow her out back.

This time, though, something's a little different. I take in a long breath, then turn to her slowly.

"Hey, Amber," I say. She flips her long blonde hair over one shoulder, her hot pink halter top cut low enough that it doesn't leave much to the imagination. Lucky for me, I don't really have to imagine it. I've seen the real deal, plenty of times.

She smiles, and her brown eyes light up under the neon bar lights.

"Hey, yourself," she says. "Got a few minutes?" She raises her eyebrows, and I know that's my cue.

Amber Cole. She was a few years behind me in school, and had a crush on me all through the years. We were in similar boats for a while, Amber and me. A lot of our friends took off after we graduated, but we stayed. And we found each other. We've been finding each other behind the bar, at her place, at mine, in my truck...well, all over Baycrest for the last few years. I would never go so far as to say we were dating...there wasn't much more to Amber and me than sex, and the occasional inappropriate text message.

Sometimes we'd meet some other friends for food, but I always found myself spending most of the meal talking to everyone else around the table. There's no substance with Amber. And I've always known it. And I've always been honest about it. Amber holds on, though. She thinks some-how, sometime, some way, the tides will change. I know they won't.

But looking at her now, I just don't know how I can say no. And I don't really know why I want to. I let Berta know I'm taking a breather, chuck my towel down on the counter, and follow her outside. Before I get a word in, she's on me like bees on honey.

She pushes me up against the side of the building, kissing my neck, nipping at my ear. It gives me a little chill, but for whatever reason, that's it.

Usually, I'm ready for action in half-a-second with Amber. It takes all of one minute, the sensation of her tongue on my skin, the slight tug as she undoes my belt. Now, I kiss her back, but only for a minute. But I'm just not into it tonight. She carries on for another minute or two, and then she pulls away, slowly.

"What's the deal?" she asks. I shrug and sigh. She raises an eyebrow, but when she realizes I won't be doing any raising of my own, she steps back. I clear my throat and re-buckle my pants.

"I'm sorry, I'm just not in my right mind," I say. "Got a lot goin' on."

"Well, that's okay. Maybe later," she says with a casual shrug. There's no denying the disappointment in her eyes. She straightens out her top and smiles at me, then glides back into the bar. I watch her go, and I know that me and Amber, whatever we are, it's coming to an end. And as much as I want to deny it, I know exactly why. It's because ever since I got cussed out by the girl with the coal-colored hair, I don't have any interest in getting off with any other woman. And it's annoying as all hell.

As I'm walking back behind the bar, I freeze when I see my phone light up with a text. It's from Rodney. And suddenly my heart's pounding a mile a minute.

6

LENA

It's early Monday morning, and even though we've been here for a few days, I'm still not quite used to how bright the sun is when it reflects off the Chesapeake. It's streaming through our windows, and before I know it, I'm wide awake. Millie and Caleb are snuggled up on the other side of the bed, curled up tight under the big, white, down comforter that Josie brought us. She also brought us a cot for Caleb, but so far, he's lasted exactly zero nights in it before crawling back into bed with us.

I get dressed and sneak downstairs. It's clear the second I reach the first floor that Josie has gone back to D.C.; there's no smell of fresh coffee wafting through the kitchen, and there's no three-course breakfast waiting for us.

There is, however, a pitcher of lemonade, and a box of waffles in the freezer. I guess he's trying, at least. Or maybe he's just so scared of his big sister that he decided it was worth making some sort of effort. Either way, it makes me smile.

As I sift through the other food in the fridge, I hear a car door slam outside. I curiously step over to one of the huge windows, sipping my room-temperature lemonade out of a mug. Jesse is climbing into the cab of his truck, lifting out two brand-new rocking chairs. He carries one in each arm—making it look way too easy—to the porch, and situates them extra close to each other. Then, he all but runs back to his truck, dragging the old, decrepit ones behind him. He closes the back of the cab, and pulls it off to the side of the house. He gets out and rushes to the barn. He goes inside, and returns moments later with a giant broom. He starts sweeping the steps, the porch—I swear he's moments away from sweeping the gravel driveway.

Then he goes back to the barn again, and returns with a tool box. He grabs his hammer and starts wailing away at random nails around the porch. After a few minutes of that ruckus—which I cannot believe my nephew slept through—I see Jesse making his way toward the front door, and I quickly tuck myself back into the living room. I grab a seat on one of the big blue couches, making it look like I've been casually sitting for a while. He almost doesn't see me, but stumbles in place when he finally does.

"Oh, uh, mornin'," he says.

"Morning," I say, taking another sip.

"There's waffles," he says, motioning to the fridge.

"I saw, thank you," I say. He pauses for a moment before heading back to the kitchen. I hear a few cabinets open and close, then he's back with a bottle of window cleaner and an old rag. He starts going to town on the windows, and I cringe at the streaks he's leaving.

"Is Monday cleaning day," I say, "or are you expecting someone?"

He doesn't stop his horrible swirling of the rag. He moves from one massive window to the other, twirling the rag in horrific circles all over the place.

"Someone's coming to look at the inn," he says.

"Someone?" My first thought is he's expecting someone, a girl maybe. Someone he doesn't want the inn to look like a total disaster. But then I remember it's barely past six in the morning, and he's moving awfully swiftly.

"Yeah. Someone who's interested in buying it. My realtor texted me last night," he says. He finishes—at least to his standards—and scurries back to the kitchen to put the cleaner away. He rushes past me again, bursting out the front door and heading for the barn. As he walks, he swiftly unbuttons his shirt, letting the flannel slide off his thick muscles as he disappears inside the big doors. I feel heat rising in my cheeks as I force myself to look away.

I hate that he's attractive. I hate that he's really, *really* good-looking, in that gruff, stubbled kind of way. He's big and broad and strong. And he's also an ass. But knowing that he's under a bit of stress does something to me—it makes me want to help.

I set my mug in the dishwasher, then grab the window cleaner from under the sink. I turn back to the windows, and get to work at recleaning what he's already "cleaned."

In a few moments, he's back at the front door, just as I'm finishing the last window, leaving it perfectly streak-free.

"Oh, I, uh, just wanted to help," I say, tucking the cleaner and rag behind my back. He takes a quick look at the windows.

"Thanks," he says with a nod. He walks past me and out the door.

I follow him outside, and start rearranging the new chairs.

"Do you need help with anything else?" I ask him. He stops plucking weeds from the front bed and turns to me.

"Ah, actually, I think that about covers it. It's an as-is

deal; I was just trying to give the place a little more umph before he gets here."

I nod and turn back to the inn. It's almost like looking at someone you love, a grandparent, maybe, as they age. Watching them slowly turn into a less vibrant version of their old self.

It's clear there was once a lot of life in this old house. It's just slowly fading away.

"When is he supposed to be here?" I ask. Jesse brushes one hand through his sandy locks, and holds up his phone the other.

"Ten minutes," he says, a nervous shake in his voice.

"Okay. I'm going to go wake Millie and Caleb, and we will get out of your hair for a few hours," I say. I swallow as I make my way into the house.

I know we've only been here for a few days, but right now, this old house is the only thing that emulates anything close to "home" for us. And I'm basically helping throw it away. Not that I have a choice. I know we can find another place by the time settlement comes around, but I...I'm getting ahead of myself. Besides, it's not like we intended to stay at the Rowan for long. Eventually, we won't be able to afford it. Single-night rates or not.

I get Millie and Caleb up and rolling, and in a flash, we're downstairs and loading into my car. Jesse's standing on the front porch, and as I'm about to duck into the driver's seat, our eyes catch each other. I give him a quick "good luck" nod, and he nods back.

We take Caleb to get some breakfast at a little diner on the highway. He's coloring away on his kids' menu while we're flipping through ours. My eyes wander out the window, and I can't help but wonder how the potential sale is going.

"So, any ideas where we should go next?" Millie asks, as if she's reading my mind.

"I haven't looked much yet. I was going to ask Jesse if he had any recommendations nearby," I say. Sometimes I'm amazed at my ability to spitball, to totally pull an answer out of my ass to avoid causing others anxiety. In our family, I'm *always* the one with the answers. Despite my internal panic, I'm quick with a comforting smile and a nonchalant wave.

"Good idea," Millie says. Her eyes drop to Caleb, and when she sees that he's still coloring, she turns back to me. "He called again last night, late."

I drop my menu.

"Why did you turn your phone on?" I ask. I was quick to monitor both of our phones when we left Boston, but I'm still paranoid. And with Tiger, there's no such thing as being too safe.

"I just...I don't know I just wanted to see if he was looking for us, I guess," she says.

I glare at her.

"Millie, why?" I ask.

"It's not because I want him to," she says, placing her hand on me to reassure me. "Honest. I don't. Not this time. Not when he..." her voice trails off as she looks down at Caleb, brushing his hair back. I remember her, just a few days ago, sitting in his bedroom. Knowing that Tiger had chased them in there, knowing that he got closer than ever before to hurting my favorite little human. A chill goes down my spine. "Not this time."

"Then, why?" I ask.

"Because. I guess I just wanted to see how much time we have before he starts moving. Starts using his dad's tools and money to find us," she says.

I nod and take a big swig of my coffee.

The Bentleys own a few restaurants in the city, and word is, they traffic a lot more than just food. Tiger's dad has connections all over the country, and I don't mean like free tickets to a game, connections. I mean like, give-me-a-name-and-I'll-give-you-a-body connections.

I take another sip of my coffee as the panic starts to settle right on my chest.

I had thought plenty about avoiding Tiger, but I didn't think through avoiding his rich father. I just knew we needed to get out, so we did.

"You turned it off again, right?" I asked. She nods. I can tell by the look on her face, she's feeding off my anxiety. I smile at her and grab a crayon off the table.

"I'm X's, you're O's," I tell Caleb, drawing a Tic-Tac-Toe board on the piece of paper. I look back up to Millie. "We're gonna be fine."

WE HEAD BACK to the inn a little bit later. As soon as I park, Caleb is running through the grass, chasing, and being chased by Coby. I smile as I watch them run—Caleb's never had this much room to himself in his entire life. To be honest, neither have Millie or I. For a brief moment, Caleb stops running, turning back to us.

"I love it here, Mommy. I wish we could always live here," he says, then turns back to run after the dog. Panic washes over me once again as I realize that this might be coming to an end.

"Don't go near the water!" I hear Millie call as she follows them around the back of the house.

I look around. There are no other cars in the driveway. Jesse's red truck is still parked off to the side. I look around, but he doesn't seem to be outside anywhere. Just as I'm about to walk up the porch steps, I hear the barn doors slide open. He's stomping out, dragging behind him a wheelbarrow full of bricks.

"Hey," I say, but he just walks on by me, dumping them in the dirt behind his truck.

"Humph," he musters up, before wheeling back into the barn. I follow him inside, but before I can speak, I lose myself inside the barn for a moment. This was the restaurant, before everything shut down. There are still a few tables set up, and the counter at the back of the room is still shiny and silver, despite the dust everywhere. I can tell the dining area had a rustic theme—rod-iron chandeliers hang from the ceiling, and artificial sunflowers sit in jars on a few of the tables. At the back corner of the room stands the long staircase that leads to what I guess is Jesse's room, and he is currently stomping up the steps. I follow him up, my curiosity getting the best of me. There's one door at the top of the stairs, and when he opens it, I see the most boring bedroom I've ever seen. There's nothing but one dresser, and an unmade bed. Funny that I didn't notice this the other day; the almost-naked man standing in it at that moment must have distracted me.

"So is this your room?" I ask, startling him. He whips around.

"What are you doing up here?" he asks.

"I just wanted to check, see how it went with the buyer."

"There is no buyer," he says, his gruff voice seeming even more gruff right now. "He said the work that needed to go into it wasn't worth the aggravation of the sale."

He digs through one of his drawers, then he turns back toward the stairs, stomping again.

"I'm sorry," I say, following him down. He actually lets out a laugh before turning back to me.

"Don't you worry, looks like your little vacation doesn't have to end anytime soon. So by all means, continue making yourself right at home," he says, his voice oozing with sarcasm.

A second ago, I felt bad for him. Now, I'm holding myself back from kicking him down the rest of the stairs.

I have a lot of four-letter words I'd like to shout at him right now. Several not-so-nice names stand on the tip of my tongue, ready to be fired off in his direction. But as I watch him bluster across the barn floor and out the big doors, nothing comes to me. Nothing but just the tiniest bit of relief that our little sanctuary can remain just that a little while longer. Jesse has no idea just how important this little "vacation" really is.

WE AVOID JESSE FOR DINNER—OR, rather, he avoids us, since he's not even home. After eating, we take Caleb outside to swing a little bit more, then settle him into bed. Millie and I curl up on one of the wicker benches on the back patio, letting the cool summer breeze blow through our locks. The only difference is that mine sit straight down my back, while hers are naturally shaped into beautiful curls, something I've always been jealous of.

"It really is beautiful here," she says after a few minutes. I look out over the water. The bay is so blue, even in the disappearing sunlight. The sky has a twinge of orange in it, and the cattails are all bowing in the wind. A few boats skate across the water way out in the distance, so small they look like toys.

"It is," I say.

"I know Caleb will be devastated when we leave," she says. "And to be honest, I will too."

I look down at the ground. Despite the infuriating company here, I will be too.

Jesse's words echo in my head.

The work that needed to go into it wasn't worth the aggravation of the sale.

Suddenly, my survival instincts kick in, and my creative juices are flowing.

I don't want to go. Neither do Millie and Caleb.

We're safe here, at least for now, and their safety just isn't something I'm willing to give up on.

"What if..." I say, gathering my wild thoughts. "What if we don't leave?"

"What?" she asks, giving me a concerned look. "You mean like, squat?"

I snort.

"No, ya dork," I say. "What if we help him fix the place up some? It would buy us some time to stay here until we figure out a solid next move, and it would help him get the house in better selling shape."

Her eyes grow wide with a mix of possibility and concern.

"I mean, I guess it could work?" she says.

"Maybe we can work out a deal. We stay for free as long as we help him," I say. She nods. "Although, I imagine if we're staying for free, he won't necessarily be too keen on feeding us every day. Even if it is just lemonade and waffles."

The wheels in my mind are spinning into overdrive. We still need money. We've been frugal, living off of snacks and mostly fast-food, but my savings and the money from Mrs.

Hinders are going to run out eventually. Probably sooner rather than later.

"I could get a job," Millie says. I look up at her. She hasn't worked since she was a teenager. After she had Caleb, Tiger forbade her to work. Just one more way he alienated her from the world, leaving her clinging to him for anything she might need.

"Mill, you don't—"

"No, Lena. If this works, if you can get him to agree to this, I'll get a job. As long as you don't mind keeping an eye on Caleb while you're working around here, I'd be happy to get one. I haven't had my own money in a long time. It will be a nice change of pace," she says. "I mean it. You're always taking care of things. Let me do this."

I smile, nod, and squeeze her hand.

"Okay," I say. "First thing tomorrow, I have to charm Mr. Uncharming."

Millie laughs as she puts a hand on my knee.

"Say what you want," she says as she pushes herself up from the bench, "but you're not exactly stealth in the way you basically drool over him every time he walks away." My jaw drops.

"I do *not*! That is bullshit. That guy is a complete asshole," I say, crossing my arms like an angry child. She smiles.

"That may be so, but it doesn't make him any less good-looking. And he might be an ass to you, but your nephew sure has taken a liking to him. I think it might be mutual," she says.

"No way. He'd have to have a heart to like a kid," I say.

"Well, you better hope he has something left of a heart, if you want this plan to work."

7

JESSE

I roll out of bed the next morning—early—and head downstairs to move more of the leftover bricks out from the back of the barn. My parents had planned to build this big, beautiful patio on the side of the barn, but it never happened before the accident. I can't bring myself to do it now.

I'm an early riser—growing up in this place did that to me. My parents were always up by 5:30 a.m. to make sure everything was ready for the guests. Comes with the territory, I guess. If only I could grow out of it, since there's not so much to tend to these days.

But almost every single day so far, that girl's been up at the same time as me. And each time I catch a look at her through her window, I wonder what gets her up so early.

Just as I'm loading up the last bit of bricks into the wheelbarrow, I hear creaking wood—it's her, leaning against the barn doors. I smell coffee instantly, and it sets my insides on fire.

"Morning," she says. "I brought you a cup."

She's holding one of the mugs out to me. I hesitate, then set the barrow down and take one out of her hands.

"Thanks," I say. She nods.

"Lemonade just wasn't doing the trick for me," she says with a sly smile. I crack a fast smile, but it disappears into my mug.

I can't make out what she's thinking as we stand here in silence, sipping our coffee. I'm desperately trying not to look at her. Her hair is wavier this morning, like she must have slept with it wet or something, and it's flowing down, directing my eyes straight to her chest. These little white strings are hanging from the hem of her jean shorts, and her tank top is tight to her body. She's got an arm crossed over her ribs, I think to keep herself warm in the chilly morning air, but all it's really doing it displaying her...assets. And it's killing me.

But as hard as I'm trying not to look at her, I can feel her icy blue eyes piercing through me. She hasn't stopped looking at me since she stepped foot inside the barn.

She clears her throat and shifts her hair over one shoulder. If I didn't know any better, I'd say she might be a little bit nervous. But why?

"Do you ever sleep?" she finally asks.

"I could ask you the same thing," I say, setting my mug down on the bar and lifting the barrow up again, pedaling it out the doors.

"Eh. I don't sleep much when I have things to figure out," she says. It feels like a bait—she wants me to ask what she's trying to figure out. But I won't. I don't have time for these games.

I move back into the barn and start straightening up the tables and chairs that have all been pushed there.

"What are you doing with all of these?" she asks.

"Movin' 'em," I say. I know I'm not the most talkative guy, but there's something about this girl that makes me never want to talk. If I'm being honest, it's because I'm a little afraid she might get too much out of me. I've never wanted to avoid someone but also see them naked so much in my life, and it's making me nuts.

"I see that. Why?" she asks.

"Rodney says it might help to show off the square footage some. So I'm movin' 'em," I tell her. She nods. She clears her throat again, and lets out a long breath. Here we go—whatever she's been dying to bring up these last few minutes is coming out.

"So, um, I was talking to my sister last night, about our...situation. And yours," she says. I glance over at her, but quickly divert it back to the barrow. Where is she going with this? "And...I sorta had a thought."

Aw, shit. What kind of thought?

I don't say anything, I don't ask...I just keep moving. Can't let her know that I'm all kinds of curious.

"For the love of God, can you just pause, for like, a second?" she asks. Her tone makes me freeze for a minute. God, there's something so damn sexy about how direct she is. It's annoying as all hell, but also really freakin' hot. I put the last chair down, and turn to her slowly.

"Yes?" I ask impatiently, feeling the tension growing in my jeans.

"So. You need a buyer," she says. I raise an eyebrow. Where *is* she going with this? "And in the best case scenario, it would be a buyer that would offer you something that will actually leave you with some sort of profit."

I cross my arms over my chest, and if I'm not mistaken,

she glances up, her eyes scanning my chest and shoulder before finding mine again.

"Wow, I didn't realize I wanted to make a profit," I say sarcastically. She ignores it and moves on.

"So, what if we...I...could help get it into selling shape?"

I rest back on my hip, pulling my arms even tighter across my chest, secretly trying to entice her to look. There's gotta be some sort of ulterior motive to this.

"Ha," I say. "And what does this have to do with you?" She swallows, and for a moment, I feel bad for asking. I don't know what the deal is with these three yet, and I have a feeling that this plan of hers has a lot to do with it.

"Well," she says, her voice getting a little shaky, "my sister, and Caleb and I...we need a place to stay."

I lean back on my hip again. What are they running from?

"So, what if...what if we worked out a deal where I help do the work around here, and you let us stay?"

"What?" I ask, a bit baffled.

"Hear me out. If you let us stay here, with no fee, I could fix it up. I can help with whatever you need. I was thinking maybe we set a timeline, like, maybe...three months or so?"

This actually makes me chuckle, and she looks surprised. Probably because I haven't given her more than a fast smirk the whole time she's been here. This chick must be crazy. She clearly doesn't realize how fast I plan on running from Baycrest...if I could just find some sucker stupid enough to buy this shithole.

"Three months? I want to be on an island somewhere floating around in three months. Not stuck here with this godforsaken piece of shit inn on this stupid inlet. Three months," I say, shaking my head as I turn back to the table.

But there's a part of me that feels this pull, this small tug, toward her. Toward her sister. Toward the kid. Why do they need a place to stay so badly?

"Well, it sure took you longer than three months to tear this place apart like you did, so I don't know how the fuck you think you're gonna sell it the way it stands now. Or barely stands, for that matter," she says. I whip my head around to her, and she's standing there, arms crossed again, giving her chest yet another perfect boost. And as the breeze blows her hair back, and I see more of her skin, I forget for just a minute that she's one of the more infuriating humans I've ever been in contact with.

And probably the most annoying thing about her is that Josie likes her. Which means my mom would, too. She's got that same sort of unstoppable attitude my mother had. And she will never know it, but it's actually a little intimidating.

I don't know quite how to respond, but lucky for me, she keeps going.

"If you want to be living it up somewhere else, you're going to have to put some work into it. If you don't, you won't even get half of what it could be worth. Or, you might not even sell it at all."

My eyes move slowly across the floor, as I actually start to hear what she's saying. If I think I'm going to be in the sea somewhere, drinking from a coconut in a few months' time, with this place looking like it does...I have another thing coming. Shit. She's right. And that's so damn annoying.

"Look, I think this place could be a freakin' gem," she says, catching my eye, "again. This place could be as amazing as it once was. If you want it to be. If not, we can still fix it up enough to where you can get what you deserve from it. What your parents would deserve."

That catches my attention.

"And what exactly would you be helping with?" I ask. I see this light in her eyes, like she's realizing that she's got me tracking her bait. But I keep playing along. I really am genuinely curious to see where this goes.

"Anything. I'm not afraid of physical work. I'm pretty handy. But I can also help with things like interior decor, cleaning, cooking, occasionally wiping down the counters…" she says with a slight smile, a dig at my housekeeping skills.

"Three months, huh?" I ask. Three months isn't *that* long. And I really could use the help. Maybe some feminine direction, like how mom used to run the place. The only downside—for a few reasons—is having to be near her for the next three months. But I think I can deal.

"Three months. Then you can put it up, and watch the buyers flock," she says.

I reach a hand up and scratch my stubble.

"And what about you guys? What will you do in three months?" I ask. She pauses, that nervous look returning to her face. I'm asking like I want to make sure they will really be out of my hair. But I'll admit, there's a small piece of me that just wants to make sure they will be okay, wherever they end up.

"I'll have it figured out by then," she says. I look at her, letting my eyes travel down her whole body before I flick them back up to her. She shifts in her shoes, but she doesn't take her eyes from mine.

"Alright," I finally say. "Three months. You guys and the kid can stay."

Instantly, I watch her shoulders drop, as if some huge weight has lifted from them. And I really want to fucking know what that weight is. But I can't get too caught up in this. I don't need this. I just need to fix this place up, sell it, and get the hell out. A shy smile forms over her round lips.

"Thank you. You won't be disappointed," she says, turning to make her way out of the barn.

As she's walking away, and my eyes are betraying me and trailing her every step, I think of something pretty damn important.

My shifts at the Shell won't exactly cover three extra people. And I need to save that money for whenever I go, wherever I end up next.

"I can't support you guys, though," I call out after her. "You'll have to deal with your own food."

She holds her hands up.

"Oh, absolutely not. My sister will get a job somewhere in town, as long as you don't mind Caleb hanging with us while she's there." I nod quickly, suddenly feeling a little sheepish for even mentioning it. I don't know her all that well, but I do know that she's not the expectant type. And it's pretty clear that she takes care of herself...and the other two. But *why?* As she turns to walk away, my curiosity gets the best of me.

"Why do you guys need a place to stay?" I ask. She freezes. She turns back to me slowly, taking in a long, slow breath.

"Let's just say that my sister and I didn't have a quiet upbringing on the bay," she says with a fast smile that never touches her eyes. "And I don't want Caleb having the same sort of upbringing. That's why we're here. And that's why we can't go back to Boston. Not right now, anyway."

I take a step back, nodding. I remember how badly Millie's face was bruised when they got here, but I was a bit of a selfish ass—too consumed in my own shit to really ask, or to even give a shit. It's healing up nicely, but there's still a small scar over one of her eyes.

"So, the kid's dad?" I ask. She nods. I nod back, looking

down to kick a pebble on the ground. Then I look up at her again. "Three months," I say.

"Three months," she says.

8

LENA

It rains a bit in the morning, and Caleb's getting restless. He and Millie are playing a board game that we found in one of the hall closets when I get up to make us some sandwiches. Ever since I told Millie the news, she seems lighter, relaxed. Which makes me feel lighter, relaxed.

Just then, Jesse makes his way through the front door, covered in mud and soaking wet.

"Were you working outside?" I ask him.

"Naw, I just sweat a lot," he says, his voice dripping with sarcasm. I look him up and down. His shirt is clinging to his muscles again, and Jesus, it's hard to look away.

"Well, if you want to go change, I'm making sandwiches. You want one?" I ask. He dries his hair with a hand towel from the kitchen.

"Yeah, eat with us!" Caleb cries.

"Alright," he says. He stomps down the basement steps to where the laundry is, and I feel a pinch on my side.

"Having ourselves a little lunch date, are we?" Millie asks. I swat her hand away.

"Stop it. We need him to like us," I say.

"No, we don't. We just need him to let us stay. You just *want* him to like you. Which is so unlike you, I must say," Millie says, leaning against the counter and snatching up a baby carrot from a plate in front of me.

"What do you mean?"

"I mean, you have literally *never* been one to give a shit about what anyone thinks of you. Especially a guy," she says, way too nonchalantly.

"Well, I still don't. I just want him to be happy enough with us to let us stay," I retort. Millie smirks as she snatches another carrot. "What?" I ask.

"You want him to like you," she says, as she ruffles Caleb's hair and sits down next to him. I want to argue—I always have the last word, and this is no different. She's not right. I don't need or want Jesse to like me. I just...don't want him to *not* like me. Ugh, okay, fine. Maybe I do want him to like me. But no other human needs to know that. And just as I'm about to point out all the reasons why I don't care what he thinks—which are surprisingly difficult to come up with—he's back in the kitchen, and I have to swallow my tongue.

I finish slapping the last bit of mayo on the last sandwich, and pile them up on a plate.

"Sit here!" Caleb says, patting the chair on the other side of him. A smile flashes across Jesse's lips and disappears as he does what Caleb says.

"These look yummy," Millie says, taking a sandwich off the pile and grabbing some chips out of a bag in front of her to put on her plate. "So, Jesse, do you have a job?"

I look up at Millie. While I'm a generally curious person, I've resisted the urge to ask too many questions of Jesse. One, because the first time I did, he responded by being an asshole. Two, because…oh, for Pete's sake. Because for some reason, I want him to like me. But I will never, *ever* admit that out loud.

But, in any case, I'm sort of glad she asked, so that I don't have to. I want to know more about him. He's so quiet, mysterious. He's just this big, hulking, brooding being that stomps around the property all day, moving heavy objects and letting the Eastern Shore sun hit him in all the right places. It's unfair.

I want to know more about him. And I wish I didn't.

"Uh, yeah," he says, clearing his throat before he takes another bite of his sandwich. "In town," he says. Ah, so descriptive. Thank you for the details, Mr. Rowan.

"Oh, nice. Doing what?" she asks, keeping it casual, but knowing damn well how intently I'm listening. I sigh. It's unnerving how well my sister knows me.

"I help out at one of the local businesses. A friend of my parents' runs it," he says. She nods. Still so freakin' vague.

"Did you help out at the inn, you know, when it was running?" Millie asks.

"A little," he says. The hardly riveting conversation stalled as the quiet sounds of chewing and crunching took their place.

"Do you know how to fish?" Caleb asks, and the relief on Jesse's face is palpable. He clearly doesn't want to talk about the inn.

"Yeah, I know how to fish," Jesse says, shooting a quick smile in Caleb's direction. "Do you?"

Caleb shakes his head, using the back of his little hand to wipe the crumbs from his lips.

"No. I never been," he says.

"Okay, kiddo. I think it's time we get outside. The rain's stopped, and you need to get some energy out!"

Millie says, standing up to grab her plate and Caleb's. I give her a glare. I know what she's trying to do. She wants to leave us alone.

Only, Jesse's standing up now, too.

"Yeah, I have some more work to do in the barn," he says, gathering his own plate. Damn. He ate that sandwich in all of two bites. He puts his plate in the dishwasher then stops at the doorway. "Thanks for lunch."

I nod as he walks away. Millie lets out a sigh as I roll my eyes. Her plan had unraveled.

LATER THAT NIGHT, as we're getting ready for bed, we hear the engine to Jesse's big red truck roar to life.

"Where do you think he goes all the time?" Millie asks, pulling off her t-shirt and pulling on her pajama top. I shrug.

"I have no clue. Probably back to his lair," I say, pulling my long locks into a braid. She rolls her eyes.

"If only you could get an invitation," she says with a smirk as she climbs into bed.

The next morning, I wake before I'm ready to a loud banging noise. I squint in the streaming sunlight, struggling toward the bay window to see what's going on. Caleb appears next to me as Millie sits up, stretching in bed. And I can't believe what I'm seeing.

Mr. Cold Heart, Mr. No Soul, is fixing the freaking dock.

"We can go fishin' now!" Caleb says, running to grab his shoes and put them on. Millie laughs.

"Hang on there, kiddo. You need to put real clothes on first," she says, snagging him by his collar and pointing him in the direction of his suitcase.

Millie stands up, pulling on a pair of jean shorts and gazing out the window.

"Man. He's got a soft spot for kids, *and* he's handy. And doesn't look half-bad shirtless," she says, making her way out the door to follow an overly ecstatic Caleb. I pause for a moment, soaking in the sight of Jesse from this vantage point.

She's right. He doesn't look half-bad.

From the looks of it, he's been working for a while. I'm not sure how it took us this long

to be woken up. He's got on another pair of baggy jeans, but whatever shirt he was wearing is lying in a ball on the shore while he hammers away, the muscles of his back glistening in the summer sun. His sandy hair is thick with a bit of a wave to it, which makes it somehow always fall perfectly into place. And I swear, even from way up here in this window, I can see how blue-green his eyes are.

Caleb's running across the lawn toward him now, and Jesse stops hammering to greet him. I can see Millie waving at Caleb to slow down and stay back from the water—the kid has no idea how to swim—and then I see her thanking Jesse. Jesse holds his hand out, letting them walk out on the dock, and Caleb's literally jumping with joy.

Then Jesse turns slowly toward the inn, and our eyes lock through the window.

I duck down like a nervous teenager.

Caught me again.

I pull on a clean tank top and a pair of shorts, and head down myself. By the time I make it outside, he's got his shirt back on—much to my chagrin; I was really hoping to get an up-close inspection. He's making his way toward the barn when I stop him.

"Hey," I say, just as he's reaching for the doors.

"Hey," he says.

"Thank you for fixing that up for him. I know he's ecstatic," I say, nodding my head toward the dock. He looks out at Caleb, and that brief smile flashes across his lips again.

"Ah, well. It was on my to-do list for fixin' anyway," he says. I smile.

"You know, you could just say 'you're welcome.'"

He turns to me slightly, before reaching his hand back to scratch the back of his head.

"You're welcome," he says. I smile again. I can't help it.

"So, when do we start on that list?" I ask him.

"What list?"

"Your to-do list. I mean, that's part of the deal. I get put to work," I say. He looks me up and down quickly before turning back to yank the doors open.

"I, uh, I haven't really thought about where to start," he says. " I just sort of work on things as I think about them."

The Type-A in me is choking on air right now. I'm picturing a million different types of lists floating around in my head. Check boxes, check marks, scratched-off items. Ah, the glory of a well-planned to-do list.

"No problem. I'll start making a list, and you can let me know what we need to add. Deal?" I say. He looks me over one more time, and nods slowly before heading into the barn.

He's a man of few words, and I'm a girl who likes a challenge. This could be interesting.

THE NEXT MORNING, I decide to make good on my word before Jesse can change his mind. I wake up with the sun like I normally do and change quickly, hoping to beat him downstairs. To my pleasant surprise, it seems I've succeeded.

His truck is in the driveway, but the barn doors are still closed, which normally means he hasn't woken up yet.

I make myself a pot of coffee, and while I'm sipping, I start digging through all the drawers in the kitchen. As I'm digging, I find some worn and dog-eared recipe books, a stopwatch that's older than I am, a business card for Chef Andres, and finally, a notepad. I pull the pad out of the drawer, but stop when I find an old, faded, photograph.

The bottom right corner is bent, but the picture itself is beautiful. There's a tall, broad, handsome man, with a square jaw just like Jesse's and a head full of thick, dark hair. He's got his arms wrapped around a petite young woman, with long, flowing blonde hair. She's got the same nose and lips as Jesse. The woman is looking directly at the camera with a smile on her face. They're standing in front of the inn, and a sign next to them in the grass reads, "VACANCY, ROOMS AVAILABLE." A small, hand-written note at the bottom of the photo reads, "opening weekend, 1980." It's the Rowans—Mr. And Mrs. They are as picture-perfect as one would imagine the owners of the "gem of the Chesapeake" might be.

The thing that gets me the most about the photo, though, is the way Mr. Rowan is looking at his wife. She's smiling, seemingly bursting with pride at their new business. But Mr. Rowan—he's staring down only at his wife, with the same full, grateful smile. The entire inn could be engulfed in flames behind him and he wouldn't even notice. He wouldn't even care—as long as he had her in his arms.

"Where'd you find that?" I hear the gruff voice ask me, and I jump in my shoes.

"Oh! Jesus, you scared me," I say, handing him the

photo. "It was in this drawer. I was just looking for a pad of paper to start making a list."

He takes the photo slowly, and it looks tiny in his hand. And I see something in his eyes that I haven't seen the whole time we've been here—a little bit of softness. His eyebrows jut up just the tiniest bit, and I watch silently as his seaglass eyes scan every inch of the photo.

"They look so proud," I finally say. He nods, reaching a hand up to scratch at his stubble. "You look a little bit like both of them."

He nods again, then puts the photo back in the drawer. I grab the notepad and a pen and start making my way out of the kitchen, assuming that was the end of that conversation —if that's even what it was.

"That photo is hanging up in the Chesapeake Bay History Museum," he says, taking a sip of water and staring out the window that's over the sink. I stop and turn back to him slowly.

"Really?"

"Yeah. They have a whole exhibit on mom and dad and the inn," he says, taking another sip.

"That's amazing. I'd like to see that," I say. I wait a beat, but he says nothing. I let out a quiet sigh. "Well, I'm gonna head outside."

I slide out the back door of the parlor, and when I reach the back patio, I draw in a long breath. I'm not sure why, but whenever we're alone, whenever it's just the two of us, I feel my chest grow tight. I feel this flip in my stomach. It's not like he's easy to talk to. It's not like he's personable, by any means. It's not like he's full of compliments, or charm, or that I should be head-over-heels with him. He's just...a mystery. He's a puzzle I really want to put together.

I look out over the bay. The sun is peeking up over the

top of the water now, way out on the horizon. It's crazy to think that the water in front of me is just a bay, a small sliver of the world's water, and that it leads to an even more massive ocean. It's framed by cattails in every direction, and you can see the silhouette of a few docks way, way out across the water. But for the most part, all you can see for miles is the big, blue bay. I take in another long breath. It's stunning here.

I make my way around the side of the house, and I start my inspection.

The white paint is chipping, from every section of the house, except from the patches where it's already gone. The shutters on some of the windows are still intact, but I imagine they will still need a coat of paint to match the replacements for the missing ones. I can tell from the survivors that they were once a beautiful emerald green, which matched the green roof. I start inspecting the windows, which seem to have been replaced somewhat recently. They're all double-paned, and God, there's a ton of them. They could stand a good washing, but they're in decent shape otherwise. As I continue around the side of the house that the kitchen window faces, I stop when I see him.

He's still standing there at the window, sandy hair disheveled, stubble shining in the morning sunlight. And he's looking right at me.

Our eyes meet, and I feel this tiny little shock. I look back at him for a moment, trying to figure out just what he sees when he looks at me. But the moment passes, and I nervously tuck a piece of hair behind my ear and keep moving. I make a full lap around the house, jotting down everything I see that needs to be fixed, painted, hammered, or just altogether replaced.

There's a *lot* of shit to do in this joint. A lot of shit to do if we want this place to resemble anything close to the "gem" in the photograph.

JESSE LEAVES FOR A FEW HOURS, so Millie and I sit on the back patio while Caleb plays with some of his toys on a blanket in the grass.

"So, did you make your list?" Millie asks. I nod, pulling it out of my shorts pocket.

"It's a doozy," I say. I watch her eyes grow wider and wider as she reads through it.

"Damn. You think the two of you can really do all of this?" she asks. I raise an eyebrow at her. She knows better than to suggest that I can't do something. She smiles. "I'm just saying. Can you do all of this *and* drool over him at the same time?"

I roll my eyes and punch her shoulder as I snatch my list back.

"On that note," I say, hopping to my feet, "I'm going to make my nephew some lunch. You, on the other hand, can starve."

She laughs as I walk inside, stopping to pat Coby's head. I've never had a pet before, but I've gotten used to his presence. It would feel weird to be here without his jingling chain and slobbery kisses every day.

As I'm standing at the kitchen sink making us sandwiches, I notice the barn doors are open, and Jesse's truck is back. I pull out two more pieces of bread, slap some mayo and turkey on them, and put them on a plate.

I add a handful of plain potato chips—not that I've been paying attention to what he eats, or anything—and make my way out the front door to the barn. As I walk, I pick up the pace, eyeing the back of the house to make sure I'm out of my sister's sight. She doesn't need to see me playing nice.

I peek my head into the doors and look around. I hear some noise from the room at the top of the stairs, and my curiosity gets the best of me. I tip-toe up the stairs, carefully gripping the wrought-iron railing to keep my steps quiet, and peek through the crack in the door. He's on his knees on the floor, his navy t-shirt pulling tight around his back muscles. He's searching for something under his bed.

I almost want to laugh—he's living out here in this barn room while we get the luxury inn to ourselves. Then I start to wonder why a man who has access to nine high-end suites, ten if you include the owner's suite, would *choose* to sleep in a barn.

"Can I help you?" he asks, and I jump.

"Sorry, I didn't mean to spy," I say, holding up the plate. "I was just bringing you some lunch."

He pushes himself to his feet, nodding. I take a step into his room, and I feel that weird stomach flip happening again. Maybe it's because we're alone together...in his bedroom. He takes the plate, mutters a quick "thanks," and then heads toward the door.

"I'll eat this downstairs," he says, and I can tell he doesn't really want me in here. I nod and follow him down the steps. He pulls out one of the chairs at one of the tables and takes a seat. He takes a bite of his sandwich, then looks back up at me. He springs back to his feet and grabs another chair off the stack, plopping it down on ground across from his own.

Wow. This is the first gesture he's ever made.

I take a seat and sit quietly while he eats.

"So, what were you looking for up there?" I ask.

He takes another bite.

"Something for you," he says. I swallow, my heart skipping a beat.

"For me?"

"Yeah. But I can't find it."

"What was it?" I ask. But he just shakes his head.

"You'll see when I find it."

I nod. My personality is pressing me to keep asking, but something about him makes me hold back.

"Okay. Another question. Where do you go every night?" I ask. He raises an eyebrow at me, and I can tell he's wondering why I care. But I don't mind. There's a part of me that wants him to know that I want to know more. There's a part of me that's hoping he might want to know a little more about me.

"Out," he says, leaning back in his chair. I lean back in my own, crossing my arms against my chest, giving my breasts a little boost. And if I'm not mistaken, his eyes travel downward for the fastest second. I raise an eyebrow at him. *One of these days, Mr. Rowan, you're gonna start talking more.*

"The Broken Shell. It's a bar in town." I nod. He stands up slowly from the table, swiping some crumbs onto his plate and pushing his chair in. He starts making his way across the wood planks on the floor and stops, turning back to me. "You can come tonight, if you want."

Then, he disappears out of the big barn doors.

I smile to myself as I stand up from my own chair. I think Jesse Rowan just asked me out.

A few hours later, I'm brushing my hair in a mirror down the hall, with my sister breathing down my neck behind me the whole time. We're whispering since Caleb is napping in our room, but I can tell how badly she wants to squeal.

"This is so exciting. I mean, it took him long enough. Geez, it's almost been what, a *month?*"

I roll my eyes, pretending like a swarm of butterflies isn't forming in my stomach.

I have on a tight black tank top and skinny jeans, paired with black sandals. It's not exactly the finest night-out ensemble, but I didn't exactly have time to plan my wardrobe when I was escaping a madman in Boston.

"It's nothing. I think he just offered to be nice," I say, pulling my brush through my hair one last time.

"Yeah, whatever. Don't think I don't notice him watching you, too. It's like the most painful, slowest romance movie in the world. One of the ones where you want to just scream at the main characters to get it on already."

I laugh and shake my head as I put on a few more swipes of deodorant, grab my little sweater, and walk toward the door. I let out a long breath and tell her I'll see her later. It's a minute before nine, when Jesse had told me to meet him down at his truck.

She smiles and spanks my ass as I walk by her.

"Don't stay out too late. And use protection!" she yell-whispers. I shake my head again and wave her off.

When I get out to the truck, he's already in the driver's seat and waiting, the engine roaring. I open the door and hop in, surprised at how high off the ground it is.

He doesn't say much, but I feel his eyes scan me up and down before he puts the truck into drive. The inside of his truck is surprisingly neat—although, now that I think about it, so was his bedroom. It's just the rest of the place that's completely falling apart.

It smells like musty cologne—it smells like him, and I'm surprised how much I like it.

"So, how far is this place?" I ask. A small smirk tugs at his lips.

"Nothing in Baycrest is further than six minutes apart," he says. "If it's further than six minutes, you're not in Baycrest anymore." I smile and nod.

He's wearing a plaid button-up shirt and a pair of dark jeans. He's got boots on still, but they are nicer, cleaner than the ones he wears around the inn.

His sleeves are rolled up to his elbows, showing off the long, thick veins that trace along his hard forearms. He's got one hand on the wheel, and the other on his knee.

Six minutes later, we turn into a small parking lot, right along the shore. A blinking neon sign above the door indicates that we have indeed arrived at "The Broken Shell," and music pours out of the open windows. The parking lot is completely packed—cars are double parked, and lining the curb. Jesse pulls the truck right up to the door, double-parks behind another truck, and hops out.

"Can you park here?" I ask. He smirks again.

"I can park wherever I want. It's Baycrest," he says. He walks a step ahead of me, but to my surprise, he pulls the door open and holds it for me. I nod and step inside, taking in the scene around me. The room is dim, but lit up by people laughing, singing, talking extra loudly to each other. The restaurant is just one big open room, with a jukebox in one corner, a stage, what appears to be a dance floor, and a bar against the side wall. The crowd includes people of all ages—maybe some who are even too young to be here, I think, wondering if they bother to check IDs in this town. I smile as I take them all in: Baycrest's finest.

The one thing I notice is that everyone looks happy to be here. It's refreshing.

As we squeeze inside, heads start to turn.

A man almost as tall as Jesse with short, dark hair slaps his shoulder.

"Jess! You're here. Who's your friend?" he asks. Jesse shakes his hand, but doesn't seem quite as excited to see the man as he was to see Jesse.

"This is, uh, Lena," he says. The man tips an imaginary hat to me and smiles.

"Hello, 'uh, Lena,'" he says. "Welcome to Baycrest. I'm Rob." I smile and nod. I guess it's easy to pick out the out-of-towners.

Another man, much older than Jesse with a long, white beard, shakes his hand as we walk by. When we finally arrive at the bar, I hear a loud, high-pitched squealing. And a half dozen girls—probably around Jesse's age—abandon their table and scamper over to the bar.

"Hey, Jess!" one busty blonde blurts out, her chest spilling out of the low-cut neckline of her white shirt.

"We missed you!" says her brunette friend, who's chest also appears to be too much for the fabric of her shirt to handle.

"Yeah, we did," adds a tall, leggy blonde, as she steps directly in front of him, giving him her best fuck-me eyes. I feel her eyes trail over to me, realizing that I came in with him. There's nothing that kills a lady boner quite like another chick who you think is a threat. "Who's this?" she asks, her eyes moving back to Jesse.

"Hey, Amber," he says. "This is, uh, Lena. She's a guest at the inn." I feel the air grow cold despite my best attempt at a warm smile in Amber's direction.

"I thought the inn was closed," Amber says, her eyes like daggers. Jesse swallows.

"She's, uh, helping fix it up some," he says. He reaches a hand behind his head and scratches the back of his neck.

I can practically see the beads of sweat forming on his brow, and it's all I can do not to roll my eyes. I wonder how many times he's done it with this girl, probably throwing her thin body all over the inn property, bouncing from bed to bed, room to room until she was completely spent.

And I hate how jealous I feel.

"I'm Lena," I say, sticking my hand out from behind him. It's time to make myself known. She looks at him, daggers still in her eyes, and takes it reluctantly.

"Welcome to Baycrest!" her brunette buddy offers, before Amber's dagger eyes fixate themselves on her.

I can still feel the nervous heat radiating off Jesse, and it's sort of satisfying. I like that I'm causing the kind of issue I'm causing. Just then, we hear the roar of a woman's raspy voice coming from behind the bar.

"There you are. I need you back here—we have a few requests for the Rowan special!" the woman says. She's tall with broad shoulders, and a long, gray braid down her back. She looks to be in her mid-sixties or so, and she's wearing a red t-shirt that says "Broken Shell" on it.

She bends over to grab a few glasses from beneath the bar, but stops when she sees me.

"Who's your friend?" she asks him. "Oh, is this the girl?"

I freeze, my eyes moving slowly to Jesse's. I'm "the girl?" Meaning, he's told someone about me?

He side-eyes me, swallowing nervously. He nods to the woman behind the bar.

"This is Berta. She owns the place," he says. Berta wipes her hand on her jeans and sticks it out to me over the bar.

"Pleasure to meet you, Lena," she says. I swallow. She even knows my name.

"You, too!" I say, trying to sound as friendly as everyone around me. If not, I'll stick out like a sore Yankee.

"Anything you want is on the house tonight," she says, lifting another crate of glasses from beneath the bar. Jesse looks down at me.

"I'm gonna help her make a few drinks," he says. "Feel free to have a seat."

I nod, taking a seat at the bar. I look around, everyone around me laughing, talking, drinking, getting back to their evenings. Amber and her friends make their way back to their table, but I catch her glancing over at me, and at Jesse, at least five times. Poor girl. She's clearly infatuated with Jesse; she watches his every move, staring him up and down with longing, mascara-clad brown eyes. And when she's not looking at him, she's looking me up and down, her eyes soaking in every inch of me, too, sizing me up. She definitely thinks I'm a threat, yet, little does she know, I have to basically squeeze the words out of Jesse every time we "talk."

Unless...I look from her, to Jesse, who is currently looking right at me, until I catch him.

Maybe I *am* a threat?

No. No way. I've only known Jesse Rowan for a few weeks now, but one thing I can tell you is that he's got no soul. No emotion. Probably never loved another human in his life.

Okay, that's not entirely true. I watch the way he is with Caleb—he's definitely got some feels. But toward women? Particularly toward the single woman who's holed up in his inn, casually dropping by his barn with food, wearing shorter-than-necessary jean shorts...nothing. I've caught him staring a few times, looking at me through the window and whatnot, but I can't tell what he's thinking. Is he wondering what I look like without a shirt on, like I've wondered about him? Or is he just wondering when I'm going to pack up my shit and get out of his hair?

The world may never know.

Just as I'm about to order another drink, I feel the warmth of another body standing closer than I was ready for.

"Hey, Jess, how about another round of tequila for me and the newbie here?" I hear the body say. It's Rob, the handsome greeter from earlier. He's tall and staggering, wearing an extra-tight t-shirt that shows off the curves of his muscles, and two sleeves of tattoos down his arms. He's got thick brown hair that's combed and styled in a messy manner, with dark brown eyes.

He pulls out the barstool next to me and takes a seat, flashing a toothpaste commercial-worthy grin. I smile back as Jesse hesitantly pours us two shots.

"Thanks," I say, holding my glass up to him before throwing it back.

"So, what brings you to Baycrest?" he asks. "Ever since the inn closed, there's not much bringing people in these days."

I look up at Jesse, who is looking down at the drinks he's making, but is definitely listening.

"Oh, ah, just needed a little getaway," I say. "I came across the inn and it just seemed like the perfect place to catch my breath." With that, Jesse looks up at me, our eyes catching for the briefest moment. I'm secretly praying that Rob doesn't ask more. I don't have an elaborate enough story made up yet. To my relief, he just nods.

"Nice," he says, looking over to Jesse. "Wish you could have seen the inn in its prime. Mr. and Mrs. Rowan really made this whole town what it was. But Jess here did the best he could."

Jesse doesn't even look up at us now, just scratches his stubble and walks toward the other end of the bar.

I can't quite get a grasp on their relationship; they seem to be somewhat chummy at the door, but there's something about the way Rob talks about the inn—about Jesse—that has a condescending undertone to it.

"So, you grew up here, too?" I ask, quick to change the subject.

"Oh, yeah, been in Baycrest my whole life. Jesse and I grew up together. I graduated with his sister a few years ahead of him. I work at my dad's auto shop in town by day. By night, I'm in a band."

I raise my eyebrows as I suck on the lime that was perched on the edge of my glass.

"A band, huh?" I ask. He smiles shyly and shakes his head.

"That's the typical response I get from people when I tell them that," he says with a chuckle. "They can't believe I'm thirty-something, still playing around in a garage band with my buds. But hey, it makes me happy. Plus I've got groupies around town." He shrugs, and I giggle.

"I actually think it's really cool," I say. He smiles at me again, and this time, I feel a little squirmy in my seat. There's no denying he's got the classic, backwoodsy, home-town boy thing going on. Pair that with a guitar and what I'm picturing is a decent singing voice, and it doesn't take a genius to see that he can probably get into any pair of panties he wants to—at least in Baycrest. But as he's talking, going on about some talent contest they won years ago, my eyes keep finding Jesse, perched at the other end of the bar. Amber's found him, and she's got her knees on a barstool, leaning across the bar, whispering something in his ear. He's got this weird, tight, uncomfortable smile on his lips, and as she's whispering, I watch as her breasts heave up and down, mere inches from his face.

Suddenly, my eyes meet his, and I don't feel like hanging around with Baycrest's finest anymore. I turn to Rob.

"Any chance you're heading out soon?" I ask him, totally cutting him off. He gives me a confused look, then nods.

"I can go anytime you need me to go," he says, standing up from the bar a little too quickly. I realize he thinks there might be a chance he's getting into *my* panties tonight. Sorry, Robbie. These Boston babies are locked down.

I smile and follow his lead, walking toward the other end of the bar. I clear my throat, and Amber slides a few inches away from Jesse to give me a death glare.

"I'm getting a little tired. Rob's gonna take me home," I say. Amber looks from me, back to Jesse.

"Home?" she asks. Then slowly backs down off her stool and spins around, flicking her long locks behind her. Jesse's eyes don't follow her, instead, he flicks them up to me. He reaches a hand back and scratches the back of his head.

"Yeah, alright," he says. "I'll probably be a while." I nod as I walk by.

"See ya," I say, making my way toward the door, and I'm a little bit angry at how big of a part of me wants him to say he's changed his mind, that he'll take me home.

But he doesn't.

9

JESSE

I pull into the driveway, a little later than usual, and hop out of my truck. My head's swirling, from all the dirty things Amber was whispering to me, and from watching Rob drive away with the girl I *wish* had been whispering to me. As I turn to go toward the barn, I freeze when I hear the creak of the screen door.

"Well, thanks for the nightcap," I hear Rob say from the porch, and it literally makes my balls jump inside of my stomach. He's still here? I turn slowly, just as he leans in to kiss her cheek. Her lips are smiling, but her eyes are not.

What kind of *nightcap?* The kind that ends in them getting naked in one of my guest rooms? Fucking Rob.

"Maybe if you're not busy next week, we can plan another night..." he says, fiddling with her fingers in his own. She looks up, her eyes catching mine in the dark. I can see her swallow, and she slowly pulls her hand from his.

"I'm sure I'll pop back into the Shell soon," she says. "But I'm going to be pretty busy around here for the next few months."

She's talking to him, but she hasn't taken her eyes off of

mine since she saw me. I see Rob nod his head, his eyes slowly trailing across the yard to me. Then he takes a step back, like he sees what's really going on here.

Although, I'm still not sure if *I* know what's really going on here.

"Right. Well, if the groundskeeper here lets ya out, lemme know if you want to get together." He says it with a smile, but it pisses me the fuck off. And I can tell it pisses her off, too.

"'Lets me out?'" she asks. She scoffs, turning back to the door. "Goodnight, Rob."

"Have fun?" I ask sarcastically, as he hops down from the porch. He looks up at me, flashing me that stupid grin.

"Well, if you're not going to, someone should," he says with a wink. It takes all my strength not to storm up to him and knock him out.

He's gonna bring home *my* guest, and screw her at *my* inn?

Fucking Rob.

But then again, I'm the asshole that let her leave with him.

A few minutes later, I'm lying in my bed in nothing but my boxers, but I'm hot as hell. I didn't even have anything to drink tonight, but I'm feeling all clammy and uncomfortable, sort of like I do when I'm wasted.

Fucking Rob. As long as I've known the asshole, he will stop at nothing to be the hometown hero, the center of attention in this shitty little town. He's been pushing his band on any out-of-towner that might happen to stroll through, and hopping from one local girl to the next since we were fresh out of high school. He's always annoying as hell, but for some reason, tonight, I had an extra urge to sock him right in the fucking face.

And for no good reason. Except that he brought Lena home. To *my* home.

I should have been the one bringing her home.

I don't know why I feel that way. We're not *together* by any means. I guess technically we're living together, although we have yet to sleep under the same roof. We're more like neighbors, I guess.

And if we're being honest, she's a total pain in my ass. A pain in my ass who is sticking around for another three months. Ninety days with the pushiest woman I've ever met. She's so in my face, asking so many goddamn questions.

I roll to my side, shoving my arm under my pillow as I try to quiet my brain.

But seriously, this girl. She's everywhere. I just want to be here in Baycrest, alone, pouting. I want to sit here until the inn sells, missing my parents in peace. But no. In she comes like a damn hurricane off the water, making me be all productive and shit.

She wants a place to stay...to take care of her sister and nephew. Why should that become my problem? Although, to be fair, I like the kid. He's a funny little guy. He's got a lot of spunk, and he's quick to make a friend. He has a lot of questions too, but I don't mind his so much. I can answer questions like, "how far can you throw this ball?" and "where does Coby poop?" a lot easier than anything Lena's ever asked me.

She wants to work on the inn...to help me sell it. She wants us to work on this damn list together, day after day, HGTV-ing the shit out of this place.

Okay, so most of what she's pushing isn't *so* bad, but she's *so* damn bossy. Pushy, pushy, pushy.

Still, I'm the one who brought her to the bar. I'm the

one who introduced her to everyone. Me. I should have been the one to bring her home.

But I couldn't man up and let Amber know she was crossing that line again. I couldn't man up and just tell Lena I wanted to take her home. To smell her shampoo when the wind blows through the truck windows, or to feel how soft her skin is when our hands brush against each other on the center console.

Fuck.

I should have brought her home.

And as one more painful vision of her clouds my brain —her tank riding up as she leaned over the bar, smiling at every single person she spoke to— clouds my brain, I hop up from my bed. I strip off my boxers and jump in the coldest shower known to man. I feel my family jewels shriveling up, but I don't care. I don't know what this girl is doing to me, but I know this flame needs to be doused before it becomes a full-blown wildfire.

10

LENA

I wake up in a shitty mood. When I got home, Millie was basically begging me for details.

"How did it go? Did he, ya know, make any moves or anything?"

I rolled my eyes at her.

"No."

"Well, did you guys talk more, at least?"

"Not really."

"Well...what happened?"

"Not a damn thing," I snapped, just before I locked myself in the bathroom to change. I got in my pajamas, squeezed into the sliver of bed Caleb had left me, turned away from her and went to sleep.

This morning, though, I wake up in the middle of the bed, with the uneasy feeling that I have way too much room. I feel around next to me, but it's empty. The sun is bright and shining through the big window, and I realize I slept much later than usual.

Maybe it was the drinks, or maybe it was the obnoxious

sexual tension between me and the jughead in the barn that will never be squashed. That might be it.

I slink out of bed and start toward the window when I hear a shriek coming from the back.

The sight I see out the window leaves me with a scrunched face of disgust. I quickly pull up a pair of shorts and throw a t-shirt over my head before running down the stairs. I freeze at the parlor window. Outside, my sister is lounging on a chaise on the patio. A few yards ahead of her, Jesse is showing Caleb how to bait his hook. The shrieks continue every few seconds, as Jesse playfully dangles the worm above Caleb's head. They're shrieks of laughter, both from my nephew and my sister. And Jesse even has a smile on his face. I angrily pour myself a cup of coffee and walk outside through the big French doors.

"Morning," my sister says, peering up at me over the rims of her sunglasses.

"Humph," I reply, seething and staring ahead at the jackass who can't take a hint, being all cute and adorable with my four-year-old nephew. It's like he's a different person. But whichever version he is, I still want to punch him in the face, and shove him up against the stupid barn he's always brooding in. Tug at his shirt, feel his muscles underneath my hands...damn him.

I gulp down my cup, then turn on my heel.

"Where ya goin'?" Millie asks.

"To start working. Some of us have shit to do around here. We can't all bait hooks and catch fish all day," I say, blasting off to the side of the house.

I take a deep breath and reach into my back pocket, pulling out the list.

One of the first things I know needs fixing is the shutters. Some of them need to be completely replaced, and they all need to be taken down before we can repaint the house. I look up at the high second-story ones. No place better to start than the top. I know I saw a ladder in the barn earlier, so I walk up to the massive doors and pull them open. I grab the tall, wooden ladder and drag it to the side of the house. I lean it up against the siding, take a breath, and start the climb.

I'm only slightly scared of heights, but I'm determined to use my frustration as my motivation today. No phobia is stopping this chick today. Nope.

When I get close to the top rung, I realize I left the hammer on the ground. Perfect. Just as I'm about to take the first step down, I hear him.

"That ladder is a hundred years' old. You shouldn't be doing this by yourself," he says, making me jump, and lose my balance. In a perfect world, I'd have some witty comeback about how I can do anything I want to, and I don't need a man to tell me what I can and can't do. But in the real world, I'm clutching to the side of a deteriorating old ladder, and it's slowly sliding across the side of an old, deteriorating house. Holy shit. I'm about to die.

"Whoa, whoa!" I hear him say, but the ladder's still sliding. Yup, I'm a goner. Goodbye sis, goodbye Caleb. Love you both.

I'm clutching on for dear life, my eyes squeezed shut, when the ladder comes to a halt. I open one eye slowly, breathing in short, panicked breaths. Then I see that Jesse is holding the side of the ladder and slowly walking it back up into place.

Meanwhile, I'm dangling off the side like a drunk monkey, still pretty unsure of how I'm going to get down.

"Open your eyes," he calls up to me. I shake my head,

squeezing them shut even tighter. "Lena. Open your eyes. I need you to look down at me."

I'm totally terrified, but there's something really calming in the way he says my name.

"You're okay. Open your eyes and look down at me."

I take in a deep breath and slowly peel them open.

"Okay, good. Now, just loosen your hands a tiny bit, careful not to let them slide too hard on the wood, and lower yourself just a bit. I can almost reach you."

"Are you fucking *crazy?*" I ask him, feeling the sweat forming on my brow.

"I'm not the one dangling twenty feet in the air. Now, lower yourself down, just a little bit," he says again. I take in another deep breath, and use all my muscle—which isn't a lot, by the way—to lower my weight down just a tiny bit. Within moments, I feel his large hands reach up and wrap around my thighs. If I wasn't fucking terrified right now, I'd be...something else.

"Okay, you can let go," he says. I shake my head. "Lena. Let go."

I take one more breath, in case it's my last—I might be a tad dramatic—and unwrap my hands from the ladder. I sink a few inches, and then I feel myself sliding down his long, hard body. He turns me around so that we're facing each other, but he doesn't set me down yet. He just lets me slide, inch by inch, my breasts inches from his nose, as my hips brush what feels like a 12-pack of abs. He freezes for a minute so that our noses are inches apart. I've never been this close to him before, and I don't hate it. His eyes are like glass, clear and blue, with this greenish tint around the edge of his irises. His sandy hair is blowing perfectly in the breeze, and his matching stubble is glistening in the sunlight. He's kind of pretty. Okay, *really* pretty. Finally, he sets me down on the ground in front of him, and I'm engulfed in his shadow.

"Thanks," I mutter, steadying myself on the ground. He looks at me for a minute, then—could it be—flashes me an actual *smile*. It lasts a third of a second, but I saw it.

"You shouldn't be doing that alone," he says, and now, I'm mad again.

"Well, we had a deal. I intend to stick to it," I say, leaning down to grab the hammer. I walk toward one of the shutters—on the first story, this time—and start using the back of the hammer to pry out the rusty nails that are holding them onto the house. He leans up against the siding, crossing his big arms over his chest, that I now know feels a little like a brick wall.

"What?" I ask him, as I catch his gaze, watching me work.

"How'd you learn to do this kind of stuff?" he asks. I chuckle.

"Uh, pull a nail out? YouTube. And common sense," I say. Now, he chuckles and shakes his head.

"Nah, I saw your list on the table the other day. You've got a lot of shit written down. How do you know to do all of that?" he asks again. I shrug.

"No one else fixed anything in our house growing up," I say, images of the tiny, decaying rowhome on the outskirts of Boston flashing through my mind. With fake green grass overlaying the front porch, cloudy windows, a screen door that always slammed shut. If it wasn't so hot out, I'd probably feel a chill down my spine. I hated that Godforsaken dump. "So I had to teach myself, if we ever wanted anything done."

For a second, I think he might ask more, and to tell the truth, I'm not sure that I want him to. There are some things about my past, namely, any memory having to do with my father, that I don't really want to discuss. He knows enough. Hopefully that's enough for now. And to my relief, it is. He just nods, running a hand through his dirty blonde waves.

"What about you? You clearly know how to do a thing or two, despite the current state of this place," I say with a sly smile. He smiles back—twice in one day, I'm feelin' lucky—and shakes his head.

"My dad taught me everything. Well, actually, both of my parents did. They were never not working on something in this place. Even when it was in the best shape of its life, they were always making improvements. Josie and I were right there with them," he says, looking up at the house now, some sort of memory floating through his mind. I smile.

"It must have been cool as hell, growing up in a place like this," I say. His eyes trail back down the house and land on mine again, then they drop to the ground. He swings his hand back to scratch the back of his head, then drops it to his side.

"Yeah, something like that," he says. "I got a few errands to run today before I head back to Berta's tonight."

Ahh, back to Berta's. Back to the leggy blonde who I'm pretty sure was trying to poison my drink with her mind last night. And Jesus, do the people in this town *ever* leave the bar?

I nod my head.

"Tell Amber I said hello," I say. He stops in his tracks, turning slowly back to me.

"I'm not going to see Amber," he says, not a crack in his voice, not a glimpse of a smile on his face. I swallow. "But I can surely tell Rob you said hello, if you'd like."

He turns back on his heel and storms off around the side of the house. I wait for a moment until I hear the grumble of his engine and see the cloud of dust forming in the drive-way. And then I smile.

Because he knows who brought me home last night. And he's still thinking about it. I'm not the only one who had to fight off some jealousy last night.

And I kind of like it.

11

JESSE

The second I walk into the Shell, I'm moving like I'm on speed. I'm cleaning glasses, stacking bottles, wiping down tables that don't need to be wiped down. I'm moving chairs around, taking out trash. I can't sit still.

It's that girl.

I watched her this morning, walking around the inn, her hair shimmering in the sunshine. She's pushy as hell, but I'd be lying if I said she wasn't also hot as hell. But the thing that really got me was the way she looked at the house. She wants to fix it up. She gives a shit, and though I'm not quite sure why, it makes me wanna let her help. It makes me wanna be around her.

And for some reason I can't figure out, I really, *really* don't want her thinking I'm with Amber. I don't want her thinking that I'm with anyone.

And that bothers the hell out of me.

I should be seeing whoever I want to, screwing whoever want to.

Lena will be gone soon anyway. And so will I—thank

God. I don't have time for this. I need to focus on getting the inn ready to sell, and then think about where I want to end up. I just need to keep my mind off the girl with the coal-colored hair that's currently living in my house.

"Where's your friend at?" Berta says as she walks in. Well, there goes that plan.

"Amber?" I ask. Berta shoots a knowing eyebrow up as she puts her purse behind the bar.

"Don't play dumb, boy," she says. I almost smile, careful not to let her see. Berta knows me almost as well as my own mother did. "I mean Lena. Ya know, the cute brunette you're shackin' up with."

This makes me laugh.

"I'm not 'shackin' up' with anyone. You're forgetting that her sister and nephew are staying there, too."

"Well, whatever. Don't think I didn't catch you watching every move Rob made on her all last night."

I feel a tingle as my blood boils a little bit.

"That guy's a prick," I say, pulling a few glasses from the crates and stacking them on the bar.

"Tell me somethin' I haven't known for the last ten years," she says. "But I don't think it mattered if it were Rob or a total stranger. You didn't want anyone lookin' at that girl last night."

I feel my eyes widen as I lean back against the bar. I'm a little embarrassed to be called out on it, and I'm also a little freaked out that Berta might be right.

"Berta, come on. It's not like that. Lena wants to help me fix the place up, in exchange for letting them stick around for a little while," I say, going back to push in some of the unruly chairs from last night.

I feel her eyes tracking me as I move about the room.

"Help you fix it up?" she asks. I nod. "Huh."

"What?"

"Nothin,'" Berta says with a smile.

"Come on now. What?"

"It's just that your sister has been trying to get you to fix that place up for a year now, but you've barely changed a battery much less picked up a hammer," Berta says with a chuckle.

I smile behind the bar. She's right again.

"Yeah, well. I figure it's time. I need to move on. It's time for me to get that place off my hands and get out of here," I say, as casually as my voice will let me. When I stand up from kneeling down to straighten up some more bottles, Berta's standing, arms folded across her chest, rag in hand. "What?"

Her head drops, and she shakes it.

"Nothin,' Jess," she says. "I guess I just...I knew this was your plan for a while, but like I said, you haven't exactly been the most motivated. I was gettin' kinda used to you being around the bar, helping out, seeing ya all the time. It's like a little piece of your mama is still hangin' around this place."

I drop my head, kicking my shoe on the wide wood planks.

"Berta, I ..."

"No, Jess, I'm not trying to make you feel bad. I just...I guess it just hit me. But the truth is, I'm ecstatic for you. Truly. You need a change. You need to find something that gets you goin,' rather than something that holds ya down."

I smile back at her, but I feel a little tug at my heart. If I'm being truthful, there's a part of me that's terrified of leaving Baycrest. The only me I know how to be is the one that's here in this little town. And the only people left in the world that give a shit about me, are right here.

But that can't be a reason to stay. I need to figure out what the hell I'm doing with the rest of my time here on this planet.

"Tell me something, though, Jess," she says. I look up at her. "How is it that they can stick around for so long? What are they leavin' behind up in Boston?"

I look down at my hands, thinking about what Lena told me.

"Something with her sister and the kid's father. I don't know much, but all I know is, they don't want to go back."

"Don't *want* to, or *can't?*" Berta asks. I shrug. She nods her head slowly. "Well, Jess, just be careful. Situations like that are never over easily. I don't want you gettin' mixed up in anything crazy."

"Aw, don't worry about that. I'm keeping my head low. I have my own plans to stick to," I say, waving a hand in her direction.

But the truth is, I want to know more. The fact that I don't know all the details sort of bothers me. Not because I don't trust her, but because I want to know what she's running from. I want to know if I'm strong enough to battle it. But Berta seems appeased by my answer.

"Huh," Berta says, perching a hand on the back of her hip as she looks around the bar.

"What?"

"If you and Lena are going to be workin' around the house, I don't know how much time you'll be able to spend here," she says. My eyebrows raise. I hadn't thought about that. The night shifts should be fine, but I sometimes help out during the lunch rushes, too. That will be hard to work around.

But then I have an idea.

12

LENA

A few hours later, I'm reading in one of the rocking chairs on the front porch. Although I've recently come into a rather large home improvement project—on a home that's not even mine—I can't remember a time in my life where I've been able to relax this much. I've been working since I was twelve—running errands for elderly neighbors, mowing lawns and babysitting until I was sixteen and finally old enough to wait tables. My parents' bills weren't going to pay themselves and I had to step up amid their constant mountainous highs and valley lows.

There's something so peaceful about this place. It's quiet; the inn is the only property on this side of the peninsula. It's warm, and though it's late in the season, it feels like summer will never end. And being here, far away from Boston, tucked away on this shore where Tiger can't find us...washes me in a calm that I've never felt in my entire life.

The only thing that raises my blood pressure is Jesse.

He's the puzzle I'm desperate as hell to put together—and I don't even like puzzles.

He's currently taking a break from housework and

brooding to throw a stick for Coby, and, in turn, for Caleb, and there's something really endearing about it. Caleb doesn't pick up on Jesse's rough, biting side. It's like he knows it's just a front and refuses to acknowledge it. Instead, he treats Jesse like he treats my sister and me. Like one more adult in his life that he can trust. One more adult in his life that he doesn't have to fear. And as much as I hate to admit it, that's just one more attractive quality about Jesse.

Like clockwork, my sister appears just in time to interrupt my hazy staring, flying down the driveway in my car, which desperately needs a wash, by the way. She slams on the brakes and jumps out. I sit up quickly, her urgency preparing me to hear of some sort of catastrophe. But she's got a smile on her face. I push myself up from the chair and run down the steps.

"What's going on?" I ask her. She races toward me, wrapping her arms around my waist, and spinning us in a circle.

"I got a *job!*" she practically screams, spinning us again.

"Hi, Mommy!" Caleb says, running over to greet her. She bends down, scoops him up, then spins him around, too. There's a lot of spinning going on.

"Where?" I ask.

"The Broken Shell!" she cries. My eyebrows shoot up. Jesse moves toward us. Millie, catching sight of him, puts Caleb down, runs to Jesse, and embraces him too. What the heck is going on here?

"So, she had somethin' for ya, huh?" he asks her, awkwardly patting her on the back.

"She did. I'm gonna help her with the lunch shifts to start, and maybe pick up a few of the nights, if we can work out a schedule with Caleb," she says, looking over at me. I nod, giving her a "you know I'd do anything for that kid" kind of look. She smiles back and clasps her hands in front of her. "Ah!" she screams, making Jesse and Caleb jump. "This is so great. I haven't gotten a paycheck of my own in...I can't even remember when. It'll be nice to make my own money. And be able to pay you back for even just a *fraction* of what you've done for us over the years. Mwah!" she says, blowing a kiss in my direction. I can feel Jesse's eyes on me, but I shy away from his gaze.

"Come on, Caleb. We're going for ice cream!"

"Yay!" Caleb cries, running to the car.

"You guys want to come?" Millie asks.

"I'm gonna hang back. You two go celebrate. I'm proud of you, Mill," I say. I can feel Jesse off to the side.

"Yeah, I have a few things I was going to work on today. I have a list now," he says with a half-smile. Millie smiles and nods, skipping back to the car.

We watch as they drive away, and I turn to him.

"So, you put in a good word?" I ask. He shrugs.

"Berta was my mom's best friend. She's getting older, but that bar is the only life left on this shore. She needs the help, and if we're going to get anything done around here, I need to cut back on my shifts," he says. I raise an eyebrow. Shifts? Picking up on my confusion, he went on, "You saw me tending there the other night. That's why I'm there all the time. My mom used to tend bar with Berta some nights when the inn was slower. And now that she's gone, I took over. But Millie needed a job, and I need some time back. So it worked out," he says, shrugging again so that his t-shirt pulls against his muscles. I thought he might have just been helping occasionally, pouring drinks for his friends. I didn't realize he was actually going there to *work*. Not to hook up with Amber. Well, at least not anymore. I look at him, his hair blowing in the breeze. And then I can't help but smile.

"Thank you, Jesse," I say, just above a whisper, refusing to let my eyes leave his. Each time our eyes meet, I feel this crashing sensation, this intense impact that shoots me forward, and then yanks me back. Finally, he breaks the gaze and looks down at his boots.

"So, back to the shutters today?" he asks. I smile again and nod.

"Let's do it."

We're back around the side of the house, working on removing the rusty nails that are barely holding the shutters to the siding. Some of shutters are rusted so badly that they have to be scraped off the side of the house, others are stuck on by paint, and some by dried mud from years and years' worth of bay storms kicking up wettened dirt. It takes longer for us to remove a single shutter than I'd care to admit. But finally, we're into a rhythm. He climbs the ladder to take down the second-story ones, telling me that I've lost ladder privileges, while I work on the bottom level ones. We don't talk a whole lot, but there's something really nice about being out here with him, getting work done, quietly catching glimpses of him in the sunlight.

"Ugh, this one's really stuck on there. I'm gonna have to get the rest of my tools," he says, climbing back down the ladder slowly. I squint and look up at him, feeling a bead of sweat forming right on my brow.

Without thinking, I reach down for the hem of my shirt, lifting it up to expose my bare stomach as I use it to wipe my forehead. When I drop it, I'm surprised to see him staring at me. But not for long. Because the shutter that was "stuck," suddenly comes crashing down from 20 feet above us, landing right on his head.

"Whoa!" he calls out.

"Oh, shit," I say, fighting the urge to laugh. He stumbles a bit, catching himself by placing a hand on the side of the house. When he finally straightens up, I take a step closer, pulling his hand from his head to survey the damage.

"You should let me clean that up," I tell him. He reaches up again, feels the blood, and nods slowly.

"I don't have anything here," he says. I smile.

"We're traveling with a four-year-old boy. We have the necessities, don't worry."

I lead him inside and pull out one of the kitchen chairs, motioning for him to sit down. I run up to our room and grab the first aid kit—which is actually a freezer bag filled with bandages, rubbing alcohol, and peroxide, and head back down to the kitchen.

"Well, at least the shutter came down," I say with a chuckle. He rolls his eyes and leans his head back slightly.

I wash my hands in the sink and make my way over toward him. There's a cut right above his eyebrow. He'll live, but I'd hate the thought of anything scarring this pretty face of his. So it feels like my duty to see that it's at least disinfected.

"Close your eyes," I tell him, taking a few steps closer. I'm standing to his side, and I force myself to get closer. As I move within reach, I'm hit by a wave of his scent again—it's sweet and musty, almost like mahogany. It's intoxicating, and I have to clear my throat to remind myself that this is not a dream.

I take one step closer, and now, we're just inches apart.

"This shouldn't sting, but it will be cold," I tell him, before pouring a capful of peroxide over the cut, and blotting at it with a towel. He squints a bit, then opens up his seaglass eyes, his long lashes batting a few times.

"Close them," I direct him again. But he doesn't listen right away. Instead, he leans back, squinting a bit, but not because of the pain, or the peroxide. It's like he's trying to read me, trying to figure something out. I raise my own eyebrows, taken aback by his, well, beauty. I'm not sure if it's his scent, or the way his eyes are closing in on me, or the fact that he just got my sister a job. But my wires are crossing and all the angst and annoyance I've been feeling toward him has suddenly been replaced by something else. Something that makes me want to step just a little bit closer, stare just a little bit longer. The corners of my lips turn up.

"Close. Them." A flicker of a smile flashes across his face, and he finally obeys.

I take my time with the rag, dabbing and blotting more than I probably need to. But there's something really sweet in caring for him, touching him like this. As I lean in a little closer, I see his Adam's apple bobbing as he swallows, nervously, his hands flat on his knees. Finally, I carefully dry his forehead and place a bandage on. It feels wrong to cover up any portion of his chiseled face, but I know it's necessary. Just as I'm admiring him for one last moment before his eyes open, there's some commotion at the front door.

"Hey, ya'll—" Berta calls, stomping through the house, and coming to an abrupt halt when she sees us. And that's when I realize that I'm standing mere inches from his face, right in between his legs, my hand still on his face. We turn to her, both of us putting a little bit of space between us.

"What's going on here?" Berta asks, putting a few brown bags down on the counter. Berta is a tall woman, and she's not heavy, but she's not skinny, either. She's got a big chest, and a long, blondish grayish braid that's always flipped over one shoulder. She's got some prominent wrinkle lines around her mouth and eyes, but her eyes are kind.

"Shutter fell, clocked me right on the eye," he says, pointing to his battle wound. She nods, her eyes scanning both of us like she's looking for some sort of evidence.

"Uh-*huh*," she says, before a brief pause. Finally, she speaks again, letting the moment pass. "We had a bunch of leftovers this morning, so I figured I'd bring some by." I smile and nod, walking over toward her to put the food away.

"Thank you so much, Berta," I say, "this is so nice of you."

I can feel the two of them giving each other some sort of look, but I'm not sure what conversation they're having in silence.

"So I'm sure you both heard that I've hired a new waitress," she says. I smile at her again.

"Yes, and we can't thank you enough," I say. She rolls her eyes and waves her hand at me.

"It's nothin', I could really use the help, and Jesse here gave a good recommendation," she says, slapping him on the back. "So, since you're gonna be cutting back on your shifts here comin' up, why don't you two come back to the Shell tonight for a little celebration of Jesse's time behind the bar?"

She looks from me, to Jesse, back to me.

"It's been way too long since this boy has had a real, fun night. What do you say?" she asks. I look at Jesse, who's awkwardly looking down at the ground. I smile.

"I'd love to. Really, I can't thank you enough, both of you, for giving her this job," I say. "You don't know what it means for us."

With that, I feel Jesse's eyes on me again.

"Great! We'll see you two kids tonight," Berta says, grabbing her keys out of her pocket and heading for the door.

"You don't have to go back," Jesse says, once Berta is out the front door. I turn to him.

"I want to," I tell him. He swallows.

"Okay," he says back. There's a long, awkward silence before he clears his throat again. "Thanks for, uh, patching me up."

I nod.

"Guess I'm not the only one who needs supervision on the ladder," I say. He smiles as he walks by me. I let out a long breath once I think he's out of the room, but then I hear the old wood floors creak beneath his feet as he turns back around.

"I'm glad you're goin' tonight," he says, his voice quiet. I blink twice, not positive that I heard him say what I think he said.

THAT NIGHT, I'm doing my hair again, and this time I'm spending a little bit more time on my makeup. Millie gave me a top to borrow—a really cute little flowy tank top. It's nicer than anything I brought with me, and makes me feel a little more fancy. She's sitting on the bed in the empty guestroom next to ours that we've slowly but surely turned into our vanity station, watching me wind my hair around the only curling iron we have ever owned.

"So, you think some other guy is gonna bring you home again this time?" Millie teases, clutching a pillow to her chest. I give her a smirk through the mirror as I grab another piece of hair.

"I don't think so. Actually, I think *I* might be the one driving *Jesse* home tonight," I tell her. She gives me a perplexed look. "I think this whole night is supposed to kind of be celebrating him. I told Berta I'd be his DD if needed."

Millie smiles and nods as she continues watching me. And for a second, I feel a wave of guilt washing over me. This is the second time that she's stayed back alone while I've gone out. I know she's a mom, but that doesn't mean she should never have a break.

"Mill, do you want to go tonight?" I ask, really, *really* hoping she says no. Her eyebrows pinch together.

"What?"

"Well, I mean, I've already gone out once, and we've been here for a while. You haven't gotten to go out at all yet. And after everything, you could probably use a night to decompress." She smiles at me, and scoots forward on the bed. She takes my hand in hers, looking down at our intertwined fingers for a minute.

"Lee, you've stopped your life so many times for us. And this is the first time in my whole life that I can remember closing my eyes at night, and not worrying about what real-life nightmare might wake me. And it's because of you. I get to sit here with my favorite little person in the whole world, in this little paradise you found for us, and just watch him sleep. Or read a book if I want to, or stretch myself out on a lounge outside and not worry. I'll get my independent time when I start this job, which I also can't wait for. In a matter of weeks, you've turned our lives around. Go have fun. I'll be here cozying up with this," she says, holding up one of her favorite old romance novels.

I smile back at her, my heart swelling in my chest. All I've ever wanted for the two of them was peace. And for right now, they have it.

. . .

A FEW MINUTES LATER, I'm downstairs on one of the porch rocking chairs, letting the cool evening breeze rustle through my manufactured waves that I so desperately want to look natural. Finally, I see the barn doors slide open, and I perk up.

Jesse is wearing a black button-up shirt with the sleeves rolled to his elbows, and a dark pair of jeans. He's got boots on his feet again, but these ones aren't dirty and scuffed. These must be his goin' out boots, I think, chuckling slightly to myself at the simplicity of men's fashion in a small bayside town. I smile when I see him, knowing he can't make out the expression on my face from so far away in the dark.

"Hey," he says, as he ambles toward the house. "You ready?"

I stand up, and I feel his eyes scouring me.

"Ready," I say, hopping down the steps. He jiggles his keys as I walk toward him, his eyes dropping to the ground, to the keys, and back up to me.

"You...uh...nice shirt," he says, before walking toward the truck. I bite the inside of my cheek to keep from smiling. I *think* Jesse Rowan just tried to compliment me. Before I have time to get there myself, he's on the passenger side. He reaches over and yanks my door open, standing by as he waits for me to climb in. I tilt my head, narrowing my eyes at him.

"Jesse Rowan...a *gentleman?*" I say, grabbing hold of the handle and climbing in. I might have...*might* have stuck my ass out just a tad more than necessary as I pulled myself up to the raised truck cab. I see him roll his eyes playfully as he fights his own smile, then shuts my door and comes around to the driver's side.

Six minutes later, we're illegally double-parking at the

Shell, and I can hear music flowing out of the windows again. Not jukebox music, though, live music. When we get inside, I realize it's Rob's band. He's actually not a bad singer, and I was definitely right in assuming he had a local posse of single women to choose from. They're gathered at the front of the dance floor by the stage, swaying their hips and even singing some of the lyrics to his songs. I recognize some of them from Amber's group, but to my pleasant surprise, blondie herself is nowhere to be seen.

Jesse holds his hand out, motioning for me to head to the bar, and I take the lead. But as we get closer, Berta lays her eyes on us. She scurries to the microphone just as Rob is finishing his song, and snatches it.

"Hey, guys and gals, the man of the hour has finally made it in!" she says, holding a hand out in Jesse's direction. The bar erupts into a loud cheer, and Jesse does that nervous head scratch thing, briefly raising the other hand in the air for a quick wave. I sneak a look at Rob, who seems less-than-pleased that he's no longer in the spotlight, and even less pleased that Jesse is the one who stole it.

"Most of you know that Jesse and his sister suffered a huge loss last year. This world, and this town, will never be the same without Jack and Scarlett, but in our time of need, Jesse stepped up. He's helped me keep this place running for over a year now, putting his own projects to the side. Jess, we wouldn't be here without ya. I know they are proud," Berta says, her bottom lip quivering. "To Jesse!"

"To Jesse!" the bar echoes, and Rob quickly snatches the mic back to pick up where he left off, nodding to me before he starts.

Berta makes her way over to us, patting us both on the back.

"Neither of you is paying tonight. And I had them save

some curly fries for you in the back," she tells Jesse. "I'm glad you're here." The two of them exchange a glance, and I see him reach a hand up to squeeze hers.

Other than with Caleb and Coby, I've almost never seen him show any type of emotion, let alone affection. It appears Jesse Rowan might be turning a new leaf. Or, I realize, maybe this side of him has always been there, he just hasn't shown it.

As the night goes on, Rob and the band finally finish their set with some long-winded, slow, somewhat-pitchy ballad. The crowd has dissipated a bit, and while some of the other locals are talking with Jesse and pouring alcohol down his throat, I can feel Rob's eyes on me from across the room. Then I see him out of the corner of my eye, coming toward me.

The first time, I was a little bit flattered. But this time, I'm just...not interested. There's nothing particularly wrong with Rob, aside from his apparent need to dominate all female attention around him, but I just really don't give a rat's ass about what he has to say tonight. I turn on my barstool, taking a sip of my soda and looking up at the wall, admiring the photos Berta has framed above.

"So, we didn't scare ya off last time, huh?" Rob asks, swiveling around on the stool next to me before throwing his foot up onto the bottom rung of mine.

"Not yet," I say with a polite smile as I take another sip.

"What, just soda tonight? Jess not letting you have any fun?" he asks with a sly smile as he takes a swig of his beer. I shoot him a look.

"*Let* me?" I ask. He's still got that dumb smile on his face.

"Nah, I get it. It's cool of you to let him have his fun. If that's even possible anymore." I raise an eyebrow at him, and he goes on. "Look, it's no secret the guy's not exactly the life of the party. And since his parents died, it got even worse. It's like he...the inn...everything about that place...was just stripped of anything happy."

I look over at Jesse. He's got a pained smile on his face, and I can see how uncomfortable he is being the center of attention. It's true he hasn't been the most accommodating host. It's true that for the first month that we were in Baycrest, I found his personality repulsive and infuriating. But not one day has gone by that I haven't felt happy since I've been here. I felt peace here in Baycrest for the first time in my entire life. At the inn. With Jesse. I take another sip of my soda and turn to Rob.

"I have to disagree with you, there, Rob," I say. Now he raises an eyebrow at me. "It might not be the place everyone here remembers, but I can tell you from personal experience that there's still some happiness left there."

He throws another swig of his beer back before slamming the bottle down on the bar. He nods slowly as he wipes his mouth on his sleeve.

"Yeah, well. If you ever want to get out of the old wood shack while you're here in town, you know where to find me," he says. He stands up slowly, clearly not taking the defeat, and begins to turn, totally unaware that Jesse is standing directly behind him.

"Hey," Jesse says, and Rob freezes in his place. "At least the wood shack offers breakfast." Then, Jesse looks up at me and winks. "Most days."

I smile as Rob's eyes catch mine. I shrug and nod, and he turns on his heel and heads to the other direction of the bar, where he has a better chance of succeeding with someone of the opposite sex.

"So, I'm not usually quick to judge, but that guy's an

asshole," I say. Jesse laughs—like, a real, hearty, out-loud laugh, and it makes my body tingle.

"That didn't take you long to figure out," he says, leaning back against the bar. Someone clicks through the jukebox, and a slow, twangy country song starts playing through the speakers. Couples make their way to the dance floor and sway to the sappy melody, including Rob and one of Amber's friends.

Jesse clears his throat, and I can feel my heartrate accelerating. He inches just the tiniest bit closer to me, and I can feel the heat coming off of his body.

"These people really like their music," I say, surprised at the nervousness in my own voice. He smiles and nods.

"Yeah, they do," he says. Suddenly, I feel my feet scooting me just a smidge closer to him. We're mere centimeters apart now, but I can't take my eyes of the dance floor. I can't look at him, because I don't know what to do next. But out of the corner of my eye, I feel his eyes drop to me.

"Lena," he says, just above a whisper. I turn slowly, looking up into his big, bay-colored eyes. I really, *really* like when he says my name.

"Yeah?"

He pauses, looking down at his hand, dangling off the bar just a pinch from my arm. He sighs.

"I, uh...good work on the inn so far," he says.

I feel my heart sink. I feel his hand retreat just a bit, and I feel myself do the same. But in the same instance, I smile. Because I'm pretty sure that Jesse Rowan wanted to dance with me tonight. We might not have gotten there, but I think we both wanted to.

"Thanks," I answer. "What do you say we go home?"

A slow smile tugs at the corner of his mouth.

"Home," he says with a nod.

He doesn't seem all that intoxicated, but I still offered to drive, and he was more than willing to hand over the keys. I've never driven anything this big before—in fact, growing up in the city, I didn't drive a whole lot in general. This felt new, and powerful, and exciting. When I turn the key, the engine roars to life, and I feel this fire in my soul kick into gear. My eyes widen as I grip the wheel, and I can hear him chuckle.

"Careful, now," he says, laying a hand on the dashboard. "This here is my baby." I smile at him.

"I'll take good care of him," I say. He gives me a look.

"Her. She's Ruby," he says.

"You named her?" I ask, one of my eyebrows pointing straight up. He laughs again.

"Hell yeah, I did. I've spent more time inside Ruby than any other girl," he says. Then his eyes widen, like he's realizing what he just said. He turns away from me slowly and stares out the front window. I erupt into laughter.

"Jesse *Rowan!*" I say with a shriek between giggles. It's hard to see in the dark, but I can tell his cheeks are flushed underneath that perfect stubble.

"Sorry," he mutters. I put my hand on the dashboard next to his.

"Ruby is one lucky girl," I say, raising an eyebrow at him again. His eyes flick to mine and I can see the bobbing of his Adam's apple as he swallows. Then, I hit the gas, and let Ruby fly us back to the inn.

I put her in park, and we both hop down out of our seats. I walk around the front of the truck, and we cross paths, but as I'm fumbling with the keys, I slam into his brick-wall of a chest.

"Ow," I blurt out.

"Oops, sorry," he says, putting his hands on my arms to steady me. I peer up at him in the bright stream of his headlights. Man, he's really nice to look at. He swallows again, his eyes quickly finding his hands, still on my arms.

"Thanks for coming tonight," he says, just above a whisper.

"I'm glad I was invited. I like those people," I say with a smile. "With the exception of Rob."

He smiles down at me, as his hands slowly slide off my arms.

"Well, uh, g'night," he says. I try not to look like I had been wishing that he might give me *something* tonight—even just a peck on the cheek. Or a freakin' *hug*.

I take a step back and wrap my arms around my body. Suddenly, the summer night's air feels a little chilly.

"Yeah, g'night," I say, turning and heading back to the inn.

13

JESSE

I'm up early, my body wired and still standing on end from last night. I wanted to grab her and push her up against my truck so fucking bad. I wanted to let my fingers get lost in her long, dark hair, wrap my fist around it and kiss her longer and harder than anyone has ever kissed her. I wanted to let my body cover hers, hoist her up...damn. It might be time for another cold shower.

I don't know what it is about that girl, but she drives me wild. She gets me all fired up, which is actually not an easy task. She lights something inside of me, and it's hard as hell to smother it.

But I keep reminding myself that I have to. This whole weird living situation, it's not permanent. She'll be gone soon. I'll be gone soon. We'll all be gone, and whatever *this* is, will be gone right along with us.

I guess I could push my chances a bit. I could move in for a quick lay—or two—but I don't want to. Not with her. The thought of screwing her and calling it quits makes my stomach ache in a way I've never felt before.

But it doesn't mean I can't think about it. And it doesn't

mean that we can't have a little bit of fun while we are all still here. As I venture out of the barn, I close my eyes for a brief second and let the warm sun crawl across my face. I breathe in the bay, let the cool morning breeze roll off my skin.

It really is a beautiful place, Baycrest. And while I haven't made it my mission to be the best host, the truth is, I want to share it with her. With them. I want her to get to see why this place was so amazing. Before she leaves. Before *I* leave.

I hear footsteps crunching around on the gravel, and I see her. She's standing in a tight tank and teeny little jean shorts, with one hand on a coffee mug and the other hand on her hip. She's gazing up at the windows we were working on, presumably making another to-do list in that brain of hers. I smile as I watch her surveying our work.

"Hey," I say, my voice a little gruff from the night before. She jumps and I smile.

She turns to face me, and the sunlight flickers off her bright blue eyes. It makes my crotch tingle, but I can't look away. She's kind of entrancing.

"Hey," she says back after a moment.

"Inspecting our work?" I ask, motioning to the house. She nods, looking back up at the siding.

"Today's task is pressure washing," she says, pulling the folded paper out of her back pocket. Her back pocket that I would so like to stick my hand into. "That way we can paint next week. It's supposed to be nice out next week, so hopefully no rain will ruin anything." I nod and smile.

She's a hard worker, it's easy to tell. And just knowing how much shit she knows how to do—she definitely wasn't a princess. She's not afraid to get her hands dirty. But I'm not really feelin' the work today. As much as I like the promise of us working closely, doing physical labor side-by-side, her lifting up that shirt again to wipe her brow...it's too gorgeous a day to spend it working, when we could be out on the water.

"What do you say we take the day off?" I say, motioning to the pressure washer that she's rolled out. She looks down at it, then back up to me, one of her eyebrows tugged up.

"But...we just started a few days ago," she says. I smile. Yeah, definitely not afraid of some hard work. And definitely a Type-A, crossing-things-off-the-list type of girl. Not that I didn't already know that. At first, I thought she was a tight-ass, a pain. Now, though, it's actually a little bit...cute. No, it's *sexy*.

"Yeah, I know. But summer's ending, and it's supposed to be a great day on the water. I was thinkin' we could, uh, take the kid out on the boat maybe?" I jut my thumb behind us to my boat tied up on the dock.

Her eyes widen at my proposal, so I keep talking before any more doubt can seep in.

"I know he can't swim, but we have all kinds of life vests. We could definitely find one that fits him," I tell her, looking down at my feet now. Suddenly, I feel a little panicky that she might reject my offer. She's just staring at me now, her eyebrows raised. I can't tell if it's because she's worried about Caleb, or if she's just plain surprised that I asked. Like I said, I know I haven't been the best host, but I'm trying.

"Oh, wow," she finally says, just above a whisper. "Caleb would absolutely love that. Are you sure?" I smile and nod.

"Let me show you guys my bay," I say, with what feels like, for me anyway, an ultra-friendly smile.

"Yeah... we'd love to go," she answers, and walk-jogs into

the house to wake Caleb and Millie. Within moments, I hear the kid's little feet scurrying out the back door and across the patio.

"We're comin' with you, Jesse!" he calls from shore, waving his little arms like a maniac. I smile and wave back.

"Sounds good, bud," I call back.

The girls finally appear a few minutes later, Millie carrying a bag full of towels, and Lena carrying a small cooler bag that I'm sure she's stocked with snacks and food. As they come down the dock, each holding onto one of Caleb's hands, I can see pure fear on Millie's face.

"I found these two," I say, holding up two small life vests I found below deck. When the inn was running, we used to rent the boat out to guests for a day, so we have supplies for just about anyone's needs.

"Slow down, sweetie, and don't let go of my hand, please," Millie says to Caleb as they get closer to the boat.

"Okay, Mommy," Caleb says, pulling on her hand as hard as he can. I hop back on the boat, then turn around to lift Caleb on board. I stick out my hand for Millie, and then hesitate before I reach for Lena. I'm preparing myself for that jolt I know will run through me the second our skin touches. She takes my hand lightly and steps on. And I was right, it feels like I've been fried. I let my arm guide her down into the boat, lingering just a little longer than necessary before she finally takes a seat next to Millie.

Millie is securing the smaller of the two vests on Caleb, pulling the straps as tightly as possible. I make sure he can't lift the shoulder straps above his ears, and then I hop off to untie the boat from the dock. I climb back on and give the boat a shove off with my foot. I hop over their feet and take my place in the driver's seat, and within moments, we're off to see my bay.

There's something so invigorating in the way the bay air tastes and feels on my face. When I turn my head slightly, I see that Lena's enjoying it, too. She closes her eyes and leans back, soaking in the sun and the whipping breeze. As we make our way to the mouth of the inlet, I look back at the inn. It really is a gem, hidden, and now shrinking each second as we speed further away.

I turn the boat, and we pull out into from the little inlet into the big, wide, open bay.

"Whoa!" Caleb says, practically hopping out of his seat.

"Holy moly," Millie says, "it's gorgeous out here."

"It really is," Lena mutters, looking around, and I can't help but smile. She likes it out here. Dozens of boats are scattered on the landscape around us, and way ahead, we see the lighthouse.

"That's the Thomas Point Shoal Lighthouse," I tell her, following her gaze. She nods.

"It's beautiful," she says.

We ride a few more minutes into another small inlet, with fewer boats. It's calm today, so I turn off the engine off for a few minutes, letting the bay rock us gently.

"Well, guys," I say, leaning back in the seat, "this is my bay."

"It's amazing," Lena says, smiling over at me. I follow her eyes as they trail out across the water, taking it all in. It's a gorgeous day on the water, but I barely notice. I can't look away from her. Finally, I shake it off and pop up to my feet.

"Well, who's up for a swim?" I ask. Millie and Lena turn their heads to me.

"No way," Lena says, "I bet that water is freezing." I give her a devious, knowing smile.

"Naw, it's actually warmer than you'd think," I say

honestly, "These little inlets actually get pretty warm. Are we too chicken to try it out?"

Caleb shakes his head no a million times. I smile. I can always trust the kid to be on my side.

"Please Mommy, please? I wanna get in!" he pleads. But Millie looks stern.

"No baby, I'm sorry. You can't swim," she says. Then she turns to me. "I'm sorry, but he can't swim."

"Well, he's got the life vest on. I'll get in with him, if you want," I suggest quietly, so the kid can't hear me. I notice Lena shifting in her seat, her eyes narrowed in my direction. I look down at her briefly, then reach down and pull my t-shirt up over my head. I yank off my belt and let my jeans drop down so that I'm just wearing the black shorts I had on underneath them. I look at Caleb, then turn around, and leap off of the back of the boat.

As my body sinks below the surface, I feel a small shock. I always forget how exhilarating this water is, no matter how many days I've spent floating around in it. When I finally come up for air, the three of them are at the back of the boat, leaning over it like they were afraid I wasn't going to come back up. I whip my soaking hair out of my face and spray them with it. Caleb laughs with delight while the girls hold their hands up.

"It feels great," I say, waving my arms around and pushing myself up so I'm floating on my back. Lena looks at Millie, who I can tell is still a little worried.

"You could get in with him," Lena suggests to her with an innocent shrug.

Come on, Mill. Let the kid have a little fun.

"Mommy, please?" Caleb asks, his big green eyes pleading. But Millie stays silent for another moment. Caleb turns to Lena. "Aunt Lee, will you get in with me?"

Suddenly, I feel that tingle in my dick again. The thought of seeing her in nothing but that black string bikini I can see tied around her neck...phew, I wish this water was colder.

"Aww, honey, I think Aunt Lee is a little scared to get in," she says. I watch as Caleb's shoulders rise and fall, any ounce of hope he had leaving his little body. I know she's just trying to make her sister happy, but I'm a little disappointed, too.

"Aww, Aunt Lee's scared of the big bad bay, is she?" I call from the water, still floating around. She cocks an eyebrow at me, and I feel another zap. But this one isn't one of sexual energy like the last. Well, not *all* sexual energy. This one is my competitive edge kicking in.

"I'm not scared of it," she says, glaring at me. "I just don't really feel like swimming."

I raise my eyebrows at her.

"You're scared, *Aunt Lee*. Just say you're scared," I say, offering a quick wink that makes her lips part slightly. She's staring at me, blinking slowly every few seconds, like she doesn't recognize me. And I realize it's because I've never been this open with her, this...friendly. But something happened last night, at the bar. And after, in my truck, and while I watched her walk back inside. I want more. I want to be *friendly*. I float closer to the boat, close enough for her to reach me. She raises one eyebrow at me, then slowly bends down over the side of the boat so that her lips are inches from my ear. I lift my eyes from the dip in her cover-up collar back up to her eyes. I swallow.

"I. Am. Not. Scared," she says slowly. I push back up a bit, peering back up at her. I smirk.

"Prove it."

Boom. I can tell the second the words leave my lips, it's a done deal. This girl isn't backing down from a challenge.

She sighs and stands back. She looks to Millie, then to Caleb, and I can see the hope slowly creeping back into his body. She reaches down and pulls off her cover-up, letting it fall beside her onto the floor of the boat. And suddenly, like magnets, my eyes start scanning her, taking in a whole lot more of her than I've seen before, as she stands right in front of me in nothing but that black bikini. She's petite, but she's strong. The lines of her toned abs cutting down the sides of her stomach contract as she takes a step closer to the edge of the boat. Finally, she rocks back on her foot, then launches off the side, landing in a cannonball directly next to me, drowning me with her splash.

After a moment or two, she pops out of the water and looks up at the boat at Caleb, who's clapping wildly. I push some water behind me, moving just inches away from her.

"Nice work," I whisper in her ear, as she splashes along in front of me, and I notice her spine go straight, even in the chilly water. She smiles briefly as she looks down at the water, her treading body bobbing slightly, and I can't help but smile back.

I swim past her and look up at the boat.

"Millie, if you want to toss us each a life vest, we can sit out here and let him jump to us," I tell her. Lena looks up at Millie, her eyes pleading. I don't want to overstep; I know these guys have been through some shit, and it's understandable that Millie is a bit overprotective. But come on, let the kid have a little fun. She taps her foot, contemplating. Finally, I can tell the moment she gives in. She tosses us each out a vest, then takes Caleb's hand.

"Jump right to Jesse, baby, okay?" she says.

"We got him, Mill," Lena reassures her.

"One, two..." Millie starts.

"Three!" Caleb says, leaping off the side of the boat and landing right in my arms. We sink down below the surface for a half-second, and I thrust him to the surface as fast as I can. I know he's fine, but I don't want to make the girls worry any more than they already have to. They've been through enough, based on what I can tell. I loop my arm under Caleb's and push us up to the top. I spin him around so he's facing me, and hold him steady while he wipes his eyes. He takes in a few deep breaths, then his face melts into the widest grin I've seen from him since we met. I watch as Lena and Millie both let out a long sigh of relief, then start clapping and cheering for him wildly, Caleb giggling to no end.

The three of us splash around, Caleb going back and forth between Lena and me in the water for what feels like hours, until the clouds above us start to grow gray and thick.

I look up at them, shielding my eyes from the leftover sun. Growing up on the water, I can recognize a storm from miles away. But today, I haven't been paying close enough attention. Something to do with the adorable kid and the sexy as hell woman I've been splashing around with for the last hour. When I look around us, I notice we're one of the only boats left in the water. Never a good sign.

"We might wanna pack it in," I say, disappointment lurking in my voice. I don't want this day to end, but I need to keep them safe. "Lookin' like a storm."

14

LENA

We help Caleb paddle up to the boat, and Jesse gives him a boost as Millie pulls him out of the water.

I put my hands on either side of the back of the boat to boost myself up, when I feel Jesse's hands gripping me around my waist. I freeze for a second, then decide not to revel in it. I feel his body close to mine, as he lifts me up out of the water. He pulls himself up, then hops down from the side of the boat and plops into the driver's seat again.

I realize after he starts the engine that he didn't bring a towel, so after I blot myself own, I walk over and hand him mine.

"Want to dry off?" I ask him, feeling my nipples stand on end underneath my freezing cold top. He nods and takes the towel, drying off his hair and back before handing it back to me. I wrap the towel around my shoulders as I take a seat at the back of the boat, soaking in the scent of him.

"Thanks," he says, then puts the boat into gear and turns back toward the inn.

As we're getting closer, big, wet drops start to fall.

Finally, we can see the inn, and Jesse is kicking up the speed to get us back to the dock. The water is choppier now, and I see Millie's grasp on Caleb tighten as we rock around, a little less gently than on the way out.

Jesse cuts the engine off as he steers the boat into its slip, and reaches out one of his long arms to grab a line and tie us down. Then he hops onto the dock, just as the skies really open up. We're all scattering about to grab our things, and Jesse's waiting to help us off. I look up to the shore and my eyes grow wide. I take off down the dock.

"What is it, Lee?" Millie calls.

"The shutters! We left them out to dry last night!" I say, running toward the side of the house where the freshly painted shutters are sitting, now streaked from the pouring rain. Jesse and I had spent hours painting them a few days before, after we got them all down. I'm just off the dock when I hear footsteps behind me, and as I bend down to pick up as many as I can carry, I see him out of the corner of my eye, doing the same.

"We can put them in the barn," he says, as he carries five of them under each arm. I'm struggling with just two.

I nod and follow behind him, letting him slide the big doors open. We lean the shutters up against the wall, and let out a sigh of relief. They will have to be touched up, but for the most part, they are still in good shape. As I turn to walk out, the pile slides off the wall, landing on the back of my flip-flop. I stumble, and the ground quickly gets bigger as my face plummets closer and closer to it.

I'm milliseconds away from scraping the hell out of my knees—a sensation I am *quite* familiar with—when he wraps his hands around my biceps, snatching me back up to my feet. He nudges the shutters off to free my shoe, and spins me around.

We're inches from each other now, and I can smell his aftershave, mixed with the leftover baywater. It's making me a little dizzy in this dark, dusty barn.

"You alright?" he asks, raising an eyebrow at me. I blink a few times before I smile.

"Yeah," I say. "Thanks." He smirks.

"You know, I haven't known you long, but one thing I have learned is that you're not
good on your feet," he says. I chuckle and nod.

"It took longer than I would have expected for you to come to that conclusion," I say. He's still smirking, his eyes peering down at me as we savor the last moment of being dry before we head back out into the rain. And suddenly, I feel myself longing to stay inside this dusty old barn. With him. For far longer than it takes for a storm to pass.

His wet hair is falling out of place at the top of his head, and my hand twitches with a desire to push it back and run my fingers through it. But just as I'm contemplating my next move—if there will even be one—we hear a bloodcurdling scream.

Before I can even react, Jesse brushes past me, bolting out of the barn. I'm following close behind when I see Millie running toward the water. And that's when I see Caleb's hands, wailing in choppy waves, a few feet away from the dock.

My heart stops in my chest.

Millie's running as fast as she can, but Jesse surpasses her in moments, hopping onto the dock and diving into the water before she even makes it to the first plank of wood.

"What happened?" I ask Millie, shouting over the rain, as she gasps hysterically, still running toward the end of the dock.

"I let go of his hand for a second to pick up our bag," she

says, her voice quivering, "and he took off. He forgot his toys on the boat and ran back to get them, but he slipped off before I could get to him!"

I take her hand and we stop at the end of the dock, waiting with bated breath. Then Jesse pops up, with a coughing Caleb in his arms. He swims the two of them toward the dock, and pushes Caleb's little body up out of the water to us. Millie and I each take an arm, and I wrap him in a towel as she cradles him.

His eyes are closed, but he's coughing and crying—both good signs.

"Honey, are you okay? Caleb, baby, can you hear me?" Millie's asking, as we sit in the pouring rain. I look back into the water, but Jesse is already pulling himself up onto the dock.

"Caleb?" Millie asks again.

"Mm-hmm," he responds, between coughs, squeezing Millie's hand. "I'm okay, Mommy."

Tears keep falling from her eyes as she rocks him.

"Caleb, baby, you can't run around the water by yourself. Promise me you won't do that again."

"I promise," he whimpers, burrowing his face into her chest.

"Okay. And Mommy promises never to let your hand go, ever again," Millie says. I see the pain in my sister's eyes and it breaks my heart. She works so hard to be a good mom, she always has, despite the chaos that was her relationship with Tiger.

I help Millie stand, and Jesse and I flank either side of her as we walk back down the dock, as if we're afraid they she and Caleb might both fall in again.

When we make it to the end, Millie turns to us.

"Thank you, Jesse. I'm sorry about that," she says. He

holds a hand up. Then she looks to me. "I think I'm going to take him into town to get looked at. Just in case." I nod.

"Do you want me to come?" I ask. She shakes her head.

"We will be alright. I'm just a little paranoid," she says with a sad smile. I touch her arm and nod.

"Call me if you need me," I say.

The rain has slowed some, and we stand in the gravel as they get in the car and pull away. I turn to Jesse.

"Thank you," I say, staring up at him, the seriousness of the situation hitting me suddenly, like a giant wave. My eyes fall to the ground. "That could have been really bad." I feel my heart pound in my chest, and I'm unable to shake the sight of Caleb's little hands flailing about in the water.

I feel Jesse's hand lay on my shoulder.

"I'm sorry about that. I should put a fence up or something," he says. I wave him off.

"No, we just need to be more careful with him."

"Well, maybe I can teach him how to swim over the next few weeks," he says, his palm hot against my cold skin. I look up at him again.

"That would be amazing," I say, just above a whisper. Slowly, his hand slides off my arm as he reaches it up to scratch the back of his head.

"I just want you all to feel...safe here," he says, then his eyes drop to the ground. He steps around me, and heads for the barn. I follow behind him. When we get inside, he immediately walks over to the bar and reaches over the side of it. He opens the minifridge that's tucked back behind it and grabs two cold beers. I smile.

"Secret stash?" I ask. He shrugs and smirks as he hands me one. We sit down at one of the tables, and I turn to him.

"We do," I say. He looks up at me. "We do feel safe here. The safest we've felt in a long, long time." Then a chuckle escapes my lips. "Maybe the safest we've ever felt." I want to stop myself, but I can't. I reach across the table, and let my hand rest on his for a moment. I can feel it twitching beneath mine, but he doesn't move. My heart is beating faster in my chest, and I can feel my breaths quickening. I so badly want to reach across this table and grab that handful of hair I was desperate to touch earlier. I want to pull him onto me, taste the beer on his lips, let his strong arms wrap around me. And as quickly as those thoughts pop into my head, they deflate like a dart to a balloon.

"Well, good. At least until we sell this place," he says. Suddenly, I feel a quick snap back to reality.

Ah, yes. As Mr. Rowan has quickly reminded me, this isn't some permanent vacation. This is coming to an end. And soon. We will be out of here soon enough, and Jesse will be somewhere far, far away. It'll be sad enough to leave this place, but the thought of leaving *him* is doing terrible things for my anxiety right now. I look down at my half-finished bottle and nod. I stand, my hand still on his.

"Yeah, of course. I guess time's almost up," I say. I turn to walk away, but just as I begin to lift my hand, I feel his thumb reach up and stroke it. I turn back to him slowly.

"I'm glad you guys found us. The inn, I mean," he says, his deep voice just above a whisper. There goes my damn heart rate again. It's really unfair. A sad smile spreads over my lips.

"So am I," I say, before turning and walking out of the barn.

More than you know, Mr. Rowan. More than you know.

15

JESSE

The rain has stopped, but clouds still swirl around inside my head. She wanted something from me today in this stupid barn. She wanted me to touch her, hold her, maybe kiss her. She wanted something more, and I wanted it, too. So fucking bad.

But as I was picturing myself pulling her onto that table and ripping the cover-up off of her, tugging on those teeny little bikini straps, I was hit with a bolt of reality.

She's leaving. She's leaving the inn, she's leaving me. And soon. And so am I. I'm leaving, too, no matter how hard it will be. It doesn't matter that I haven't been able to sit down long enough to make a solid plan. I'm leaving. I have to. We will go our separate ways, and she'll forget about the few months she spent on the Chesapeake. She'll forget about me.

And even though I know I could do things to her body that would be *awfully* hard for her to forget, I'm worried I won't be able to forget it, either. That's what scares me the most.

I go outside once the sun starts peeking back out to work on my truck some. I need to change the oil, wax her down. Old Ruby's my main girl. She'll never leave me.

Just as I'm about to pop the hood, I feel my phone ring in my jean pocket.

"Hi, Jo," I say, trying not to let my voice drip with the disappointment and disdain I feel every time my sister's name flashes on my screen. It's not that I don't love my sister. In all honesty, she's the best friend I've ever had. The four of us, the Rowans, we were a tight-knit group. We were the toughest on each other, but also a force to be reckoned with when we worked together, on anything.

When I was fifteen, Hurricane Edna swept through Baycrest. She was a quick-moving storm, one that we weren't fully prepared for. We were supposed to be hosting a wedding that day at the inn, a big one. The wedding party bailed, of course, but the big white tent had already been staked into the ground. Docks were floating down the bay, houses and boats were destroyed. And as the worst was hitting us, my dad took off out the back door. We followed behind and watched as he wrapped himself around one of the poles of the tent, trying desperately to hold the gigantic tent steady, keep it from hitting the house.

Without hesitation, my mom, sister and I took off after him, each grabbing a pole and bearing down. Dad hollered at all of us to get back inside, but I'm sure he knew deep down we weren't going anywhere.

We managed to carry that thing a hundred yards down the shore in seventy mile-per-hour winds, just the four of us. It got destroyed, but it never even came close to the house.

That was the day that we became "The Fource." Dad always said the four of us could do anything together. Until he died, I didn't think he was wrong. But now, with just

Josie and I, things aren't as strong. There is no "Fource," it's just the two of us. And we can't move a tent by ourselves.

"Hey," she says. I can hear her heels clicking across the D.C. pavement as she walks. "I'm getting ready to go into court. But I wanted to check in and see how the renovations are coming along."

I roll my eyes. She can't resist being in control. Just like Mom. And like someone else I know. Someone small and strong, and maybe a little bit broken.

"They're fine. Lena and I have actually gotten a lot done. Got the shutters all painted, although they got caught up in this rain, so we will have to touch those up. Washed all the windows, finished the porch steps and the dock. Gonna work on power washing the house this week, and working on the front and back beds," I tell her.

"Wow," she says, and I can tell it's genuine. She's actually impressed. Or maybe just surprised. "You guys have been workin' hard. Have you been nice to her?"

I smile.

"Yeah. We're fine. She's actually...she's pretty cool," I say, scratching the back of my head as I picture her, in that tiny black bikini, staring down at me in the water.

"Hmm," Josie says, and the daydream quickly evaporates.

"'Hmm' what?" I ask.

"Nothing. I just wasn't expecting this," she says.

"Expecting what?"

"That you'd end up liking her," Josie says, so matter-of-factly that it makes me grind my teeth.

"I don't *like* her. Jesus, what are you, twelve?" I ask, hoping the irritation in my voice will cover up the concern. Concern that she might actually be right.

"Jess, I don't care how many miles apart we are. You

ain't gonna lie to me, kid," Josie says. "I like her, too, ya know." I raise my eyebrows. My sister is not one to play nice with others, particularly other women. Particularly other women who show *any* kind of interest in her little brother. Bringing home girls as a teenager was a nightmare, and it had nothing to do with my parents, and *everything* to do with Josie. Don't even get her started on Amber; Josie's eyes seem to be permanently rolling whenever they are in the same vicinity.

"You do? That's a first," I say. "But I didn't say I liked her. I said she was cool."

"Yeah, well. Your head's been up your ass since mom and dad died," Josie says. Her words straighten my spine. "You can't focus on anything, you're...you're lost, Jess. This is the first time I've heard you so much as *speak* about a girl since they died. I love that. I love that you have some people around. Just...just be careful," she says.

"Be careful of what?" I ask, her words hitting me like a ton of bricks.

"She's leaving soon, Jess. Don't get caught up, okay?" she says. "I can't bear for you to have another heartbreak, when you're there all alone."

I know she's just being a big sister, but her pity makes me ill.

"I'm fine, Josiane," I say, sternness in my voice. I need her to know that no girl, not even Lena, has that kind of power. I need to remind myself of that, too.

"Okay, little brother. Whatever you say. But you know I'm right," she says. "Anyways, before I go, I just wanted to let you know that I might have someone interested in the inn."

"You...you *what?* Jesus, Jo, you couldn't start with that?" I ask.

"Well, I don't always get to chat with you. Had to make sure I covered all the bases. So anyway, this guy here at the firm, his grandfather just passed and left him a *huh-yuge* inheritance. Like, *way* more than mom and dad could have ever dreamt of leaving us. They are looking to invest, and they want to get into hospitality. I told him about the inn, and he's really, really interested. He will be traveling for work over the next few weeks, but I told him the inn would be in top-shape within a month."

"A *month?*" I ask, exasperated. Suddenly I feel the dead weight of panic crushing my chest.

"Well, yeah. Isn't that when your little deal is up, anyway? Aren't they leaving in a month?" she asks.

I stare out of the window of the barn at Lena tossing a frisbee across the lawn, Coby and Caleb both chasing it. She's smiling, laughing, catching the little boy in her arms and smothering him in kisses.

Damn.

One month.

One month left, and then she's gone.

"Yeah, yeah. One month," I say.

"Okay, cool. I'll call you later this week with more details. Gotta go," she says.

"See ya."

I hit "end" and lean up against the window, just watching them play. The way she cares for her sister, the way she looks at Caleb like her own, it eases some of the crushing weight that's parked itself on my windpipe.

Suddenly, she looks up, and our eyes catch. Normally, I'd step back, duck out of sight like she's done each time I've caught her looking out at me. But I don't want to. Not this time. I want her to catch me watching them. Watching her. I want her to know I'm looking. I want her to know that I know just how much time we have left together, how fast it's slipping away. I want her to know that I need to do something about it. I just don't know what.

16

LENA

I woke up this morning with a knot in my belly, and for the life of me, I couldn't figure out why. It wasn't until breakfast, when I caught a glimpse of the *Baycrest Journal* on the counter, the date on its corner staring me straight in the face, that I realized why.

One month. Jesse and I have one month left of these renovations, these little projects, this dependable time together. And then he leaves, we leave, and I have to figure out a whole new life for the three of us—a life without him.

I haven't turned on my phone in over a month, either, and I have to say, it's been pretty freeing. To be totally closed off from Boston, from the nightmare of a life that made us, and the nightmare of a life that we landed in there. In the short time I've been here, I've become a little more carefree; a lighter version of myself than I've ever been.

As I stare down at the adorable little hometown paper, reading about the Millers' fruit stand, I hear the clanking of metal outside. I lean toward the window and lay my eyes on him. He's carrying three cans of paint in one hand, and a few paint brushes and rollers in the other, as he treks from the barn to the side of the house. When he sets them down, our eyes meet through the window, and I can't stop my lips from responding in with a slow, sweet smile. Seeing him first thing in the morning is better than a cup of coffee, or two. Those bay-colored eyes, that hair shining in the earliest rays of the day. I can't look away. And to my surprise, he's smiling back, nodding his head good morning. I throw back the last sip of coffee in my mug and head out the parlor door toward him.

"Paint day," I say. He nods.

"Paint day."

We each dump a gallon of paint into a fresh tray and start rolling. We paint in silence for a while, him up high on the ladder, and me, of course, down low on the ground where I'm safe. I smile at how simple it all is, the two of us, out here painting away in the early morning light, the breeze keeping us cool, and my thoughts of him warming me from the inside out. Every chance I get, I steal a peek at him, the muscles and veins in his arms protruding with every wide stroke he makes.

"You gonna get any painting done," he says, "or ya just gonna keep lookin' up here?"

I feel the heat rush to my cheeks, knowing instantly that they're pink. Caught me.

"I can't help it. Your stroke is all wrong," I say, trying to salvage my dignity by sounding as nonchalant as possible in my teasing. He glances down at me, then slowly climbs down the ladder, never taking his eyes of me. I swallow and turn back to the house. I'm not fazed. Nope. Not one little bit.

He dips his roller down into the tray, rolling it back and forth, back and forth, and I can see out of the corner of my eyes that his are still on me.

Before I know it, he's taken two giant steps toward me, holding the dripping roller dangerously close to my head. He reaches down with his free hand and grabs my wrist, spinning me around so that my back is now against the house, inches from the wet paint.

"Hey!" I say, becoming exceedingly aware of how close our bodies are. He's pinned one arm above my head, and is holding the roller above me.

"What was that you were saying about my stroke?" he asks. He tauntingly inches the roller closer and closer to me until it's nearly touching my face. I burst into uncontrollable laughter as a smile spreads across his round lips and he drops the roller to his side.

"I was saying," I go on, pushing myself off the house and very much into his personal space, "that your stroke is all wrong."

He draws in a long breath and takes one step closer to me, our chests inches from each other.

"What do you know about my stroke?" he asks, his voice low, and a little less playful. I swallow and feel my eyebrows jump involuntarily.

"Apparently not enough," I say, my voice just above a whisper. Now his eyebrows jump as he slowly lowers the roller to the ground. He steps closer, and I can feel his heart beating in his chest. It's beating almost as fast as mine. I can feel something big. Something big's about to happen between us, and my stomach is swirling with beautiful anticipation. He's gazing down at me, and just as the air between us is getting warmer, we hear the front door slam open against the house.

"Aunt Lee, wanna play frisbee?" Caleb's calling, hopping down the front porch and making his way around the side of the house.

My heart drops to the ground as Jesse takes three giant steps back from me, bending back down to reload his roller once more. I let out a long sigh, the steamy, altogether inappropriate vision I just had in my head totally dissolving into the wind.

"Hey, bud," I say. "Good morning. Jesse and I have some work on the house today, but I'll come around the front and play with you in a little bit. Sound good?" I ask.

"Coby could use some exercise," Jesse says. "Wanna play with him instead?"

Caleb nods his head wildly as Jesse whistles. Coby appears instantly from the back of the house, panting and bouncing wildly, just like I had been moments away from doing just seconds ago. The two disappear as they run back to the front of the house, and Jesse and I exchange a look before getting back to our painting. It seems the moment has gone.

After another hour or so, when we've almost finished this side of the house, and I stand back to look at our work. Once we've put the shutters back up, this side will be just about in selling shape. And I'm damn proud of it. We've been working our asses off these past few weeks, and it's finally starting to show.

"Wow," Jesse says when he's back on the ground. "We're kickin' ass." I smile.

"We are," I say, leaning on my hip to gaze up at the house. It really is beautiful. On top of the sheer size of the inn, the view, the land around it, everything about it exudes charm. My heart aches for its earlier days, the days when it hosted weddings, harbored honeymooners, and opened its doors for all the others just looking for a little bit of solitude. Like us.

I turn to Jesse slowly.

"How much work do you think the barn needs?" I ask. He raises an eyebrow at me.

"The barn? I mean, not much. It's just a barn. Why?"

"Well, I was thinking it might be nice to spruce up the inside of the house a bit," I say. "But I know we need some...uh...funds before we take on any more projects."

He just stares at me quizzically.

"What do you think about having some sort of...event? Some sort of fundraiser, right here, in the barn?"

He still doesn't say anything, just reaches back to scratch his head.

"I was thinking like a concert, or a dance of some sort. Maybe we charge admission, see how it goes? We don't have much to lose, and if we make enough, we could give this place the full facelift it really needs."

I see the wheels turning in his head, but there's still doubt in his eyes.

"A dance?" he asks. I nod.

"We could have some food, drinks, maybe find a local band—" I say, but stop myself. His eyes dart to mine. "Not Rob's," I quickly add. He nods slowly.

"I...I dunno," he finally answers, glancing over at the barn. "I don't know if people would come."

I take a few steps closer to him.

"Jesse, I've seen the way the people in this town love you and your family. People would come."

I can tell he's taking the bait. I can tell he's intrigued, but he's afraid.

"I'll plan the whole thing. I really think this could be fun," I reassure him.

"Let me think about it," he says, his eyes trailing back over to the house. I nod. That'll do for now. We stand in silence for a few minutes, surveying all the work we've put into the inn. Then I turn to him again slowly.

"Ever think about getting this place up and running again? You know, instead of selling it?" I ask him. His eyes drop to the ground, but he doesn't turn to me.

"Nope," he says, kneeling down to pick up a can of paint, and heading toward the back of the house.

"Why not?"

"'Cause I don't want to," he says, matter-of-factly. I know he's done with this conversation. We've been here before. But I'm not finished.

"I just think we're doing so much. It's looking so good. I think this place could really—"

"It's not gonna happen. The Rowan Inn is closed for good," he says, dropping the can to the ground with more force than necessary. He pries it open and dumps some into the tray, then starts painting the backside of the house with angry, pressured strokes.

"But—"

"I said no!" he cuts me off, louder than I was expecting. So loud it actually makes me jump. We stand in silence for a moment, my chest heaving.

I give us each a minute to recoup before I step directly into his line of sight, forcing him to stop angry painting.

"Just because you're afraid of letting this place crash and burn ...again...doesn't mean you have to be a complete ass to someone who's trying to help you," I say, crossing my arms over my chest.

"Trying to help *me?*" he asks. "You're joking, right?" I raise an eyebrow at him.

"No. I'm not joking. It's not my name on that sign out there, it's yours," I say. He scoffs.

"Please. You're just trying to figure out where you'll live

after this place sells. You'll do anything to keep it from going on the market," he says. I feel a pound to my chest. He's not 100% wrong. But he's 100% a dick.

"I'm not the only one afraid of this place selling," I push back, my voice getting louder. "You have no fucking idea what you're going to do with yourself when this place goes, and you know it. You have no idea how to live a life that hasn't been designed for you by your parents!" His eyes trail across the ground, then up to me slowly. I realize that I've stepped closer to him so that our chests are inches apart, once again. Only this time, the air between us is thick and cold. He's glaring down at me, his chest moving up and down with such ferocity, I think for a moment it might actually explode.

"You have *no* idea what the fuck you're talking about," he says, his voice loud and gruff. "Did you ever think that maybe I *have* tried? And that it didn't work? You don't know anything about me, or my family, *or* this inn. Leave it alone.
"

I can't remember the last time I've been so mad. And also a little bit ashamed, because he did sort of put me in my place. But mostly, so fucking pissed off. The heat in my body is rising to the surface, and I think I actually see a shimmer of fear in his eyes as he notices the physical effects my anger is having on my body. But just as I'm about to lose it, to fully go for it, to bite his fucking head off, we hear a soft cry.

Our heads whip toward the front of the house, where Caleb is peeking out from the side. Tears are streaming down his face, his knuckles white from clenching the side of the house so hard.

"Please just don't hurt her, okay, Jesse?" he whimpers, his voice broken and shaky. My heart shatters completely in my chest, my face dropping when I see him. I flick my eyes to Jesse for a moment, in total shame, then run to Caleb. I wipe his tears and hold him close to me.

"Oh, baby, no," I whisper to him. "We were just talking, okay? No one is hurting anybody else."

Not physically, anyway.

I take his hand and usher him back around to the front of the house, never once looking back.

17

JESSE

I drop all the painting shit and stomp back to the barn. I slam the doors behind me and begin pacing.

I feel like a fucking monster.

I mean, what I said *was* partially true. She didn't know my family, she doesn't know much about how this place was run. But there's one thing I said that wasn't true—that she doesn't know me.

She *does* know me. She's been around a while now, but even early on I realized she's also one of those people that just always digs down deep until she understands another person. And she's done that with me. She wants to know so much. I just haven't let her. And despite that, she figured out a lot more than I wanted her to.

But the kid.

He was terrified of *me*. I knew their situation was rocky, but I had no idea how bad. To see him cowering, crying, practically breaking a sweat in fear that his aunt was going to be hurt. By *me*. I feel sick to my stomach. I'm still angry. But I'm also really, really fucking sad. I'd never lay a hand on a woman—in fact, it takes a lot for me to lay a hand on another dude.

I'd *never* hurt a woman. Especially not her.

I storm back out of the barn and get in my truck, speeding off in the direction of the Shell.

I barely put Ruby in park before I hop out, stomping into the bar like some sort of animal. Berta looks up at me as she's drying glasses, her eyebrows knit together. She can smell my bad moods from a mile in a way.

"What's got your boxers in a bunch?" she asks. I don't answer her, I just kick one of the barstools out before slamming myself down onto it.

"I need a beer," I grumble. She puts the glass down and perches a hand on her hip.

"First of all," she says, "I don't know who you think you're talking to, but you know damn well you ain't gettin' nothin' from me askin' that way." I feel my face unscrew as I become more aware of my childish behavior. I let out a long sigh. "Second of all," she says, "start talking."

I let out another sigh before I flick my eyes up to her. I don't have to apologize to her, even though I should. She knows I'm saying sorry without actually saying it.

"Can I please have a beer?" I ask. She smiles before popping the top off a bottle and sliding it down to me.

"Lena and me, we were arguing outside," I start to say, after a long, drawn-out swig of my beer. Berta hasn't taken her hand off her hip. She's just staring at me. I go on. "Just about the inn and—"

"What about it?"

"She started saying something about a fundraiser. She wants to have this dance thing at the barn to raise a little more money for renos," I say. Berta's eyebrows shoot up and she nods in approval. "But then she started on about how she really thinks the inn could make a comeback."

Berta's eyebrows stay risen.

"She's right," she says. I feel that anger swirling in my belly again. Only, it's not really anger. It's actually fear and anxiety.

"Berta, please...you know I can't do this on my own. And that's beside the point."

"Well, maybe doing it on your own would be tough. But that girl seems like she'd make a good teammate."

Now I have my eyebrows raised.

"Berta, come on."

"Okay, okay, alright. I'm just saying, she's not all the way wrong. But continue."

"Well, anyway, we were sort of in the heat of it. We were raising our voices, and the kid heard us."

She nods slowly.

"Berta, he started crying. He thought I was gonna hurt her."

When I say the words out loud, it hits my gut even harder. The thought that someone, especially a kid, could ever think that of me, be scared of me, is still making me sick. I start bouncing my knee nervously.

Berta drops her towel on the bar and takes a seat on the counter.

"Damn," she says. "The kid's dad?"

I nod.

"I don't know the whole story. But I know that for him to be that scared of me, it had to be bad."

Berta whistles, her eyes floating up to the ceiling.

"That shit is tough, Jess. I won't lie. That kid might have issues with that kind of stuff for a while. But the good news is he's still young. It's a cycle that *can* be broken. Especially," she says, reaching out a hand to my shoulder, "if he's around the right examples. Men who show him how to treat women. How to treat people in general."

I nod slowly, swirling my bottle around.

"I don't even know what to say to him," I say. "He was so scared." Berta pauses for a moment.

"What would your dad say?" she asks. My eyes jump to hers. If she only knew how many different times I've asked myself that over the past year. I nod slowly and finish the last sip of my beer.

"One more thing," Berta adds before I turn to leave. "It's important to talk to the kid. But you might also want to make sure he's not the only one listening when you do. Those girls probably need to hear what you're gonna say almost as much as he does." I nod again, my heart wrenching in my chest.

"Thanks, Berta." She nods back.

Six minutes later, I pull Ruby back into the driveway slowly.

When I get inside the house, it's quiet. They're not in the parlor, not in the kitchen, not in the living room. I think to check upstairs, and as I start to climb the steps, I hear whimpering coming from their room. My heart sinks again, but I know I need to be strong. For him, for her. I lift my hand slowly, take in a breath, then rap my knuckles against their door three times. The room grows silent, then the door opens slowly and I let my long-held breath out. Millie stares back at me. Behind her, Lena sits on the bed, Caleb between her legs holding a book.

"Hi," I say, keeping my voice as low and gentle as possible.

"Hi," Millie says.

"Look, uh, can I talk to Caleb for a minute?" I ask. She

swallows, looking back to Caleb and Lena. "You can come with us. I just want to explain some things."

Millie looks back to Caleb one more time, then reluctantly nods her head.

"Come on, Cay," she says, holding her hand out. He looks up to Lena, then slowly climbs down off the bed, reaching for his mom's hand and clutching it tightly. Lena hasn't taken her eyes off of me, but I can't bear to look back at her. Not yet.

I lead them downstairs and out back. When we reach the patio, I look down to Caleb.

"Caleb, can I talk to you, man-to-man?" I ask him, reaching out a hand. He looks up at me, then to Millie. She nods at him, and he slowly lets go of her hand to take mine. As we're walking down toward the water, I can hear the back door open and shut again, and I know Lena is watching, too. But this, right now, is about Caleb.

We've walked a few yards when I hear Berta's words ringing in my ear.

Those girls probably need to hear what you're gonna say almost as much as he does.

I stop walking and sit down on the grass, motioning to him to sit down next to me. He does, all the while, looking back to his mother every few moments.

"So," I say, embarrassingly nervous for someone who's talking to a child, "I scared you today, huh?"

Caleb looks up at me, his big blue eyes wide. He looks just like his mom, but he has his aunt's eyes. He nods slowly.

"You saw your dad hurt your mom a lot, huh bud?" I ask. He looks down at the grass, and nods again, slowly.

"Well, I need you to understand something," I say. He's staring right up at me. "No matter how angry I get,

I would never, *ever* hurt your Aunt Lee. Or your mom. Or any lady. Or any*body*," I clarify. He nods slowly, wrapping his little arms around himself. "See, bud, we don't hurt women—especially the women we love, like our moms and aunts. No matter how mad or sad we get."

I can hear sniffling, and I look up to the patio to see Millie wiping her eyes. Lena's a few feet behind her, her arms wrapped around herself just like Caleb's. She's staring down at me, her eyes narrowed. I look back to Caleb and keep going.

"I'm sorry I scared you," I tell him.

"It's okay," he says.

"Sometimes, we get angry. And that's okay," I say. "It's alright to feel mad sometimes. And sometimes we say things we don't mean." I look back to Lena now. "When that happens, we should say sorry."

She takes in a long breath, her eyes drilling holes right through to my soul.

"It's okay to feel a certain way. But it's never okay to hurt someone. Does that make sense?" I ask him. He nods again. "If I ever make you feel scared or sad again, I want you to tell me. That's what friends do. Deal?" I ask, holding out a fist. A meek smile appears on his mouth, and he fist-bumps me.

"Deal," he says.

"Frisbee?" I ask.

He hops to his feet.

"Frisbee!"

Millie makes her way down to me, wrapping me in a long, tight hug.

"Thank you," she whispers.

I wrap my arms around her, but I'm staring up at the

patio. Lena has disappeared back into the house, and every part of me is aching to follow her.

LATER THAT NIGHT, I'm lying in my bed in nothing but an old pair of worn basketball shorts, tossing one of Caleb's nerf balls up into the air. I can't stop picturing her on that patio, wondering if she believed the words I was saying. Because damn, I've never meant something more in my life.

I toss the ball up one more time, and then I hear the barn doors opening below. I hop to my feet and open the bedroom door, when I see Lena walking toward the bottom of the steps. She's carrying a plate full of cookies, and her eyes are carrying something heavy in them. I step down the stairs slowly, our eyes never leaving each other's.

When I get to the last step, she hands me the plate. Her gaze drops to the ground, and I'm frantically searching for the right words. Finally, she speaks.

"I need to say something."

"Okay," I say, feeling my heartrate pick up. She takes in a long, slow breath and closes her eyes for a moment.

"My dad was like Caleb's dad. Only, he didn't stop with my mom. He hit us, too."

I swallow.

"It was bad. She was constantly beaten and bruised, and we weren't much better off. We actually got taken away by CPS a few times, but it never stuck," she goes on. I feel my heart thudding behind my ribs. "He killed her."

My eyes grow wide, and I'm not sure I heard her right.

"What?" I ask. She nods.

"When Millie was 19, and I was 16. They were fighting at the top of the stairs, when he grabbed her and threw her down. Broke her neck. She was dead almost instantly."

I don't have any words. I don't know what to say, and she can tell.

"It was a nightmare, losing the only parent who loved us. But in the end, he went to prison where he will spend the rest of his miserable life. It was tough, but we took care of each other. For a little while, I thought we were going to come out of all of it stronger. Until Millie met Tiger. And the cycle started all over again," she says.

She looks down at the ground, wrapping her arms around her body.

"One of the scariest thoughts for me, aside from Tiger eventually killing my sister, is that one day, Caleb might grow up to be that kind of a monster to someone. No man in his life has ever done what you did today. I don't...I don't know what to—"

Her lip is quivering now, and my body reacts. I set the plate down on the step next to me and reach out, pulling her into me. She wraps her arms around me, burying her face into my chest. She's silent, but her shoulders are shuddering with quiet sobs. I rest my chin on the top of her head, and let my fingers slide through her long black hair. After she calms down a bit, I reach my finger down and tilt her chin up.

"I need you to know that I meant every word I said to him today," I say, just above a whisper. A sad smile sweeps over her lips, her eyes still glossy from the tears.

"I know you did. And I need *you* to know that I wasn't afraid of you today. I knew you could never be that kind of man. I never thought that for a minute. He's just a kid, and he's seen a lot," she says, and I feel this wave of relief crash into me. I nod again before I realize that our arms are still around each other. At the same time, she realizes it too, because she quickly unlinks hers from around my waist and takes a few steps back.

"I'm gonna go make sure he's sleeping," she says, turning toward the doors. At the very sight of her walking away from me, I feel this inexplicable rush of sadness. But just as she reaches the doors, she pauses and turns back.

"Thank you, Jesse. In a weird, roundabout way, that was the nicest thing anyone has ever done for us."

I nod in return, watching her take the last few steps out of the barn. As she closes the doors, I look down the see the last of her tears rolling down my bare chest. I press my hand to them, that hollow sadness forming a huge pit in my stomach again.

I would rather die than hurt her, or even let her *think* that I could.

And I'm pretty sure I'd kill anyone else who tried to.

18

LENA

I barely slept a wink last night, and I don't think my sister did, either. The talk Jesse had with Caleb could be life-changing for him, but the more I thought about it, the more I realized that it was probably life-changing for Millie and me, too.

I've never been in a serious relationship, because I refuse to become my mother, or sister. I know it sounds silly, but I've seen it happen where a woman is certain it would never be her—that she'd never put up with it, that she'd leave if it ever happened.

But then I've seen a man take away all of her lifelines. I've seen a man force her to be totally dependent on him for survival. I've seen her feel there is no other option but to accept the sick brand of "love" he's offering, fists and all.

And I know that if it happened to them, it could happen to me. So it's easier if I just avoid the situation as a whole. I don't trust easily, and I keep my circle small.

But these few months, and those words I heard Jesse say today, they earned him a spot in my circle.

It may have been Caleb's first talk with a man who

wasn't physically abusive. But it was also one of the first for Millie and me, too.

Telling him about my parents wasn't easy by any means —it never is. But it felt effortless compared with any of the other times I've had to tell it. Because he wasn't expecting anything from me, he wasn't staring back at me with pity. He was listening, taking it all in, letting me know just by the expression on his face that he heard me, and that my mother's love, her life, and ours, weren't in vain.

As if listening so intently and saying all the right things weren't sexy enough, he stood there in those shorts, his broad chest exposed, holding in it all the warmth I didn't know I needed as I clung to him.

And damn, did he look good.

It was an intimate moment for innocent reasons, but still I couldn't help but fight off this intense urge to run my fingers up and down his back, tug his hair, run my fingertips over his soft, round lips. I wanted more last night, and that seems to be a theme whenever I spend any time with him. And as the time we have left grows shorter, my need to touch him, to let him touch me, grows stronger. Not a great correlation.

I don't know exactly what I wanted from him, but all I know is, I can't wait to get out of bed and see him today. Millie and Caleb are snuggled up next to me, and I slip out of again hoping to steal some more one-on-one time with Jesse this morning. But just as I'm approaching the last step, I hear the familiar sing-song sound of Josie's voice.

I'm hit with this simultaneous wave of excitement and disappointment. I like Josie, but her presence means I'll get no alone time with Jesse. When I enter the kitchen, she's sitting across the table from Jesse, sipping a cup of coffee and talking. She really is stunning. Her long, sandy hair is curled, and though she's not in her normal attorney attire, she just has that dignified look of someone who does important shit every single day.

"Ah, morning!" she says when she sees me in the doorway. Jesse looks up at me, a sad smile forming over his lips as he nods in my direction.

"Coffee?" he asks me, standing up to get me a mug. I nod back and take a seat.

"Thank you," I say. "Hey, Josie. You must have left D.C. early to get here at this hour." She smiles.

"Yeah, well, first you don't sleep in law school. Then you don't sleep when you become a lawyer. Your body adapts, and soon you can survive off just a few minutes a night!"

I laugh and reach up to take the mug from Jesse.

"Thank you," I say again, nodding in his direction.

"So, I just cannot get over how much work the two of you have done to this place," Josie says smiling at me. "I mean, Jesus, where have you *been* all our lives?"

Jesse's eyes flick to me at her question, like he wants me to answer it. Like he wants to know why it took me so long to find the inn. And him.

"Well Jesse has been a great reno partner," I say shyly, looking down at the coffee in my cup. I feel Josie's eyes bounce from me, to Jesse, back to me. She doesn't make a comment, she doesn't ask anything. But I can tell she's curious. She's picking up on something. She's bright.

"Did Jesse tell you that we have a potential buyer?" she asks, taking a small, delicate bite of the muffin on her plate. My eyes find his.

"No, I don't think he mentioned that," I say, still looking at him. *How long has he known this?*

"I, uh, meant to mention it yesterday, but we were a bit

busy," he says, nervously scratching the back of his head. I nod slowly. *Ah, yes. Yesterday.*

"Well, that's great. Someone you know?"

"Yeah, a friend of a friend at the firm. He's really interested, and wants to come out in a few weeks to look at it."

I nod, taking a long sip from my mug. I feel knots forming in my stomach, even though that's ridiculous. I shouldn't be this invested in the inn, or Jesse, or anything Rowan. I can't be.

"There's a few more things I'd like to work on," Jesse says quietly, his eyes finding me again from across the table. "If you're up for a few more projects." I nod.

"Anytime," I say.

"We're just running low on reno funds," Jesse adds. Then he turns to Josie. "Lena has this idea for a dance."

Josie turns to me, her eyebrows pulled together skeptically.

"A dance?"

My eyebrows raise as I look at Jesse. I can't tell if he's pitching it for her approval, pitching it for her resistance, or pitching it because he actually likes the idea and believes in it.

"Uh, yeah. I was just thinking, it might be good to make a few updates to the interior, and maybe the barn. But I know Jesse doesn't really want to use his inheritance if he doesn't have to, so I thought we could turn this barn dance thing into a fundraiser."

Josie looks from me to Jesse, then back to her muffin. She starts nodding slowly, then leans back in her chair.

"Tell me more," she says.

"Well," I say, clearing my throat, "I thought maybe we could find a local band—" with this, her eyes find mine, and I make the same quick addition that I made with Jesse. "Not

Rob's." She nods in relief. "And I thought maybe we could have some light food, some drinks, and just invite people to come have a good time. We could charge a small cover and after we pay the band, we can bank the rest for the renovations."

I look up to Jesse slowly.

"Plus," I add, "if this seller really does come through, this could be sort of the last hurrah at the Rowan Inn."

Jesse's eyes narrow at me, then he slowly looks to Josie and waits. She nods again, then a huge smile spreads across her lips.

"I love it. I think it could be a great turnout," she says with an excited chuckle. "Seriously, where have you *been?* God, if I knew all it would take to light the fire under my brother's ass was some tough chick from Boston, I would have found you years ago!"

She reaches out and squeezes my hand, and I force a smile. But really, I'm wishing that I had found this place all those years ago. I wish I found *him* all those years ago.

"What do you think, Jess?" Josie asks.

His eyes are still narrowed at me, but a slow smile finally tugs at the corner of his mouth.

"Why the hell not?" he asks with a shrug, and I can't help but smile back at him.

"Yay!" Josie says, clapping her hands and jumping to her feet. "I'm gonna run into town for a few things. But later, we can all sit down and go over some plans. This is going to be great!"

We both smile as Josie leaves, and then I finally break our staring contest to take my mug to the sink. As I'm scrubbing it, I can feel him behind me.

"You doin' okay today?" he asks, leaning against the counter. I turn off the water and look to him.

"Yeah, I am," I answer with a quick smile. "I really am." He smiles back and nods.

"Good. Josie's excited about the dance," he says. I look up at him.

"But you're not?" I ask. He sighs and crosses his arms over his chest.

"I am, I guess. I just don't know if I'm..." he pauses, his voice trailing off.

"If you're what?" I ask. He looks down at me.

"I don't know if I'm ready for this place to take another hit. Another failure."

My heart feels heavy. I feel the weight of his fear on mine. I slowly reach out a hand, letting it stroke his for a moment.

"It's not going to fail," I say. Then I take a step closer to him, so our faces are inches apart. "*You're* not going to fail."

I look right into his eyes when I say it, making sure he feels how much I mean it. There's a long moment of silence between us, then he smiles.

"Wanna get some breakfast?" he asks. The question actually knocks me back an inch or two. I give him a suspecting smile.

"We just had breakfast," I say, pointing to the table.

"Well, technically, you just had coffee," he says.

"True. And I am pretty hungry," I say, letting him lead the way to his truck.

Even if I wasn't, I'm pretty sure I'd say yes to doing just about anything with him. He smiles as we hop into Ruby.

After a few minutes, we pull into the lot of Daisy's Diner, a small place I've noticed a couple of times since we've been in town. It's essentially a double-wide trailer with a red aluminum roof, but it's totally adorable. When we get inside, the waitress behind the counter nods in our direction as Jesse gives her his most winning smile.

"Mornin,' Mr. Rowan," she says. "New friend?"

Jesse nods, and I feel my body tense as he places his hand on the small of my back, urging me forward, closer to him. I look up to him, unsure if it's getting warmer in here, or if it's just the heat created by our bodies touching. It's the smallest, simplest gesture, yet, from him, it feels massive. Like he's laying claim, letting others know that I'm with him, and at the same time, letting me know he's with me. I'm not sure what it was, but something happened in that barn between us last night. He felt my tears, saw me crumbling. But somehow, today, I feel stronger in front of him.

"This is Lena," he says, "she's staying at the inn, helping me through some renovations."

The woman nods slowly, grabbing a few menus from the hostess stand and heading our way.

"Lena, this is Edith. She was another good friend of my mother's," he says. I nod and smile.

"Hi, Edith," I say.

"Hello, dear," she says, leading us to a small booth at the far side of the restaurant. "What kind of renovations we talkin'?"

"Ah, just about everything. We're updating the exterior, painting, reshuttering, fixing up the inside, fixing up the barn. Lena has an idea for just about every inch of that place. Helpin' me get it into selling shape," he says, his eyes finding mine as we take a seat. I give a curt smile and nod. I'm not sure how he wants me to respond to that. Edith puts a hand on her hip and lets out a slow sigh.

Actually, that's the exact response I wanted to have.

"Damn. I was really hoping Lena here was helping you fix it up so that you'd stay," she says.

Jesse's eyes drop to his menu as he flips it from front to back, clearly not reading a damn thing on it.

"You know that's not happening, Edith," he says. "I need to get out of this place." His voice is hushed, and he isn't making eye contact with either of us as he talks.

I want to press him on the issue, Lord knows, but I can tell that right now, he needs me not to. In fact, he might actually need some backup. I clear my throat and turn to Edith.

"Actually, Jesse and I are throwing a bit of a fundraiser in a few weeks over at the inn," I say. Edith raises an eyebrow. "It's going to be a barn dance; live music, some food and drinks, hopefully just a laid-back good time. We're hoping to raise a little bit of money for the last of the indoor updates we want to make."

"Wow," Edith says, pursing her lips out in surprise.

"Would you mind hanging up a few flyers in here, if I drop some off later this week?" I ask. She nods.

"Absolutely," she says. She sighs again and turns to Jesse. "I know your parents would be so sad to see that place go." She reaches out a hand to Jesse's cheek. "But I know more than anything, they'd just want you to be happy, Jess. It's what we all want. This whole dang town."

He nods and lets a nervous smile flash over his lips before turning his menu. Again. Finally, Edith walks away.

"Jeesh," I say. "People really love that place, and your family. Talk about pressure." He lets out a low laugh and smiles.

"You got no idea," he says. I smile back at him.

"What's good here?"

He scoffs.

"Anything. Everything," he says. "But the cream

chipped beef is the best on the bay. Probably on the whole shore." I smile.

"Cream chipped beef it is," I say.

We eat mostly in silence, but it doesn't feel strained. It feels almost content. And I realize how much I enjoy being near him, even if not so much as a syllable is spoken between us.

As we get ready to go, Jesse pays the bill before I can even reach for my wallet—something I'm not sure how to respond to—and we walk back to his truck.

"Mind if we make one more stop?" he asks.

"Sure."

A few moments later, we're pulling into the Broken Shell parking lot. When we get there, it's still closed, but some of the waitresses are inside getting tables set up for the lunch rush. Jesse takes me around to the back door. Berta is sitting in a chair next to the door, smoking a cigarette and reading the morning paper.

"Afternoon, Berta," Jesse says. She jumps when he scares her, quickly throwing her cigarette to the ground and stomping it out. Jesse puts a hand on his hip. "You ain't hidin' that from me. I saw you spit out the death stick."

She gives him a nervous look.

"You've been telling me you were gonna quit since I was twelve years old," Jesse adds, the disappointment still all over his face. Berta breaks into a smile.

"Well, then, I guess you should know by now that it's most likely not going to happen," she says with a chuckle and a shrug. "What are you two up to?"

"Just had a late breakfast at Daisy's. Listen, Lena here had an idea that I wanted to run past you."

Berta puts down her paper and pushes herself back in her seat, like she's readying herself for the proposal.

"She wants to throw a barn dance," he says. "Music, food and drinks, just a social event. We were thinkin' we'd charge a cover and use it to pay the band, and then use what's left for renovations inside."

Berta raises her eyebrows and clasps her hands in her lap.

"Whoa, sounds like you two have really thought this through," she says. Then she pauses for a minute, tapping her lips with her index finger. "I like it. And I think other people will, too. This town hasn't had much fun in the last year or so. I'd be happy to do the bartending. In fact, I'll donate some finger foods and drinks to the cause," she says. Jesse smiles, and I can't help but reciprocate.

"Thanks, Berta!" Jesse says, leaning down to squeeze her hand. She smiles quickly, then turns to look up at me.

"Great idea you got there, girl," she says. I smile back.

"Thanks, Berta. I just want to help Jesse get the most out of the place, after all he's done for my sister and me."

I feel my cheeks get hot the moment I say it. Berta's eyes narrow a bit, but she's still smiling. I feel Jesse's eyes on me, but I can't look in his direction.

"Well, you should know that we all appreciate what you're doing to help him," Berta says, looking back to Jesse. "We just want our boy to find some joy again."

Jesse slowly lets go of Berta's hand and clears his throat, his fingers scratching the back of his neck.

"I'm gonna, uh, grab my paycheck from last week," he says, motioning to the back door. "I'll meet you at the truck?" he asks. I nod as he disappears inside.

"Well, thanks again, Berta," I say. "I'll be back later this week with some flyers and we can go over some of the details."

I turn toward the exit, but before I put any distance between us, she calls my name. I turn back around to her.

"I know you know we all want him to stay, keep that place running," she says. I nod. "I'm not sure exactly what you want for him. But whatever it is, whatever's going on between the two of you, however long it lasts, thanks for making him smile again. Even if it's only for a little while."

I nod and smile back at her. Then my eyes follow his trail to the back door.

"He's not the only one smiling," I say, wrapping my arms around my body. "See ya, Berta."

As he gets back into the truck, I turn to him.

"What are the chances you have a computer and a printer at home?"

He turns to me and gives me half a smile.

"I barely had electricity when you got here," he says with a chuckle. I roll my eyes. "The cafe has a computer though; I'm sure Mike won't mind you using his."

"Okay, cool. Gosh, this place is certainly back in time, isn't it?" I say, looking out my window. He chuckles again.

"Yeah, I guess it is," he says. "But lately, I've been wanting it to freeze."

His face grows a little more serious now, as his eyes flash from me, to the road, back to me. I swallow and slowly slide my hand across the empty space on the seat between us.

"I know what you mean," I whisper.

19

JESSE

It's just before dinner, and Millie insisted on making a pot of clam chowder after I told her I'd never had any. I have to admit, the kitchen smells amazing when I step inside.

"Dang, that does smell good," I say, nodding toward the pot on the stove. She smiles at the sink. "I know it can't beat some good old-fashioned Maryland crab soup, but it is enough to make my mouth water."

She rolls her eyes as she dries her hands on a dish towel.

"Just you wait, Mr. Rowan. You haven't tasted it yet," Millie says. I smile. Millie looked so worn down when they first got here, with fresh bruises on her face and a thick fear in her eyes. But now, she seems calmer, like she's finally taking full breaths after running for years on end. She's got the kindest soul; like Lena, only, without Lena's sharp edges —which I don't mind so much now. It makes me happy that she feels at home here. I want them all to.

"Where's Caleb?" I ask, hoping her answer will also give me Lena's whereabouts. I want to see her all the damn time, but not everyone needs to know that.

"He's upstairs looking at some books," she says. I nod, and Millie smiles. "My sister's down doing laundry. In case you were wondering."

I can't help but smile back. Damn, Millie's good.

I slowly leave the kitchen, trying to hide the fact that I want to race down the cellar steps to see her again. But once I'm out of Millie's sight, I do just that.

I find Lena in the washroom, bent over pulling some clothes out of a basket, and it hits me like a ton of bricks. She's wearing a pair of those short jean shorts again, the ones with the strings hanging down, and when she bends over like that it knocks the air out of me. I want to push myself up against her so bad; I'm fighting every urge not to lift her onto the washing machine right now.

She's humming something, I can't make out the tune, and I swear I could sit here and watch this all damn day. But as she pulls out a pair of jeans, something falls from the pockets and shoots across the linoleum floor in my direction. I see that it's a cell phone, and I bend over to pick it up and hand it back to her.

"I didn't know you owned one," I say, handing it back to her. "Come to think of it, weird not seeing one of you millennials on one of these things all the time."

She smiles and rolls her eyes, reaching back out for it. She hesitates for a moment as she looks down at it, then turns on the power button.

"'You millennials?'" she mocks. "You're a millennial, too."

"Barely," I say. She nods slowly, and I see her wheels turning. It's the first time we've acknowledged that there's a bit of an age gap between us, but nothing about this girl feels childish. She's all woman. If anyone's a kid here, it's me, with the way I can't keep my damn jaw off the ground when I'm around her.

The screen of her phone flashes with light in her hand, and she freezes as she stares down at it. Her eyebrows knit together.

"Everything okay?" I ask, feeling a knot form in my stomach. She nods, her face relaxing immediately as she holds the power button down again.

"Huh? Oh, yeah. Just forgot I even had one of these," she says with a nervous laugh as she tucks it into the back pocket of her shorts. "Millie and I sort of went off the grid when we left Boston."

I nod slowly.

"Is someone trying to reach you?" I ask. I can hear her swallow and she continues sorting the clothes.

"Nah, no one important." She closes the machine and walks past me, back up the stairs.

THE CHOWDER IS DELICIOUS—I have to admit it.

"Well, Millie, you've made me a believer. Maybe you Yankees know a thing or two about seafood," I say, laying a hand on my stomach. She sits back in her chair, satisfied.

"Told you. No one can beat us," she says.

"Yeah!" Caleb says in agreement, chowder dripping off his chin.

"Okay, okay. But before we can truly decide on a winner, you all have to come to a crab feast."

"A crab feast?" Caleb asks. I smile and nod.

"Yep. Not just any crabs. Bay crabs," I say. "You haven't lived till you've tried one. With Old Bay." I close my eyes and lick my lips. When I open them, Caleb's smiling, his eyes wide.

"I wanna try one!" he says.

"There's a crab feast in town tomorrow," I say. "We can all go. And you can decide which state knows their seafood better."

Millie smiles and nods.

"You're on," she says. I look down the table at Lena. She's got a shallow smile on her face, her spoon swirling slowly around her bowl of untouched soup.

"Lee, you okay?" Millie asks, beating me to it. All I can think about is that phone. I need to know what she saw.

"Huh?" Lena asks, her eyes raising to us, realizing she's the center of attention. "Oh, yeah, sorry. I'm not feeling great. I actually might go up to bed soon," she says.

"You sure? What's wrong?" Millie asks.

"Nothing, nothing. Just feeling extra tired," she says. "Thanks for dinner, Mill. Goodnight, everyone."

I help Millie with the dishes.

"She's okay, right?" I ask. Millie shrugs.

"I'm not sure. This isn't really like her," she says. "I'm going to take him for some ice cream. I'll check on her when I get back." I nod and wave as they head out the door.

I walk toward the front door, getting ready to head over to the barn, but I stop. I can't leave her like this. Not after seeing that look on her face in the laundry room. I turn around and start up the stairs, taking them two-by-two. I take in a breath and knock a few times on her door.

She opens, and I instantly go weak. She's got on short little pajama shorts and a flowy tank top—and, clearly, nothing underneath. I shake my head to clear it of any intentions.

"Uh, hey, I just wanted to check on you," I say. She reaches a hand across her body and holds onto her arm.

"Oh, thanks. I'm okay," she says, looking down at the ground. I know she wants me to turn and leave, but I can't.

"You sure? 'Cause I saw that look on your face when you saw something on your phone. And you sort of haven't been the same since," I say.

She lifts her eyes slowly to me, tapping her foot nervously on the floor. She bites her lip—eliciting an insane response from my dick—then steps back into her room. She returns a second later with her phone. She turns it on, pulls something up, and hands it to me.

I look down at the text message.

It won't be long now. I'll know where you took them soon enough, it says. I read over it a few times, then slowly hand the phone back to her.

"Caleb's dad?" I ask. She nods. I feel my blood start to boil beneath my skin. I clench both my fists involuntarily, "That's why you didn't say anything to Millie." She nods again.

"I can't. I can't worry them like that. I just need to…I just need to figure this out." She wraps her arms around her body tightly, her eyes never leaving the ground. I run a hand down my face, and take a step closer to her.

She fumbles to turn the phone back off, tossing it onto the bed.

"I have to figure this out," she says again. "I have to take care of them. They are all I have."

I look down at her, and reach out a hand to her arm. She shudders gently beneath it.

"Look," I say, "he can't possibly know where you are, right?"

She shrugs.

"We've been keeping our phones off so he can't track us," she says, "but he's figured out things like this before.

He's got connections. I just don't know what—" she stops, and I can see she's trying desperately not to cry again in front of me. And just like that, a pain strikes through my chest. I have to make this better. I have to take some of this unbelievable weight she has on her shoulders and carry some of it for her. It's clear that no one else ever has.

"Look, I don't know this guy," I say, "but I can tell you that while you're here, in Baycrest, you're safe. The people here, they aren't going to let him near you. Any of you." I step closer to her, and I wrap an arm around her, pulling her into me. It feels so good to have her head on my chest again. "And I won't, either."

We stand like that for a long time, and as I run my fingers down her long hair, I realize that she'll be gone soon. Out of my sight.

And maybe back into Tiger's.

20

LENA

I know I should be worrying about Tiger right now, but after last night with Jesse, I'm having trouble focusing on the danger at hand.

He was such a gentleman, holding me in his arms until I felt calmer, saying goodnight at my door without even so much as a peck on the cheek.

There's still a wall between us that he puts up, but every single time I'm near him, it takes every ounce of my strength not to scale it. I want him, in a lot of different ways. I want to know more about him, his parents, his life before the accident. I want to know what he likes, what he doesn't like, what he's afraid of. And I want his body.

God. I want his body.

Every moment I'm in his presence, I'm fighting myself not to go back to basic human instincts and let out some sort of freaking mating call.

It's ridiculous.

When Millie and Caleb wake up, I'm already in the kitchen flipping pancakes. I'm bright and cheery as ever, as if I didn't receive a threatening text message from the man who has come close to killing my sister several times.

"Feelin' better?" Millie asks.

"Oh, yeah, much," I say, plopping a big stack of pancakes onto her plate and Caleb's. "Must have just been a 24-hour bug."

She nods, but I can see she's suspicious. But after a bite of my famous pancakes, that look slowly fades away from her face. I'm pouring Caleb a glass of juice when the front door opens and shuts. I hear his boots along the wood floors, heavy but somehow gentle, and I can't help but smile. And when he lays those seaglass eyes on me, I forget a Tiger even exists.

"Mornin'," he says, "glad to see you're up and moving."

"Yep," I say, holding up my spatula, "and I made pancakes. Have a seat."

I walk him over a stack before taking a seat myself.

"So," he says, before shoving a forkful in his mouth. He stops mid-thought to savor the bite. "Damn, those are good. Anyway, the crab feast is at a little park in town today. They get pretty busy, so I was thinking we should head over there fairly early. Jo's getting in today a little before lunch, and then I thought we could head over?"

"Yeah! Bay crabs!" Caleb says.

"Great," Millie says. "Then we can all be there when you admit that Boston's better at seafood."

Jesse chuckles.

"We'll just see," he says. "I'm telling you. Old Bay. Life-changing."

A LITTLE LATER THAT MORNING, we're upstairs getting ready for the feast. I'm spending too much time deciding on an outfit, and I should have known that my sister would notice.

"You're eating crabs," she says. "Not going to a wedding."

I roll my eyes.

"Well, I just wanna look nice in case..."

"In case Jesse decides to *finally* make a move?" she asks with a smile. I look in the mirror at Caleb behind us on the bed, blissfully oblivious to our conversation as he makes his T-rex eat a truck.

"*No,*" I say. "In case anyone wants to talk about the dance or anything. I just want to look presentable."

I pull down the blouse I have on and turn to the side to check my butt in the jean capris I chose.

"Mission accomplished," Millie says, tucking a stray hair back into her bun. "Ready?"

I nod.

Just as we're headed downstairs to meet Jesse, we hear a car door shut outside.

Josie hops out, in a blue sundress and an adorable floppy hat, with big, round sunglasses. As always, she looks completely flawless.

"I hate judges, courtrooms, and anything that *remotely* has to do with the law. I need Old Bay, and I need it *now,*" she says, marching toward Jesse's truck.

These Marylanders and their Old Bay. They think it's some sort of magic fairy dust.

"Uh, hey, Jo," Jesse says, a perplexed look on his face. Josie stops in her tracks, like she just realized that they weren't alone. She turns to us slowly.

"Oops, sorry all. Week from hell—*heck,*" she says, correcting herself and eyeing Caleb. We smile.

"Sorry, Josie," I say. "We're glad to see you."

"Oh, you have no idea," she says back, rustling a hand through Caleb's hair.

We pull up to the park a few minutes later, and like Jesse said, it's already crowded with people. Tents stand over long, paper-covered tables, each adorned unceremoniously with wooden mallets and plastic knives. At least a dozen massive pots are scattered around between the tables, a wooden basket sitting on the ground next to each one. People are pouring drinks and chatting. The bay is big and blue behind us, and I smile at how simple things are here in Baycrest.

"Jesse!" someone calls as we walk in further. "Josie!"

They stop to hug and catch up with multiple people, introducing us to every single one of them. Despite the heat and the fact that the rest of us are speckled in sweat, Josie looks exquisite as ever. She's a damn professional, the way she smiles, makes small talk with just about everyone. She so could have totally owned the inn. She has the perfect personality.

Jesse, on the other hand, has a different vibe. Quieter, subdued. Polite, of course, anytime anyone else acknowledges him. But never the first to start a conversation. Never one to draw attention to himself.

And yet, I know now that he'd still be perfect to run the inn. His heart, how badly he wants to carry on his parents' legacy—he could do it, if he wanted.

Finally, after all the pleasantries are over, we find a table at one of the back tents and sit down.

"Oh," Josie says, reaching into her oversized Coach bag, "these are for you."

She lays a pile of flyers in front of me on the table, the ones Jesse and I had drafted at the cafe.

"Jess sent them and asked me to print them."

"I thought we could hand some out today," he says with a shrug. "Basically all the town will be here."

I smile.

"Perfect. Thanks," I say.

"Best clear everything off the table, miss," a man says, coming toward us with a huge platter of steaming crabs. We do as we're told and scoot back as he sets it down. I have to admit—they smell amazing.

"Whoaaaa!" Caleb cries. "How do you *eat* those?" Josie and Jesse both laugh, but Millie and I are both wondering the same thing.

"Lemme show you," Jesse says, grabbing a crab off the platter, and putting one in front of Caleb. He nods to Millie and me to each take one.

"Maryland Living 101," Josie says. "Always test for weight."

She picks up a crab in each hand, moving them up and down in the air to see which one is heavier, the she sets one on the table in front of her.

"Start with the claws," Jesse says, twisting them off, "then each of the legs. If you got a good one, you'll get an appetizer." He twists off one of the hind legs and a giant lump of meat from the body comes out with it. He sucks the meat off the leg, showing Caleb the empty vessel that's left.

Caleb shrieks with delight as he figures out how to follow along.

We watch as Jesse and Josie fly through their picking, stopping occasionally to check in on us newbies.

I have to admit, these crabs are *damn* good.

And I sort of get the obsession with Old Bay.

After what feels like years of picking and eating ourselves full of crabs, we all sit back, wiping down with the towelettes that lie in little baskets on the table.

"Hey," Jesse says to Caleb, "you wanna see what these guys look like before they're cooked?"

Caleb's eyes grow wide.

"Did you know that before they're cooked, they are actually blue?"

Caleb blinks, and we smile.

"I wanna see!"

Jesse hops up from the table and pulls Caleb's chair out.

"Come on," he says with a smile. I smile and nod in his direction, silently thanking him for continuing to be the best male role model Caleb has ever known. I'm hit with a wave of sadness when I realize how devastated Caleb will be when we do leave Baycrest.

Maybe as devastated as I will be.

"He's so good with him," Millie says, watching the two of them as they play with the live crabs.

"He is," says Josie. "Actually, he's good at a lot of stuff. But you'd never know." I turn to her.

"What do you mean?" I ask. She sighs, loving eyes still on her brother.

"I love my baby brother, but it's no secret that since we lost mom and dad, we lost him, too. Our whole lives, he wanted to take over the inn. My dream was law school, his dream was running the inn when mom and dad got tired. We both loved growing up here, but he has always had this...connection with the shore that I didn't always feel. That's why everyone is so shocked that he's leaving," Josie says. I swallow.

"Then, why *is* he leaving?" Millie asks.

"Well, you saw how the inn looked. I mean, the truth is, parts of the inn were starting to fall apart while mom and dad were still alive. They had these grand plans with Jesse to start renovating it, sort of like what you two have been doing," Josie says, nodding in my direction. "But then, they died before they got started, and he just felt like he couldn't do it without them. He felt like it was their dream and they didn't get to see it through. And instead of doing it in their honor, he sort of panicked, I guess. He has this horrible guilt about their death."

My eyes shoot to her again, my eyebrows synching together. Josie looks down at her plate, as if she realized she'd said too much.

"Why would he feel guilty about that?" I ask. She sighs again, leaning back in her chair.

"The night of the accident, they were coming home from a dinner in Annapolis, and there was a bad storm. They stopped when they got a flat tire. My dad was having trouble changing it and called Jesse a few times. He was at the Shell with some friends and never heard his phone. By the time he looked at his phone, he had another missed call —from the police. They'd been hit by an out-of-control tractor trailer while they were pulled over. Pushed their car off the side of the road and flipped it over the guardrail."

I feel this weight pound down on my chest, my eyes trailing over the grass to Jesse. He looks so happy, so content when he plays with Caleb, but it's not hard to see there's a thick layer of pain in his eyes.

"Poor Jesse," Millie says. "He can't blame himself for that, though. They still could have been hit either way."

Josie nods.

"I know that, you know that, the whole town knows it. Jesse's the only one who convinced himself that it's his fault. And what's worse, that guilt has trickled down into this never-ending abyss of self-deprecation. He doesn't think he's capable—or worthy—of anything these days. It breaks my heart," Josie says, and I swear I hear a crack in her voice.

I reach out instinctively and grab her hand.

"I wish I could be here for him more, but I just...this isn't the life I wanted. And I know mom and dad would want me to..." she says, her voice dying down into a whisper before trailing off completely.

"Your parents would want you to keep living your dream," Millie says, reaching across the table to take Josie's other hand. "You worked so hard to become a lawyer, I'm sure."

I agree with my sister; Josie can't just throw away her life in D.C. to get Jesse back on his feet. But my heart is pulling toward Jesse; I hate the idea of him living here on this shore, all alone on the inn property, destined to spend his lonely days cursing himself for not pulling his damn phone out of his pocket, or picking up a hammer every now and then.

"I'm so glad you two showed up," Josie says, collecting herself a bit. "And you," she says, looking at me and placing her hand on my knee, "you've been an incredible help. I haven't seen that spark in him—that pride he has in the inn —since before they died. Even if he does still want to sell it, at least he can be proud of what he's leaving behind."

I nod and force a smile, patting her hand on my knee.

"I'm proud of it, too," I say, my eyes trailing back across the lawn. "And of him."

I feel both of their eyes on me as I stare at him like a buffoon, but for some reason, I don't care. I don't feel as compelled to hide what I feel for him anymore—whatever those feelings may be. Maybe it's because I know how badly he might need to know.

Josie fans her face for a moment and straightens out her dress, then stands up from the table.

"Should we go ahead and hand these out?" she says,

splitting the pile of flyers and handing some to me and Millie.

"Oh, yeah," I say, pulling my attention away from the gorgeous man who's currently winning over my nephew's heart.

We each take a stack and disperse amongst the tents. Jesse wasn't kidding when he said most of the town showed up to these things. Baycrest is small, but when the whole town is in one park, it looks like a sea of people.

I smile and nod as I hand out the flyer, explain the details, and invite people to come. Everyone seems pleasantly surprised that there's some sort of happening at the inn again, and it makes my heart happy. This could actually work.

I lean over one table to lay down the last few flyers and spin around to head back to ours, when I stop in my tracks.

"Oh, hi, Amber," I say, tucking a piece of hair behind my ear. I grab a flyer from the table where I just left it and hold it out to her. "We're having a barn dance—" I say. She crosses her arms over her chest.

"Yeah, I've seen those things everywhere," she says, clearly unamused.

"Oh, okay, cool," I say. There's a long, awkward silence, and I scoot to the side to make my way around her.

"You know it's a lost cause, right?" she asks. I freeze and turn around to face her.

"What is?"

"Trying to get Jesse to stay."

I swallow.

"I'm not...I'm not trying to get him to stay. I'm just trying to help him out," I say. She scoffs and rolls her eyes.

"Help him out? By shacking up with him for free? Please," she says, pulling her arms over her chest tighter.

"Take it from me. Nothing is going to keep him here. Nothing's stopping him from selling that place. You're not the first girl to go making a fool of herself trying to get him to change his mind."

Something in her voice changes when she says that, her eyes dropping to the ground, like it's the first time she's heard the words, and I actually feel sorry for her. It's pretty clear that what she felt toward Jesse—maybe what she still feels—is a lot more than he felt for her.

I sigh, and stick out a flyer toward her again.

"I'm not trying to stop him from doing anything he wants to do. He's done my family and me a big favor these last few months. I'm just trying to return it," I say. I catch her eyes. "I hope you come to the dance, Amber."

She looks at me, her eyes wide. Slowly, she takes the flyer out of my hand.

As I walk back to our tent, I see Jesse chasing Caleb with a live crab, Millie and Josie laughing hysterically as they look on.

But all I can hear are Amber's words echoing in my ears. *Nothing is going to keep him here.*

And I know she's right. Not even me.

It's been a week since I saw Tiger's text, and I'm still not quite over the initial panic. I hate how even after this long, even hundreds of miles away, tucked back on this peninsula on the Bay, he still haunts me. He still holds power over me, and I'm not even the one he put his hands on.

But this time, I had someone to tell. This time, I had Jesse. And since I told him, and since I know a little more about his own demons, there's been this strange feeling I've never felt before—I think it's relief. Even if he couldn't do a damn thing to stop Tiger—which, judging by Jesse's sheer size, would not be the case—just knowing that he knew, that *someone* knew, is making me feel even just a tiny bit better. The fact that I'm not alone in knowing Tiger's still looking for us takes a load off my shoulders that I didn't even realize I was carrying.

Most of my focus lately has been on the fundraiser. I've been running around the inn like a madwoman trying to get things tidied up for the dance. It's less than a week away, and I'm suddenly starting to feel a hell of a lot of pressure. Mostly because this whole thing was my idea, so if it flops, it's on me. But also because if it fails, it's just one more kick in the ass to Jesse—just one more point he needs to back up his seemingly unrelenting self-disappointment.

For some reason, restoring a little bit of Jesse's faith in the inn, and himself, means more to me than I was counting on.

I'm on my hands and knees rearranging a few of the tulips that Caleb haphazardly "planted" with me yesterday, when I'm covered by a shadow. I hear him clear his throat behind me, and instantly, the hairs on the back of my neck stand up.

"Lookin' good," he says. I smile to myself as I turn around slowly, squinting in the bright sunlight. "The plants, I mean." He hits me with one of those rare, yet absolutely devastating smiles, and I can feel the heat rush to my cheeks, then flow down my body to a spot that has been recently reawakened, only by being around him.

"Is that so?" I ask, taking my gardening gloves off and putting a hand to my hip. I use my other hand to wipe my forehead, and I can feel his eyes on me as I do it. I know exactly what I'm doing, but damn if I'm going to stop. It feels good to be wanted by anyone, but to be wanted by *him* feels so *damn* good. He takes a step closer to me, the expression on his face growing a little bit more serious. Suddenly, my confidence is slipping away a little bit, and nervousness is taking its place. He's towering over me now, so that my nose is just inches from his chest. But I won't take my eyes from his. He squints a little bit, then raises his hand, bringing it closer and closer to my face. He takes his thumb and sweeps its across my forehead.

"Got a little somethin' there," he says, his voice quiet.

"Thanks," I mutter. It's hot today—one of the hottest days since I got here, despite the fact that fall is on its way—and 've been working my butt off these last couple of days getting everything ready for the dance. Suddenly, I can feel his eyes on me again, then they trail to the water, then back to me. I raise an eyebrow.

"What?" I ask. That same smile tugs up on one side of his lip.

"Caleb?" Jesse calls, his eyes still on me. "Don't you think Aunt Lee looks a little dirty?" he asks.

Caleb trots around the side of the house to inspect. He looks me up and down, then looks back to Jesse.

"She could use a quick dip, don't you think?" he asks. Suddenly, a tiny little devilish smile crosses Caleb's lips, and he begins jumping up and down. He knows exactly what's about to happen, and now, I do too. I drop my gloves to the ground and hold my hands up, as if they'd be able to do anything to stop Jesse.

"No, no, no, come on now," I say, waving my hands in his direction. But Jesse takes another step closer to me, that smile killing me, making me boil over from the inside out. I am trying desperately to keep this stern look on my face, but I know it's no use. None whatsoever.

"I don't know, Aunt Lee, you've been workin' like a dog for these last few days, and you're starting to smell like one, too," Jesse teases, walking toward me more swiftly now. He reaches those long arms out, and suddenly, they are wrapped around me. I press my hands against his chest, but like I said, it's no use. It's like trying to hold off a brick wall.

"Jesse!" I cry out in between bouts of hysterical laughter. Caleb is shrieking and giggling, following behind us closely. Jesse swoops me up and hoists me over one shoulder, then turns to Caleb.

"Help me count it down," he tells him. I hear the back door open as my sister steps onto the patio.

"One," Jesse starts.

"Two!" Caleb continues.

"Three!" They say unison, along with my sister. Traitor.

Jesse takes off toward the water, flying through the grass and onto the dock. When we get to the end, he shifts so that he's holding me in front of him now. He smiles down at me as I clutch onto him, squeezing my eyes shut. I'm not getting out of this one. I take a deep breath as he launches us off the end of the wood and into the chilly bay.

When we plunge underneath, I feel him reach for me again as the water pulls us apart a bit. He pulls me into his body so that no part of us isn't touching, and even though I'm under water, it feels like a breath of fresh air. He pushes us to the surface, still holding me close. He reaches a finger up and slides a loose piece of hair out of my face. We're treading the water, our chests still touching, when I feel his other hand land on my lower back, then slide, painfully slow, down to the crest of my ass. I raise an eyebrow at him.

"Now who's the dirty one?" I ask him with a smirk. He narrows his eyes at me and smirks right back.

"You have no idea," he says, and I feel that electric zap shoot back down to my nether regions.

"Aunt Lee! Jesse! Are you guys okay? Can you do it again?" Caleb asks from the shore. I turn to swim back, but before I do, I let my hand slide down his chest, across his abs, right to the rim of his jeans. I slip three of my fingers into his pants, tugging at his waistband, and I feel his whole body tighten.

"Careful, Mr. Rowan," I whisper, then I quickly retreat my fingers and swim back.

I mean it in so many ways.

Because if he gets me going, I'm not going to be able to stop myself. For months I've been forcing myself to keep my distance, to keep my hands off of him. But I'm realizing now how quickly that can be undone.

And because if he takes it there, I'm never going to want to turn back.

21

JESSE

After practically drowning myself in another freezing cold shower, I'm finally lying in bed. I can't stop picturing how she looked in that water, completely soaked, perfectly drenched. Her eyes were so bright against the Bay, her black hair pushed back out of her face. Her nipples pointing through the thin cotton of her tank, so hard I swore they were going to cut through. And when our bodies touched...I swear to God if we had been alone, I wouldn't have been able to stop myself from doing whatever she wanted to her body. I wouldn't have been able to stop myself from showing her how badly I want her.

Not a fucking chance.

I could feel how bad she wanted it, too. That look she gave me, her fucking hand practically in my pants. Jesus Christ. I'm gonna have to get back in the shower again just thinking about it.

I know our time here is limited, but it doesn't make me want her any less. In fact, I think it makes me want her more. It feels urgent, like I need her or I might suffocate. She's so fucking beautiful, and she has no idea. I wish I wasn't such a pansy ass. I wish I could get my shit together, just grab her one day and pull her into the barn with me, show her how bad I want her. How much she's made me feel like my old self. How badly I need her to understand that in these few short months, she's changed me a little bit. Maybe a lot.

Tomorrow is the dance, and I'm nervous as hell. I haven't put myself out there—or put the inn out there—since mom and dad died. But I'm also nervous for her. She cares so much about this place; I just want her to see her hard work pay off.

And if it does, I'm a step closer to being rid of this place. To being out of here.

Which is definitely what I still want.

Most of the time.

I WAKE up the next morning to the sound of a hammer downstairs. I walk groggily to my door and open it. I look down the stairs and see Lena on the floor of the barn, pounding away at the legs of a chair.

"Is all that necessary this time of morning?" I ask, squinting in the sunlight that's streaming in from the windows. She barely acknowledges me as she whacks at it a few more times, then checks to see if it's sturdy before flipping it back onto its feet.

"It is if we want tonight to go well," she says, rolling over her hip and hopping back to her feet. I can't help but smile at her. She does remind me of my mom in a lot of ways, with her no-bullshit, get-it-done attitude. I make my way down the steps, aware that I'm in nothing but shorts, and reach for her arm as she's walking toward the doors.

"Hey," I say, looking down at her. I can see the frantic

thoughts in her head, every second she's not doing some-thing feels like a waste. So I wait a moment until our eyes meet, until I know she actually sees me. Her face softens a bit, her eyebrows pointed up to the sky. "Tonight is gonna go great."

She draws in a long breath, then finally, cracks into a small smile. She nods as she reaches her hand up and squeezes mine. Then she turns and walks out the barn doors.

I pull the tables out and place the chairs around them, spreading them out evenly toward the back corner of the barn. I wipe down the bar and start unloading the beers that Berta's delivery guy dropped off into the coolers behind the counter. Then I start unwinding an extension cord, making sure the electric reaches to the makeshift stage we built in the front corner,

Millie comes in a few minutes later with some string lights, and I hold Caleb up on my shoulders as he "helps" us hang them. I'm sure Lena will redo them later, but he's not bad for a four-year-old.

All day long, I'm taking orders from Lena and Josie, and Berta when she's around, but I don't mind it. There's life in this place today, and I'm diggin' it.

"Hey," Berta finally says, nodding in our direction as I nail the last corner of the banner Lena had printed into the wall above the door. I hop down off the ladder and we all gather around her, Caleb playing with dinosaurs in the far corner of the room.

"I'm gonna hang behind the bar with the tenders for the first little bit," she says, "but then I was thinkin,' I could trade places with you." She motions to Millie, whose eyes grow wide.

"I'm too old to be out here partyin' with all you kids,"

Berta goes on. "So I thought I'd kick back and watch some T.V. inside the inn while the kid sleeps, and you can hang out here with the youngsters. You need a night of fun, too."

Lena smiles widely, and throws her arms around Berta. Millie's eyes are still wide, and suddenly, I see tears prickling in them. Aw, hell. I hate when women cry. There's almost nothing I wouldn't do to stop a woman from crying.

"Thank you, Berta! That would be amazing!" Lena says, answering for Millie. Finally, Millie smiles and nods.

"Yes, thank you so much," she says, "but are you sure? If he wakes up..."

"If he wakes up, I'll just call one of these two," Berta says, motioning to me and Josie, "and they can send in mama bear. Don't worry. I used to watch these knuckleheads all the time when they were kids. And they turned out okay. Mostly."

Josie and I both chuckle and nudge her. Millie smiles again, but I can still see the worry in her eyes. Berta walks out of the barn, and as the rest of us return to our to-dos, I gently nudge Millie's arm.

"Don't worry, he'll be in good hands," I tell her. "And we'll be right here if he needs anything."

She nods and smiles.

"Alright, troops," Lena finally says, clapping her hands together. "I think we've just about done all we can do. Let's go get ready, and pray people show up!"

IT'S A QUARTER TO EIGHT, and I'm sitting in the parlor of the inn waiting for the girls to make their grand entrance. I decided to step it up a notch. I'm wearing khakis and a nicer button-up; I probably looked more dressed up than Lena's ever seen me. But this is a big night. For me, for the inn, and, mostly, for her. I decided to give it a little extra umph. I even combed my hair after my shower and decided against my staple Baycrest baseball cap.

Josie's the first one downstairs, and not shockingly, she's dressed to the nines. You'd think she was going out for a night on the town in D.C., rather than a dance in our dusty old barn. But that's Josie for ya.

Millie follows close behind after finally getting the kid down, wearing a flowy skirt and white tank, with her dark hair twisted into a bun. She looks a little flustered, but she looks ready. I want her to have a good time tonight. I want her to breathe, relax, have a drink or two. I want her to have one night to herself. One night.

"Looking beautiful!" Josie says, taking Millie's right hand, then motioning for her to do a spin. "Care to join me in the barn for a quick pre-party shot? It'll take the edge off." Millie pauses for a moment, then I watch as her face relaxes. Berta's already perched up on the couch in the living room with a stack of magazines and a soda. Finally, Millie nods, taking Josie's outstretched hand again.

"Let's do this," she says. I chuckle and shake my head as the two of them giggle out of the house like a couple of teenagers and disappear toward the barn.

I hear some stumbling down the steps, and then she turns the corner, where I spot her before she's noticed I'm there. She's got on a flowing baby blue sundress with extra-skinny straps and some sort of heeled, strappy sandals. Her long, coal-colored hair is curled, and pulled to one side. She's even wearing a little makeup, and her eyes are shining like freakin' sapphires.

She looks a little flustered, but she also looks like she's on a mission. She's about to fly around the corner toward the kitchen, but stops in her tracks when she sees me.

"Damn," I mutter without even thinking. It just slips out. I see her bite her bottom lip to hide her smile.

"It's Josie's," she says, tugging on the bottom of the dress. "I didn't have anything nice enough. Guess I forgot to pack my barn-dance attire when I left Boston."

I smile and take another step closer to her. I have to take a deep breath to keep myself calm. She looks fucking amazing. My eyes travel up and down her body like a car that's lost on a street. Like they don't know where to land, because every inch of her is perfect. The sweet smell of her hair is intoxicating the closer I get to her. Her skin is tanner than it was when she first got here, and I know it's from all her work in the summer sun. A few freckles splay across her shoulders and chest, and it's taking all the restraint I have not to pull her in and kiss every single one of them.

The closer I get to her, the harder the pull becomes, and the more I know I should walk away. She clears her throat nervously, tucking a stray strand of hair behind her ear. There's something so sexy about the fact that she's done all this for the inn. For me. I'm amazed by her, but also a little bit of afraid of her. Afraid of what she could do to me.

"I...uh," I stammer. I want to say something so fucking bad. I want to tell her how thankful I am. But I can't. "You...you look great," I manage to get out like a nervous teenager laying eyes on his prom date.

She swallows, her eyes dropping to the floor.

"Thanks," she says. "Should we go out? See if anyone's gonna show up to this thing?"

I nod and gesture toward the barn with my hand, letting her lead the way. And all the while, I wish I could kick my own ass for not saying anything else.

We walk back through the foyer, but as we reach the

front door, she pauses with her hand on the handle. I see her shoulders fall and rise a few times.

"You okay?" I ask. She nods before slowly turning around to face me. She presses her back up against the door and closes her eyes. "Hey, what's up?"

Finally, she opens them again, her long lashes fluttering.

"I'm just...trying to prepare myself for no one to show," she says with a nervous laugh.

I step closer to her and put my hands on her shoulders. She blinks a few times, then looks up at me.

"I've never met anyone like you," I say. She cocks her head to the side, giving me a half-smile.

"What do you mean?"

"I mean...I've never met someone who just goes for it. For anything. For everything. You don't wait to take chances...you just *do* it. It's kind of amazing," I say, letting my hands drop slowly from her skin as I look down at the ground. She smiles again, shrugging slowly.

"I guess it just comes from years of not having an option. There wasn't a lot of time to weigh my options in between my mother's beatings and then my sister's. I just had to act as soon as I had an opportunity," she says. I want to pull her into me again, hold her so tight against me. Let her know, yet again, how safe she is—how safe they all are—here with me. Protect her from those memories that I can't even bring myself to think about.

But instead, I just nod.

"Well, shitty circumstances have turned you into the most stubborn," I say with a pause, "strongest person I've ever known." I give her a sly smile, and she returns the favor. I feel my knees go weak at the sight of her biting her lip again.

"Well," she says, clearing her throat and stepping off from the door, "I guess it's time."

I nod and follow her out the door. We walk across the gravel driveway in silence, but we stop when we see the lawn, flooded with headlights. Car doors opening and shutting, groups of people shuffling through the barn doors.

The band is already set up and has started playing as we make our way in, and people are ordering drinks at the bar, where Millie looks a little more relaxed after that shot. I look at Lena, whose jaw has dropped.

"Well, well, well," I whisper in her ear. I watch as goosebumps rise all over her skin. "Look at what you've done."

I smile against her hair, then slip past her and into the barn.

Josie and Millie are mingling already, talking it up with the locals, helping serve drinks and appetizers. A few people are sitting at each of the tables snacking and chatting, while others have already gathered closer to the stage, and some are even starting to dance.

Suddenly, there's life at the Rowan again.

I wander around the barn, saying hi to everyone I know —which is, well, everyone—and chatting it up as much as I can. All the while, I keep my eye on Lena, watching as she effortlessly makes friends with every person she talks to, filling the role of server, bartender, hostess. The fabric of her dress flows out every time she spins around, and she looks like an angel.

After about an hour, I find her at the bar. I want her. I want to touch her, feel her, let her know how proud I am of her. But, like clockwork, my sister comes crashing in, cockblocking as adeptly as she has since we were teenagers.

"Guys, pardon my French, but this is fucking amazing," she says. I can smell the tequila on her breath as she slams her glass down on the bar. "I've had five people tell me they'd stay here. I had another two ask when we were reopening. Lee, I think you might be right."

I turn to Lena and raise an eyebrow.

"Right about what?"

Her eyes drop sheepishly to the ground.

"I just...I mentioned to Josie earlier that if this worked, it might give us an idea as to whether or not the inn might ever be operational again," she says. Then her blue eyes flick up to mine. "I know you're not interested in staying to run it, but the next owner might be."

Normally, I'd be defensive of my decision to sell, to get the hell out of Baycrest and leave all of this on the shore. But right now, my chest is swelling with so much pride and joy for this place, and for this girl, that I can't even bring myself to be mad. I smile, but before I can respond, I hear him. Nothing gives you limp dick quite like Rob Mills.

"Well, well, well," he says, sauntering up toward us as he throws back a sip of his beer. "Interesting little shindig you guys got goin' on here. And interesting music."

I roll my eyes. I want to sock him in the face, just for existing.

"Rob," Lena says, her voice as unenthusiastic as possible without sounding completely and utterly disappointed, "you came. Good to see you."

He steps closer to her, and I feel all my senses heighten.

"You too, little lady," he says, and again, I can't help but roll my eyes so far back into my head that I can see my fucking brain. "Pretty impressive that a girl like you can just roll in and get this place off the ground again, while Jess here's been letting it drown for years."

That's it. I feel my chest swelling as I take three quick

steps closer to him. But Josie puts a hand to my chest, and Lena steps in front of me.

"We did a survey, actually," Lena says. "Most people said they'd come as long as we got a better band to play. So we did." She shrugs her shoulders sarcastically and holds her hands out, and I've never wanted to kiss someone so bad. I watch as Rob's jaw drops. He looks from Lena, to Josie, to me, then scoffs and turns on his heel. And we all bust out laughing. Damn, my girl is funny.

My girl.

As if she's mine.

As if we're going to be together.

As if either of us will even be here in a month's time.

As if any chance I ever had of being with her, of making her mine, isn't slipping through my fingers with every day that passes.

22

LENA

The party has been going strong for two hours now, and it doesn't show signs of slowing anytime soon. The band is killing it, much to Rob's chagrin, and so are Berta's bartenders. Millie disappears into the inn every hour or so just to check in with Berta, but for the most part, she seems to really be enjoying herself. I've seen the lead singer of the band, someone Josie and Jesse know from high school, whisper to her in between songs, and I see this smile turn her cheeks red every single time he does it.

Josie is a little tipsy, but she's definitely enjoying seeing the inn busy. And Jesse. I've seen that killer smile of his more times tonight than the whole time I've been here in Baycrest, and every single time, it makes my heart jump in my chest.

Even though it's a full house, my nerves have yet to settle. I know tonight is going well—we made enough to cover our expenses with the first few people who arrived, and have definitely made enough to do some more reno-vations.

But that's not why I'm nervous.

I'm nervous for what comes *after* the renovations are made.

Our time here is running out faster than I was ready for.

I do a lap around to all the tables, grabbing empty glasses and plates, making sure everyone has enough of what they are eating or drinking.

"Are we finished here?" I ask at one table, not bothering to look up as I sweep some crumbs onto a napkin.

"Nah, but you will be soon," I hear Amber say. I look up, a smug smile on her face as her girlies all smile and giggle around me. This girl. This poor girl wants a fight with me so bad. She wants a fight over Jesse, because she thinks that if I weren't here, she would have a real chance with him.

I don't want to fight with her. I don't have the energy.

"Amber," I say, collecting a few of their empty shot glasses. "I'm really glad you came."

That's all I say, my eyes drilling into hers. Because as unpleasant as every single one of our encounters has been, I mean it. I'm glad she's here. At the very least, she's one more person paying the cover charge. She clearly needs a positive interaction in her life, and Lord knows I need more of them in mine.

She doesn't say anything back, but I see her eyebrows raise in surprise. Kill 'em with kindness. Just kill 'em with kindness.

I walk back to the bar and put everything down, then I turn back around to sit at a table at the back of the room. I rest for a minute, giving my tired feet a break. They are about two sizes too big for these wedges that Josie lent me, but she's right, they totally "make the outfit."

People are dancing and laughing and clapping with the band, and then the song changes. One of the band members strums his acoustic guitar nice and slow, and couples start gathering on the floor, swaying back and forth to the sweet, sad notes coming from the stage.

"Hey," I hear Jesse say as he steps next to my chair. I look up at him.

"Hey," I answer. Suddenly, he holds his hand out, and I find it hard to take a deep breath.

"Dance with me." He says it like a statement, but that nervous look in his eyes tells me it's more of a question. It's more of a hope, a wish. I narrow my eyes at him, and a smile tugs at one corner of my mouth. I can feel eyes on us—particularly my sister's, Josie's, and Amber's, but I don't care. Not tonight. I slowly slip my hand into his and let him pull me to my feet.

"Hold on," I say, kneeling down to unbuckle these godforsaken shoes. He pauses, holding me up as I wobble, then smiles as I sink down to my normal height. He leads me to the back corner of the floor and quickly places his hand on my back, pulling me into him in one fast movement, like he's afraid I might change my mind. We begin swaying to the music, and I'm impressed with how well he's moving. I didn't pin him to be a dancer. Mr. Rowan is full of small, sexy surprises.

We don't speak for a beat or two, but with every passing moment, I feel him pull me a little bit closer to him. His thumb strokes my bare back through the keyhole opening in Josie's blue dress, and even though the barn is toasty in the summer heat, his touch leaves a trail of goosebumps all over my skin.

"I can't believe you managed to get so many people here," he finally says, smiling down at me. I smile back up at him. He pauses for a moment, then goes on. "Look, I know I, uh, I know I'm a man of few words."

I swallow and nod.

"But I just, uh, I just want to thank you. Seriously. Even if this doesn't work out...the inn, I mean, thank you for believing in it enough to at least give it a try. For the first time in a long time, it feels likes someone has a little bit of faith in me."

My eyes flick up to his, but they are staring down at the ground between us, like he's nervous to make contact. My heart is twisting inside my chest as I think of all that Josie told me; his guilt over his parents, about letting the inn fail, about not knowing what to do next. I want to take it all away for him. I want him to know that I really do believe in him. I step a tiny bit closer to him, and I let my hand slide up his shoulder and gently onto his neck. I let my fingers glide through his hair. Our eyes meet, and I can't hear the music anymore. I can't hear the people around us, the glasses clinking, the snarls from Amber's table. All I can hear is my own heartbeat, the bass from the band, the blood rushing through my ears. And all I can feel is his grip around my waist tightening. I can feel his breath on my lips as our faces get closer, and closer.

And then, out of the corner of my eye, I see a tall figure post up against the wall of the barn, positioning itself perfectly in my line of vision.

I'd know that tall, slim, dangly figure anywhere.

Our past has finally found us here in Baycrest, in the form of a Bentley brother.

23

JESSE

We were about to fucking kiss.

Mere centimeters from it.

So close, I could practically taste her.

And then she took off, bursting out of my grasp right when I thought I actually had her. She rushes toward the back wall where I see a tall, scrawny man posted up, with this crazed, demonic look burning in his eyes. I take off after her, but she reaches him before I can reach her.

She gets to him, and this demented smile crosses his lips. As she's closing in on him, I see her searching the room frantically, and the pieces start fitting together. She's looking for Millie, who happens to be in the house doing one of her routine checks on Caleb right now.

Holy shit. *Is this Tiger?*

"What the *fuck* are you doing here, Micah?" she asks. *Wait, who's Micah?*

The dude's still smiling like some sort of rabid animal, and I can feel my fists clenching. I'm about to intervene when she steps closer to him.

"Outside," she says, pointing to the door. She marches

out, and he's close behind her—too close. My instinct is to follow her, but before I do, I have to find my sister. I have to tell her to keep Millie in the house until this Micah character is gone.

Of course, Josie's in the dead-center of the room, surrounded by at least a dozen locals, laughing and totally enjoying the attention. But I have no time for it. I storm through the crowd.

"Jo," I say. Nothing.

"Jo," I say, a little louder this time. Still no answer, just a roar of laughter in response to whatever story she's telling them.

"*Josie!*" I finally scream. All heads turn to me, and I don't give a damn. She perks up, stepping out from the crowd, and I know she can see the worry in my eyes. "I need you to go to the house and make sure that Millie stays inside. I think someone close to the kid's dad is here."

Josie's eyes widen into big saucers, and her chest begins heaving up and down. She blinks once, twice, then slams her glass down on a nearby table and takes off for the inn.

I follow her out the barn doors. I don't see Lena anywhere, and I start to panic. She's not down by the water, not by the house.

Finally, I can hear her voice from the other side of the barn, somehow shouting and whispering at the same time. I back up to the wall, listening for a moment.

"How the fuck did you find me?" I hear her ask, and I do a little jog around the side of the barn.

"Cell phone signals are strong, even if they're only on once in a blue moon," he says. "Plus, you know dad's got the hookups. He had a PI on it as soon as you guys left town." Dammit. Fucking technology. And stupid fucking rich kids.

"It's time for you to leave," she says. "Now." I hear

gravel crunch, and I slink around the corner of the barn. I lay eyes on Micah, just as he's gripping her arms and slamming her up against the wall.

A fire burns in my belly, and I'm pretty confident it would take an entire army to stop me from reacting. I take off in a dead sprint down the length of the barn.

"Hey!" I call. But just as I'm about to grab him and beat the living shit out of him, I see her wriggle from his grasp. She grabs his scrawny shoulders and jerks her knee up, jamming it right into his groin. He collapses to his knees, gasping for air, and for a moment, I freeze in my tracks, in awe. But then a switch goes off and my protective instincts kick in, and I find myself stepping between the two of them, pushing her back behind me.

I kneel down so that I'm at eye-level with him, the wind still knocked out of him.

"I don't know who the fuck you are," I whisper to him. Icy light blue eyes flick up to me, a flame burning in them. "But you have sixty seconds to disappear."

His eyes twitch a bit, and I can see the fear in them despite how desperately he's trying to hide it. He slowly climbs to his feet, and I reach a hand behind me to tuck Lena into my grasp. Micah takes in a few slow breaths, his eyes drilling into me, then looking around me to find her.

"I know they're here," Micah says, his voice breathy, "and now, Tiger does, too. You can let Millie know that he wants to see his son. And he will, soon enough."

"He'll never see them again," Lena says, her voice stern and unwavering behind me. I can feel her breath, steady and even on the back of my arm. Micah straightens himself out, his eyes piercing through me to her. Then he storms off, getting into a black sedan parked—probably some sort of hired car from their father—on the lawn, and speeding off.

It's too dark to make out the tags, but I memorize the make and model of the car. I won't forget it.

I turn around to face Lena , slowly, expecting to see that fierce look still in her eyes. But it's gone.

Instead, she's crouched against the wall of the barn, her arms wrapped around her knees, her head in her lap. I can see her chest heaving, and she's sucking in air like she's suffocating.

"Hey, hey," I say, kneeling down toward her. I sit in the grass next to her, leaning up against the barn, then wrap my arm around her heaving shoulders. I pull her toward me lightly, wrapping my other arm around her as she leans into my chest, and brush her hair back off her shoulders. "Breathe. He's gone. Just breathe."

Her breath eventually slows, in through her nose and out through her mouth. She's laying on me now, her head in the crook of my neck. If I wasn't so emotionally charged right now, I swear I could get high off the way she smells. But my chest is pounding wildly and I'm all riled up. I wanted to crush that guy's face, slam him into the ground. I wanted her to know that he'd never bother her again. I want her to know that I'll take care of her.

But if we are all leaving, I can't be that guy. I can't make those promises, and it makes me feel like a fraud. Even more so than when I put up the facade of an innkeeper.

"Hey," I say, after a few moments pass. She looks up at me. "You okay? Who was that?"

She pulls her head off my shoulder, and I can't help but feel disappointed as I realize this moment is passing. She stands up slowly and straightens her dress out.

"Micah Bentley. Tiger's younger brother, and his little bitch. He's basically a henchman," she says. "Tiger used to have him watch their apartment sometimes, so that if he beat Millie really bad, she couldn't leave to tell anyone. Micah would keep watch to make sure she didn't get out while the proof was still left on her face."

My stomach flips inside my body. It's unfathomable to me that there are still men in this world who can do such heinous things to women. But it's almost even *more* unfathomable that others are willing to act as an accomplice.

I want to kill them both, and I don't even know them.

"Jesus Christ," I mutter, pulling myself to my feet. "Well, at least he's gone." She scoffs.

"For now," she says. "But he will be back. And with Tiger." After a beat, her eyes lift to mine. "They will toy with us. They won't come back right away, because we would be expecting that. They will wait a little bit so that we have no idea when to expect them. I think we need to leave."

I feel that pounding in my chest again.

Not yet. It's not time yet. It's too soon.

I step toward her, reaching a hand out to grab hers.

"Let's talk to Josie," I say. "Let's see what can be done legally first." Her eyes drop to the ground, and I know what she's thinking. "I know restraining orders haven't worked in the past, but there might be more we can do so that you don't have to keep running."

She looks to me again.

"'We?'" she asks. I take her other hand.

"We," I say. As far as I'm concerned, this is "we."

She nods, and I feel a little bit of relief.

"Okay, good. We'll talk to her first thing tomorrow. Do you want to go into the house, and I'll finish up out here?" I ask her. She shakes her head.

"No. I don't want to let him ruin the night," she says. "Let's get back in there."

I nod, and slowly let her hands slip from mine. And as she leads us back to the barn, a rush of panic washes over me. I wonder if this might be one of the last moments we share alone.

Millie refuses to come back out to the party. She says she just wants to stay with Caleb and try to sleep. But Berta stays to keep the house, promising she won't leave until we were all done for the night, until Josie and Lena were back in the house.

And out in the barn, you'd never know the party planner's worst fears had just come to life on the other side of the wall. Everyone is dancing, laughing, drinking, having a great time. The band is on their last song, and people are slowly starting to trickle out. After the last of them leave—including Amber, who is not happy that I have been MIA all night—it's just me, Josie, and Lena. The bartenders have closed up shop, the band left us their card, and there's nothing left but a few bags of trash and some glasses on the tables.

"Man, what a night," Josie says, scraping some of the empties into a trash can that she's carrying around to the tables. "I mean, aside from the psycho dipping in for a hot sec, that actually went *really* well."

Lena laughs nervously.

"Yeah, I'm really sorry about that," she says, bending over to pick up a few cups.

"Don't be sorry, hon," Josie says. "You have nothing to be sorry for."

"Actually," I cut in, "we wanted to talk to you about that, Jo."

"Sure, absolutely. Anything you need," Josie says, turning to Lena. Lena sighs and looks at her with those sweet, sweet eyes.

"Thank you, Josie. I'll take you up on that. But do you mind if we save it for tomorrow? I'm just a little spent."

"Sure, hon. Absolutely," Josie says, putting a hand on Lena's shoulder. "I heard you were sort of a badass tonight, with the nut-kick and all."

Lena looks up at me, and I shrug innocently.

"I couldn't help but brag," I say. "You kicked ass. Or, well, nuts."

We all laugh, and it feels good to see her smile.

"Alright, guys. I'm beat. I'm gonna head in, but I'll come back out tomorrow morning to finish with the clean-up," Josie says.

"Night, Josie, and thanks for your help," Lena says. Josie pulls her in for a long hug.

"You're thanking *me?*" she asks. "You kidding? Girl, we should be thanking *you*. The inn was alive again tonight. All because of you. Night, guys."

"Night," we say in unison.

I move some of the stray chairs back to their tables and sweep some of the bigger debris up off the dance floor. Lena's wrapping up the cords on the stage, and putting all the glasses into a bin.

After I move the last of the furniture into its rightful place, I turn to find her. She's in the small washroom behind the bar, and I can hear the soft sound of her humming as she washes the glasses. I peek my head in through the door and lean up against the jamb, watching her as she cleans, humming away again effortlessly. I can't help but smile.

"Another original song?" I ask, and she jumps.

"Oh, didn't hear you," she says with a shy smile. "You been there long?"

"Just long enough to hear the last few verses," I say. She

smiles again, turning back to keep washing. "You doing okay?"

I lean up against the counter next to her. She nods, slowly.

"To be honest, I haven't felt that scared in a long time," she says. The bluntness of her answer hits me harder than that damn shutter did a few weeks ago. She's so strong, so tough, so determined to get things done. Hearing her admit that she wasn't ready for something, that it frightened her, frightens me.

"I'm sure that was scary for you. But I want you to know that I wouldn't have let anything happen to you." She turns the water off and looks over to me.

"Thank you, Jesse. I know," she says. "But it wasn't that I was afraid of him hurting me. It's that the second I saw him, I knew we were done for. I knew Tiger had us. Had them. That's what scares me."

I push off the counter so that I'm standing directly behind her, my front to her back. She turns slowly to face me, and I reach a finger down to lift her chin.

"Hey," I whisper. "This isn't how this ends. We're going to talk to Josie. We're going to figure out how to keep you guys safe. They're done making you run."

Her eyes are floating back and forth between mine, searching for any hint of fabrication, but I know she won't find any. Because I mean every fucking word.

Tonight was the last time one of the Bentley brothers threatens Lena, or Millie, or Caleb on my watch. Whether I'm here with them on the shore, or thousands of miles away somewhere in the tropics. This whole game Tiger is playing ends before any of us go anywhere.

"It's funny," she says, "because tonight I faced one of

my biggest fears. But right now, all I can think about is you. And I don't want to stop."

My eyebrows jump at her words, my dick following suit. My heart is beating in my stomach, and I know this is it. I'm not backing away this time. I'm not letting her slip by me again. I'm not letting her go without telling her, showing her, what she's done to me.

24

LENA

Maybe it was the thought of us all leaving sooner rather than later. Maybe it was seeing Micah and feeling like our safe haven wasn't so safe anymore. Maybe it was an adrenaline rush. But I want Jesse, and I want him *now*. I want him to understand how badly. I want him to know how insane I've been going over these last few weeks.

I start to tell him, just after he swears he's going to help us figure out the Tiger situation. "It's funny, because tonight I faced one of my biggest fears. But right now, all I can think about is you. And I don't want to stop."

And I mean it. I'm done playing games. Done dancing around this inn without letting him know how fucking crazy he makes me, in the best way.

He takes a step closer to me so that our hips are flush against each other, and I can feel a bulge behind his jeans. He kneels down slowly, tucking a stray strand of my hair behind my ear.

"Then don't," he whispers, and every hair on my body stands on end. His fingers slink through my hair, wrapping tight around my head, and he pulls me up to him so that our lips crash together. He tastes better than I'm ready for, and my body reacts by pulling him even closer. I reach my hands up and tug his sandy hair, letting my fingers swim through it like fish in the water. Holy shit. I want to kick myself for not doing this weeks ago.

I wrap my arms around his neck, pulling myself up onto my tip-toes, and he reaches his arms around my waist and lifts me up. I wrap my legs around his waist, nothing between him and me but the thin lace of my thong under Josie's blue dress, and all the heat in my body rushes to the most delicate spot between my legs. He steps over and sets me on the counter, and the cool sensation of the counter's surface on my bare ass makes my body buck in his direction. He slides his fingers out of my hair, and lets them tug on one of the straps of my dress. He pulls one down, laying long, slow kisses down my neck, across my collar bone, and onto my shoulder. Then, he does the same on the other side, and all I can do is clench my legs around him tighter. I let my hands slide down his broad shoulders until I reach the bottom button of his shirt, then quickly work my way up to the top. I push the button-up off his big shoulders, and he's in a tight undershirt. I tug the undershirt out from the waist of his jeans, and admire his big chest while I let my fingers get to work on his belt.

He moans under his breath as I do, the anticipation of what's coming killing us both. As I undo his belt and jeans, he slides his hands up my thighs, letting his fingers dance along the teeny straps of my g-string. But instead of pulling them down, he traces my panty line with one finger, then two. He pulls me in for another kiss, our tongues lashing together, searching one another wildly. Then he lets one finger glide down into my panties, another going with it. He feels how wet I am and his eyes widen in surprise, looking hungrier than ever.

"Damn," he whispers, and it's so sexy that I can't stop myself from biting his lip.

"I told you," I whisper into his ear, "all I can think about is you."

He pushes his groin into my hand, letting the bulge press up against me.

"Right back at you," he says. I smile, tugging on his bottom lip with my teeth again before sliding my hand down into his boxers. I take his whole length in my hand—and Jesus *Christ, why* didn't I do this weeks ago?

I start stroking him slowly at first, letting myself get familiar with every inch of him. Then I push down his jeans, and slide my hand up and down wildly, squeezing him as I go. His head drops back with pleasure, and I pull him into me, letting my tongue draw trails up his neck. When he gets himself together, he continues his own work, letting his fingers dive deeper into my panties. He plays with me a little bit, letting his fingers explore my most sacred parts, sliding and gliding around in the moisture he's made.

Finally, when I can't take anymore, he plunges two of them into me, pumping in and out, causing my legs to spread involuntarily.

"Fuck, Jesse," I cry out, clutching onto a lock of his hair as I throw my head back. My hand is still working in his pants, but it's slowing down as I lose all control. He leans down to me.

"We're getting there," he whispers. Slowly, he slides his fingers out of me and wraps his hands around my thighs. He pulls me to the edge of the counter, pushing my dress up over my knees. He bends down, leaving small kisses on my calves, knees, and thighs. He pushes my dress up, higher, higher, until all of me is exposed. His eyes flick up to mine, and there's this flare in them, like he's urging me to watch. His eyes still locked on mine, he reaches a finger up and gently slides my panties to one side. He lets a hot breath cover me, and my legs spread even wider. Then I feel his mouth on me, his tongue swirling, investigating like it's going to draw a map. I say his name once, twice, three times, and I feel myself getting closer and closer to the edge.

He stops finally, coming up for air, and I'm panting like a fucking dog. He shakes his hips so that his jeans fall further, but then looks to me in worry. And I realize just what he's thinking.

"I'm on the pill," I tell him quickly, careful not to let any of this phenomenal energy go to waste. He nods slowly, then steps back to push his boxers down over his hips. When he springs free, my jaw drops. I felt him, but I didn't *see* him—-all of him, anyway—until right this moment. And holy. Fucking. Shit.

He moves in on me again, twirling my hair around his hand and gently pulling my head back so that he can kiss me again.

"My God, Lena," he says, resting for a moment to put his forehead to mine, "I've wanted you for a long time now. So fucking bad."

I scoot my ass closer to the edge of the counter, urging him to keep going.

"Then do something about it," I whisper back, my hands gripping his ass and pulling him to me. In one quick, magical move, he reaches down, sliding my panties over to one side again, then thrusts into me, and my entire body reacts to him. It feels like every cell in my being is clenched around him, begging him not to leave.

Our eyes lock for a moment, then he moves, faster, and faster, lifting me off the counter so that he's totally supporting my weight.

He's pumping into me, harder, faster with every thrust, and I can't get enough. I wrap my legs around him tighter, pulling on his hair, biting his neck.

"Harder, Jesse, harder. Show me how bad you wanted this," I whisper, and I'm almost surprised at myself. I've never been one for dirty talk, but I can't help it with him. I'm only saying what my body feels. It's the God-honest truth.

It makes him moan with pleasure, and the next thing I know, we're up against the wall behind us. He has one arm around my waist, the other pressed up against the wall above my head. He's moving harder, faster, and I know I'm almost there. Finally, he carries me back to the counter, laying me down slowly. He lowers my head down in his hand, and kisses me again, hard. Then he drives into me again, over, and over, and over.

"Lena," he groans, and I feel the veins in his forearms push out as I'm clutching onto them.

"Yes," I moan back. "Yes."

Finally, in one more quick motion, he pumps into me one more time, and we both explode. After a few moments of heavy breathing, he finally lifts himself off of me.

"My God, Lena," he says, breathless. "I've wanted so much for so long now. So much."

And I wonder if he just means the immensely sexy scenario we just found ourselves in, or if he wants even more. If he wants what I want.

After a few more minutes of basking in our glow, he helps me off the counter and straightens out my dress for me. His bare chest is glistening in sweat, and it's all I can do not to lick it off.

He kneels down for another kiss, but this one is long, and sweet, and slow. He goes around the back of the bar and brings out a roll of paper towels for me to clean myself up with, and bends over onto the floor to grab his shirt. He tugs it on over his head and shakes his sandy hair back into place.

"Can I show you something?" he asks. I nod and take his outstretched hand. He leads me out of the washroom, up the stairs, and into his bedroom.

We walk up to his room, and he motions for me to have a seat on his bed. I sit down cross legged, making sure my dress is covering everything—even though we've crossed that bridge now. He kneels down and pulls out a bin from under his bed. He lifts the lid and pulls out a dark brown leather photo album. It's thick, with pages and corners of photos sticking out from every angle. He sits down on the bed next to me and takes in a long breath.

"What's this?" I ask. His green-blue eyes lift to mine.

"This," he says, opening the big book, "was my mom's. It was her scrapbook, all about the Inn. Starting from the first day they bought it, up through her very last renovation."

He slides it over onto my lap, and I start staring at the pages. I see photos of his parents running all over the property, smiling in one of the big trees, holding hands down by the water. They look to be taken around the same time as the photo that I found in the kitchen drawer that day.

Then there's a photo of his mother in front of the inn with a big, round, belly. The inn appears to be freshly painted, and the flower beds are filled with color. The next page is a photo of Mr. and Mrs. Rowan, with a baby Josie between them. Then, there's a photo of Josie on the porch, holding another baby in her arms.

"Aw," I say, "baby Jess."

He smiles.

In some of the next photos, there's new furniture on the patio. Then new bedding in the rooms, and the updates to the kitchen and bathrooms. The Rowans had proudly documented every improvement made to their home and business.

There are photos showing the construction of the dock, and a few of the barn getting a facelift, the "Restaurant" sign being lifted into place.

There's a few photos of Josie and Jesse during their late teen years, sitting on the front porch with a very young Coby. There are photos of guests on the porch, smiling as they hold up glasses of lemonade.

There are photos of Mr. Rowan and Josie in a kayak, Berta and Mrs. Rowan on the dock sipping margaritas, and Jesse with his arm around Mrs. Rowan's neck, kissing her forehead. There was so much love here, once. And when I look up at him, I feel a lump rise in my throat. Because I know that now, there's love here again. And I'm just not sure how long it can last.

I swallow back my tears, letting my fingers glide over the faded photos.

"You guys had such a beautiful life," I say. I can feel the tears welling in my eyes. Somehow, even after the night I had tonight—before Jesse gave me the most toe-curling pleasure I've ever felt in my life—my heart is still breaking for him even more than myself. I see all that they had—all that *he* had—and now it's gone. He's big and tall and broad and strong, but meeting that vulnerable side of him, the side that feels like he let down every last person he loves, makes him seem like a little boy.

And yet, he's so much more.

He's so kind, and gentle, and fun. He's loving toward Caleb, nurturing, even. He's reassuring toward Millie. And to me, he's everything. He's big and bold and brave, but warming up to the idea of being open with me on a regular basis. He feels like the home I never knew I was missing.

"Hey," he says, covering my hand with his. "Don't be sad. I'm not showing you this to make you upset. I just wanted you to see what you're doing."

I look up at him.

"What I'm doing?"

He nods and smiles, sliding the book back over to his lap.

"You crashed into this place like a hurricane, and I wasn't ready for you. But I'm glad you landed here, because you kicked my ass into gear. All of these updates, projects on the inn that my parents did over the years, that was my childhood...these last few months with you reminded me so much of those times. You reminded me that I *can* keep this place running. I can make it that gem again. I can make them proud, even if they can't be here to see it."

I stare at him blankly, blinking. Is he saying what I think he's saying?

"You've done so much for me and this place since you've been here, so much that you don't even realize. And since you were willing to take a chance on the inn, and on me, I want to take a chance and open it back up."

I blink a few more times, my chest heaving up and down. I throw my arms around his neck and kiss his cheek.

"That's amazing, Jess," I whisper. "It's going to be great. I know it will."

He wraps his strong arms around my body, pressing me harder into him. I want him to ask me to stay. I want him to ask me to help him. To run it together. But if he does that, I might not be able to say no. And with Tiger on the hunt for us now, I know that's not an option. I'd have to say no. I'd have to choose them, because they are my family. They've been all I have for so long, that I'm not sure where Jesse fits into that. And that very thought is making it hard to breathe, because it feels like he's the missing piece to my puzzle. Without him, it won't ever be complete, and yet, I see no other choice than to move on with that hole in my heart.

M y arm is completely numb. She's curled up on it, has been for hours, but I can't bring myself to move it. She looks so peaceful right now, the most peaceful she's looked since she got here. Like she knows that because I'm here, keeping watch, she's okay to just be. To just rest, not think. And I love that. I love that I can give her that peace. I don't ever want her to be without it again.

After another half-hour, the bright morning sun creeps in through my window, and she squints and begins to stir. She rolls over to look at me, her coal-colored hair splayed out all over my pillows, and when the early-morning fog in her eyes clears, she smiles at me. I make a note to myself that going forward, I want to limit the number of mornings in my life that don't start this way. Because I can't think of a single thing more beautiful than this.

She's swimming in the t-shirt of mine that she's wearing, the blue dress lying in a heap on the floor next to us. After I showed her the book last night, we couldn't keep our hands off each other. She makes me higher than any drug ever would—like some sort of human endorphin. And now that I've had her, I can't stop. I want her in every single way.

I told her I wanted to bring the inn back to life, to open it back up for guests. I wanted to run it like my parents did. Because of her.

I wanted to ask her to run it with me. But I'm not good at this shit. I've never been any good at anything but a quickie in the parking lot. But with her, I want to be. I want to be next to her while we put this place back together. I want to watch her eyes light up when we finish a project, or when the rooms fill up for a weekend.

But after Micah's unwelcome surprise appearance, I'm scared to bring it up. Suddenly, my heart starts racing in my chest. I want to lay here with her all day. But I also want to get to my sister. I want to talk about options, ways to keep Tiger and the rest of the Bentley assholes out of here. Away from Lena, Millie and Caleb once and for all.

"Morning," she says groggily, blinking a few times and rubbing her eyes. She looks so hazy and peaceful that I feel myself melting. I want to rip that shirt right off of her and pick right back up from where we left off last night. And I happen to know that she doesn't have any panties on. Easy access. But suddenly, her eyes grow wide, and she jumps up from bed. "Holy shit. It's morning!" she says.

She scrambles out of my bed, searching for her clothes. She pulls my shirt up over her head and tosses it to the bed, and pulls the dress back on, making my insides do all kinds of crazy things. She slips her panties back on, and every part of me sinks, knowing the chances for a morning repeat are officially out the window.

"What's wrong?" I ask. Then we hear laughter coming from outside, and we turn to each other, "Shit. The kid's up."

"Yeah," she says. She turns to bolt out the door, but stops. She scurries back to me in the bed, pushing me up against my headboard. She straddles me for a moment, and dips her head down to cover my lips with hers. Her tongue slides on top of mine, reminding me that she's my favorite flavor of anything. Ever. She pulls away slowly, those starry eyes staring into mine. She winks, then hops off and runs out the door. I give myself a moment to get collected, and ...ahem, softer, then hop up and pull a shirt on. I follow her down the steps and out the barn doors. As she jogs up the steps to the porch, Caleb's running back across the lawn toward us. Millie's on the front porch, one hand holding a mug, the other arm crossed over her chest. Josie sits in one of the rocking chairs. Their expressions are identical: one eyebrow raised, and a sly smile on their lips.

But before they can make any sort of smart-ass, big sister remark, Caleb comes crashing to us.

"Did you guys have a sleepover? Cool!" he exclaims innocently, staring up at Lena and me as he munches on a pretzel in his hand. I swallow and look at Lena. She smiles nervously, then looks back up at the sisters on the porch.

Millie looks to Josie, and the two of them burst into laughter. I clear my throat anxiously, just as a shy smile tugs on the corner of Lena's mouth.

"Zip it, you two," she says, just above a whisper, trying to stifle her own laugh. I want to go jump off the dock. But I'm also relieved to find a moment of laughter in what is sure to be a stressful day ahead. We've yet to bring up the Bentley brothers, and it's a black cloud that is sure to turn into a storm.

When they finally gather themselves, wiping tears of laughter from their eyes, Josie stands up from her chair.

"I gotta get back to the city tomorrow," she says, her face

growing more serious. "Did you guys want to talk about last night?"

There it is. The reminder of Micah. All the lightness in the air is crushed, pressed to the ground by something heavier, something that we were avoiding altogether just a few hours ago, when Lena and I were buried deep inside of each other.

I see Lena's back straighten, and Millie's expression changes instantly. I can tell Josie feels bad for darkening the mood, but I know she's right. We need to talk.

Lena clears her throat, looking to Millie, then back to Josie.

"Yeah," Lena says, tucking a piece of hair behind her ear. "But can we make it a little later?"

Josie's eyes catch mine, and I shrug behind Lena's back.

"Yeah," Millie says, her voice hushed as her eyes find Caleb running through the yard. "I have a lunch shift at Berta's. Can we talk tonight?"

Josie nods.

"Sure, of course," she says.

Lena nods and thanks her, and they both walk into the house. I want to follow, make sure she's okay, press her to talk to my sister. But I feel restrained by the wall she's just put up, barricading her and Caleb and Millie. It feels like we need to be handling this sooner rather than later. It feels like we should be planning how to protect them from whatever move Tiger is planning. But Lena and Millie seem to want to put it off for now, and Lord knows, they are much more familiar with these types of situations than I am. But man, I wish they weren't.

I plop down on the porch steps, watching Coby and Caleb run from one side of the lawn to the other. I can't help but smile when I watch them. It's like they were made for each other. Coby changed, too, when my parents died. He lost his morning walk partner, my mom. He lost his best belly rubber, my dad. Even *he* looked at me with soul-crushing disappointment when it all landed in my hands.

I sigh. I'll miss this kid, too, if they leave. *When* they leave. Josie takes a seat next to me, her long legs dangling off the second step.

"So," she says, squinting in the sunlight.

"So," I say.

"How deep in are ya with her?" she asks, without bringing her eyes to me.

"Pardon?"

"You heard me. How serious is it?"

I look down at my hands on my knees. I know what the sane, sound answer should be. And I know that it's the exact opposite of what I'm actually feeling.

"I don't know, Jo," I say. "I know I want her—them—to be safe and done with this shit. I want to help them. I need to."

She nods slowly, folding her hands in her lap.

"Jess, I know you care about her. About all three of them. Hell, I think we all do. Me, Berta, the whole damn town. Except maybe Amber," she says, nudging me play-fully. I roll my eyes. "I'll talk about this all they want to. I'll do everything I can to help them. But in the end, they have to know they're safe. And they know this Tiger guy, we don't. They'll know whether or not a few words on a piece of paper will keep him away—which, judging by his idiot brother, I'm assuming they won't."

I look up at her, my eyebrows knitting together.

"What exactly are you trying to say, Jo?" I ask. She sighs again.

"I'm just saying that even if I say all the right things,

make all the right moves, get them the right help...they might still go. They might have to. And I just want you to be ready for that."

She stands up slowly, and puts her hand on my shoulder before she goes into the house.

"I just don't want to watch you fall apart again," she says.

And as she walks into the house, my big sister has no idea how those last words crush me, pinning me to the ground beneath me.

For the rest of the day, Lena's following Caleb around the property, playing catch, helping him fish—or, at least, trying to—and reading to him on the patio. Each time I find them, I feel the resistance of that protective force field she has up, that she won't even let *me* get through right now. And I fucking hate it.

When I insert myself in a frisbee game, she gives an awkward smile with zero eye contact, then excuses herself to go sit on the patio. And every single time she avoids me, my stomach flips in this out-of-control way, Josie's words echoing in my ears.

They might still go. They might have to.

No. No one is going to force them to run again. I won't let it happen.

Finally, after what seems like years, Millie gets back from her shift. Caleb runs around to the front of the house to greet her, and I can't help but feel relieved that I have a minute alone with Lena. Only, when I turn back around, she's taking off, power-walking down to the water. She continues briskly down the dock, arms wrapped around her body, till she reaches the end. I take in a long breath, watching her take a seat and dangle her legs off the edge. And I wonder if this is a preview of what I'll be doing again sooner than I think—watching her walk away.

I make my way down the dock slowly, purposely hitting the wood on all the creaky spots so I don't scare her. I take a seat next to her, leaving a little bit of space between us, despite how badly I want the exact opposite. I don't say anything, I just stare out over the water, watching the fading sun pull closer to the horizon.

After a moment, she scoots closer and turns toward me. She reaches a hand up into my hair, tugging on it gently, and pulls me into her for a hard kiss. Her other hand strokes my jawline gently, and when we finally pull apart, her eyes are still closed, her face looking almost pained.

"You okay?" I ask her. "I was beginning to think maybe you forgot about last night."

She smiles, her hand still in my hair, our foreheads pressed together. Her eyes flick up to mine.

"I couldn't forget about last night if I tried," she whispers, and my whole body melts in her hand. Slowly, the smile fades from her face, and her eyes fill with worry again.

"Hey," I say, nudging her, pulling her into me. I stroke her knee with my thumb, as my other arm holds on tight to her waist. "What's going on?"

Slowly, she looks back up at me again.

"I don't know how else this can end besides us leaving," she whispers, and I see her trying to hide her tears. Suddenly, I'm fighting back my own.

"Hey," I say again, this time, wrapping both of my arms around her. "Josie's gonna figure something out, okay? Don't give up. We're gonna figure this out."

She looks up at me slowly, and a half-smile appears.

"'We,'" she says. I smile and kiss her forehead.

"We," I say.

LATER THAT EVENING, Millie carries a passed-out Caleb up to his bed after a filling dinner of Josie's crab cakes. When she gets back downstairs, we all look at each other, and without saying a word, proceed into the parlor. We all know it's time to talk.

I sit on the loveseat, and to my surprise, Lena sits next to me, pulling one knee to her chest. She settles in against me, leaning back and resting her head on my shoulder. Our sisters don't even acknowledge it, and they don't look surprised. There's something about it that feels so natural. Like they almost expected it. They expected us. Like they could see us coming from miles away, destined to collide and become something better together. I wrap my arm around Lena's shoulder and kiss the top of her head. Our eyes dart from each other, then to Millie, to Josie. Finally, Josie begins.

"So, tell me about Tiger. Tell me what you've tried before," she says.

Millie draws in a slow, shaky breath, and Lena reaches out to squeeze her hand.

"Well," Millie goes on, "we've been together since high school. But he only started hitting me when I got pregnant."

I feel my whole body tense up as Millie tells us about Tiger, about how he alienated her from her family, how he cut off every other lifeline she had. About how she became so dependent on him that she would rather take the hit—literally—then worry about her child's welfare, and whether he would have food to eat and a roof over his head. The only person Tiger couldn't completely cut out was Lena.

"He knew Lena would never leave us," Millie says,

looking over at her sister and squeezing her hand. "But there wasn't a ton Lena could do. I wasn't ready to go, until the last time. And you," she says, turning to look at Lena dead-on, "you just waited. You did everything you could until I was ready. I'm sorry I wasn't ready earlier. I'm sorry I put you through that exact same nightmare all over again. I'm sorry I became Mom." Tears are streaming down her face, and down Lena's and Josie's, but she doesn't break. Lena is still holding her hand, and Millie keeps talking. She lets it all out, giving Josie as much information as she can. And as she speaks, my grip on Lena tightens, my other hand balling into a fist that I desperately want to unleash on Tiger Fucking Bentley.

"I tried filing for a restraining order two times," Millie goes on. "The first time, his dad knew the judge, so it was denied."

My knuckles are turning white.

"The second time, he threatened to kick me out and keep Caleb," she says, her voice catching in her throat. "And I knew he meant it. So that was it. There was no other option. But the last time he hit me, right before we came here...that last time he dragged me into Caleb's room. Normally, he'd send Caleb in there before he even touched me—at least he had the decency to protect him from seeing it all. Although, Caleb always came out when he heard us. But the last time, he didn't. In fact, Tiger dragged me in there and knocked me out in front of Caleb, telling me before he did that 'the kid needed to understand what his mom did wrong.' Turns out, what I did wrong that time was say hello to Matty Shiner, a guy we both knew from high school. Who knew."

Lena looks over to me and rubs my knee, clearly sensing how tense I am. How angry I am.

"Caleb begged him to stop, and ended up jumping on his back. And that's when I saw something that terrified me. Tiger turned to him and gave him that same look that he always gave me, right before the storm hit. It was like a resurrection of the demon inside of him each time. And I knew that we were playing a game with the devil. I knew there might be a chance that Caleb was next. And I'd rather die than let that happen."

Josie clears her throat after a few moments and smooths out her skirt. She leans forward to sip her tea, which has gone cold on the coffee table in front of us, and she sits back.

"Well, since he's not here to stop you right now," Josie says, crossing one leg over the other, "we can file a restraining order against him for temporary purposes. That's step one, although, I know you think it won't do much," Josie says. She reaches down on the ground and pulls her laptop out of her briefcase.

"Then we can file a petition for sole custody, stating child endangerment as the main reason. We can also show record of you having sole financial responsibility for Caleb for the last few months while you were here. Now, this might be rough, but do you have any photos of any of the...uh...damage done to you? We could—"

"Sorry to cut you off," Millie says, scooting to the edge of her seat, "I really appreciate the legal advice, but this feels like it's going to take a lot of work on your end. Unfortunately, I can't afford to pay you for your services."

I feel Lena's hand tighten on my knee. She's staring at her sister, and so am I. I look to Josie with a plea in my eyes. *Please, Jo. Help my girl. Help her sister. Help the kid. For me. Please.*

But my dear old sister doesn't even need to see it. Because we have similar hearts, Josie and I. The perfect combination of our parents'. She shakes her head and holds up her hand.

"Even if you could afford it, I'd refuse to take the money," she says. I let out a sigh of relief. She might be the biggest pain in my ass, but right now, I freakin' love my sister. "So, like I was saying, do you happen to have any photos of yourself, hospital records, anything?"

Millie shakes her head, but Lena swallows audibly and looks down at her feet.

"Lena?" Josie asks. Slowly, Lena lifts her eyes.

"I have a few photos saved on my phone from some of the times I came over afterwards," she says, her voice quiet. She looks to Millie slowly. Millie's eyes are wide.

"You...you do?"

Lena nods.

"Yeah," Lena says, her voice cracking. "Something inside told me I should, just in case we ever needed them for something like this."

"Great," Josie says, clapping her hands together like she just got great news. I look from Lena, back to Millie, back to Lena.

"I'm sorry," Lena says, "I should have told you, but I thought you'd make me get rid of them. I was just thinking back about all those times we took Mom in, and—"

"Thank you, Lee," Millie whispers, her jaw trembling. "You can share them with Josie. But I don't want to see them."

Lena nods.

"Any hospital records, anything like that?" Josie asks, her fingers moving a mile a minute across her keyboard. Millie shakes her head.

"None that will have anything to do with him," she says. Josie cocks her head, looking for an explanation.

"I only let Lena take me if I couldn't get the bleeding to stop on my own. So it was only a handful of times. And when I did, I always said I slipped, or something fell on me, etcetera. Never mentioned a thing about Tiger."

Josie nods, looking unsurprised. She's heard these same types of cases before, unfortunately. After typing away for another few minutes, she closes her computer.

"Alright, let me call my partner and see if there's anything else we might be able to do," she says. "I'm thinking a letter to him, filing for permanent restraining orders, if sole custody is granted, visitation *only* in a public place with supervision—"

"No." All three of us whip our heads to Millie. It's the first time Josie and I have heard any amount of defiance in her tone. And judging by the expression on Lena's face, she hasn't heard it before either.

"No visitation. If it's over, I need it to be *over*. We both do," she says.

Josie nods slowly, then reaches out a hand to touch Millie's shoulder.

"We're gonna stop him, Mill," she whispers, then walks out of the room to call her partner.

Lena stands up slowly and walks over to her sister, sitting on the arm of her chair. She wraps her arms around Millie and pulls her head into her chest, stroking the long, coal-colored hair that matches her own. Suddenly, Millie bursts into tears again, turning to hide her face in Lena's shirt. Lena sits calmly, rubbing her back, kissing the top of her head.

"Mill," she says. "Mill."

Finally, Millie looks up at her.

"This is good. This is a good thing. We're going to figure out a way to stop him, once and for all," she says, smiling and wiping the tears from her sister's face. Millie smiles for half a second, then stands.

"I love you for doing this," she says, then she looks to me. "All of you."

She takes a few steps toward the foyer, then turns around again slowly.

"I know what you guys are trying to do," she says. "And I'm so grateful. But we know how this goes. Either we get him behind bars, or someone...someone doesn't make it through this."

She turns and disappears from the parlor. Lena and I sit in silence for a moment, listening for Millie to reach the top of the steps, then go into the room. I stand up from the couch and walk over to her, placing my hands on her shoulders. Her breaths are long and drawn out, and I can feel her heart pounding through her chest. I kneel down to kiss her shoulder, then wrap my arms around her and clutch her to me. She turns, burrowing her head in my chest. She's silent, but I can feel her tears soaking through my shirt. Finally, she pulls away and looks up at me. I use my thumbs to wipe the last tears from her cheeks.

"I should stay with them tonight," she says. I nod, even though the words are an unexpected blow to my gut.

"Of course," I say, stroking her hair. Her hands land on the back of my neck, and she pulls me down for a long kiss. Our foreheads press together, and she takes in one more breath. She turns to walk toward the steps.

"This has to work," she says. "We have to make this work."

As she's walking away, I lunge for her hand. She turns back to me.

"Hey," I say. "We've got this. Josie is going to figure

something out. We are going to help you guys take care of this."

She stares into my eyes, and a slow, sad smile crosses her lips, as though she wants to believe me, but hasn't been convinced quite yet. She lifts my hand up and kisses it, pressing it to her cheek.

"Goodnight," she says.

"Night," I say.

She's a fixer of everyone else's problems. She's never had anyone to share the burden. But as she walks away, carrying my heart with her, I know I want to be the person who changes that, forever.

26

LENA

Weirdly, it didn't take Millie long at all to fall asleep. I guess fear and never-ending anxiety can either keep you up for days, or make you crash. I watch my sister and her son from the window seat, Millie clutching onto Caleb for dear life as they both dream. I've been going back and forth for hours about all of Josie's suggestions, and Millie's doomsday declaration at the end of it all. There has to be a way to end this misery Tiger has created, but I don't have the answer.

Well, in truth, I do know the answer, but it's not one I can say out loud, even to myself. In reality, I know we'll have to move again. Soon. Caleb, Millie and I will need to pack up, and keep trekking on to the next stop, hoping Tiger eventually gives up.

In reality, I know I'll be leaving the Rowan Inn, and its keeper, behind.

It was so easy to leave the first time. There was nothing left to abandon. There was no piece of life that I dreaded being without.The only two people I truly loved were with me. They were my whole life, my reason for living.

But now I have another reason. He's tall, with sandy hair, and eyes that match the Bay. He's rough around the edges but soft at the core, and he knows me in ways that no one in my past ever cared to explore.

I'm sure we will have to leave Baycrest. How can we not? I sigh as I look over at my sister again. I know she's right. Maybe someday, Tiger will get bored. He'll find someone else to control, and that poor soul will distract him from chasing my sister. But until then, it's on us to keep each other safe. To keep Caleb safe. To let him grow up. We'll listen to what Josie has to say tomorrow after she's talked it over with her partners at the firm. But in all actuality, Millie and I both know where it will lead. And that's far, far away from here.

I'm exhausted trying to figure it out, and yet I know I'll be awake for hours longer. The moon is so bright over the Bay tonight, and the water is eerily calm. Just as I'm about to pull myself up and schlep over to the bed, I hear footsteps outside. My breath catches. And then I see Jesse, marching down the length of the dock.

I smile.

We're always on the same schedule, he and I.

I hop off the seat and pull a sweatshirt on over my head. I sneak out of the bedroom and down the steps, making sure to close the parlor door as quietly as possible. I slide across the grass and tip-toe onto the dock. As I get closer, he whips around to see me.

"What are you doing up?" he asks, standing to greet me. I don't answer him. Instead, I press up onto my toes and lunge for him, wrapping my arms tightly around his neck. I let my lips cover his, let my tongue lead the way. He moans softly at my touch, and it turns my insides to flames. I can feel the heat gathering between my legs, and right now, nothing matters but leading him back to that spot.

I sink back down to my heels, catching his eyes with mine. I step backward toward the boat, keeping my eyes on his. Then I slip my sweatshirt off over my head, pulling my shirt with it and letting them land next to me on the dock in a heap. I'm not wearing a bra, and my nipples stand on end as the cool nighttime breeze blows by. His eyes widen, his hand reaching back to scratch the back of his neck. I slowly, agonizingly give my pajama shorts and panties a tug, tossing them aside to meet my shirt on the wood below. I take a step closer to him. His Adam's apple bobs in his neck, his eyes still saucers.

I slowly take his hand, guiding it to the center of my chest. I let his fingers trail down the middle of my body, leading them to the center between my legs.

"Lena," he whispers, and my whole body reacts to the perfect sound of my name leaving his lips. Just as I'm about to press his hand to the spot that wants him most, I step back, jumping off the boat into the black bay. When I rise to the surface, he's kneeling down.

"Are you nuts?" he asked.

I smile, letting the water bob me up and down.

"Care to join?" I ask. He looks around slowly, as if anyone else would be outside the Rowan Inn during the wee hours of the morning. Then, as if he can't get to me fast enough, he strips down to his boxers at the edge of the dock. As my eyes scour every inch of him, dying to see the last bit, I feel the playfulness slowly recede. I need him, right now.

Finally, he lets his boxers wriggle down his legs, and does a perfect dive into the water. He finds me almost immediately, letting his lips find my navel under water. As he breaks the surface, we collide, kissing, touching, treading.

I feel his fingers trailing back down my body, slowly leading to where they left off before I jumped. I pull away from his kiss, bracing for it, just as he plunges a finger inside of me, letting it explore me. I know we're underwater, but I also know he can tell that I'm wet regardless. I dip the back of my head into the water, letting my breasts break the surface. His mouth finds one, then the other, as his fingers continue their dance inside of me. He tugs with his teeth, his fingers finding every inch of me that's been left untouched. My eyes open, and I grip the back of his head forcefully.

"I'm almost there," I whisper, unable to grasp how quickly this explosion is coming on. I entwine one of my legs with his, both of us still treading, even as he's working me to my max.

"Jess," I whisper again. "Jess."

He pulls me into him, kissing my neck, biting my bottom lip with his teeth. Then he presses his cheek to mine, his stubble gripping the side of my face and his hot breath caressing my ear.

"Let it go," he whispers, his voice gruff and dripping with sex. "Let yourself have it, baby."

He pumps his fingers into me again, but this time his thumb is stroking my throbbing bead on the outside. And that's all it takes for me to come apart in the middle of the bay, in his arms. I pound a fist against his chest, panting like an animal. He retreats his fingers, then pulls me into him for a long, slow kiss. He leads me to the ladder of the dock, guiding me up with a gentle hand on my ass. He pulls himself up after me, bending down to hand me my clothes. He's about to pull them on, when I stop him.

"I want to sleep in your bed tonight," I say. He nods, and I take off running, butt-naked down the dock, toward the barn.

What's the use in putting clothes back on, when I have no intention of wearing them the rest of the evening?

When we get inside the barn, he slides the doors shut behind us. He's covering his package with his clothes.

"It's cold out there," he explains, shrugging. I smile, sauntering over to him. I can't remember a time in my life where I've felt this comfortable being completely naked with someone. When I reach him, I drop to my knees in front of him. His eyebrow shoots up. I tug at his hands, pushing them away. But to my surprise, he stops me. He reaches down and pulls me up by my arms, bringing me to my feet.

"You don't have to do this," he says. Now I raise an eyebrow at him.

I also can't remember a time when I'd been with a guy that refused a blowjob.

"Well, you took excellent care of me in the water," I say with a sly smile. "It's payback time." As I start to kneel again, he grasps me harder.

"It doesn't have to be like that," he says. My eyes widen. "It's not a play-for-play, Lena. I wanted to make you come. I wanted to watch it, selfishly, yes, but I also wanted to take care of you. Of your body. I wanted you to be able to come undone. I didn't do it expecting anything in return."

I step back from him, tilting my head to the side.

Jesus Christ. Mr. Rowan is a fucking gentleman.

I spring onto him, wrapping my legs around his waist. He catches me, dropping his clothes in the process. When he does, I squeeze my thighs around him, letting my middle rub against his hard core. I kneel down and gently tug on his earlobe with my teeth.

"Well then," I whisper, "I'm gonna need you to take me upstairs and take care of my body. Again."

He smiles, then invades my mouth with his. He takes the stairs two-by-two, bursting into his bedroom like he's been celibate for a year. As he moves, I squeeze my legs around him, letting my wetness spread across his body. The way my body reacts to him is foreign to me.

When we get to his room, he lays me on the bed, breaking our lips apart and leaving a trail of kisses down my neck, to each breast, and then to the sweetest spot. He gently pushes my legs apart, and I reach my hands back to clutch onto the sheets.

He takes a finger, slowly sliding it in and out, all around my folds, letting it explore every surface of my most delicate places. He works so slowly, it's almost painful, but I grit my teeth, knowing how amazing it's going to be. I buck my hips in his direction, and he smiles.

"Patience, Lena," he whispers, his voice low and raspy, making me hotter and wetter by the second. I moan in response. He bends down, his mouth centimeters from me, his eyes still on mine. Finally, his tongue and lips find the space between my thighs, swirling around, sucking and licking me up until I'm sure I won't last another moment. I'm squirming around on his bed, trying desperately not to come too soon.

When he can tell I'm at the brink, he stops, flipping me over onto my belly. I pull myself onto my knees, sticking myself up into the air, giving him easy access to what I so desperately need him to take. He grabs my hips, pulling me back toward him, and I can feel my heart beating like a drum.

"Please, Jesse," I whisper. "Take me."

He groans as he reaches a hand around, kissing and biting my neck. I reach a hand back, cradling his sac, and I feel his tip touching me.

"Damn, Lena," he says, his body jerking back.

"I need you," I whisper. He leans around, kissing me hard.

"Oh, baby," he whispers, and I feel his head pushing into me slowly. I reach my hand back, grabbing his shaft and giving it a few hard pumps. Then I guide him into me so quickly it makes us both gasp. I fall forward onto my hands, clenching the sheets so hard that my fingers begin to tingle. He's moving in and out of me with such impeccable rhythm that I can no longer speak. He reaches around, letting his fingers pull and pluck one of my nipples, the other circling my clit with the same amazing rhythm. Finally, he comes out of me, gently flipping me to my back. He yanks me down so that I'm at the edge of his bed, and pulls my legs up onto his shoulders. He scoops one hand under my ass, then plunges into me again. The angle makes me moan as he moves.

He pumps in and out, in and out, as I tug his hair and scratch at his back. He moves back again, and this time, he comes all the way out of me.

"Tell me what you want," he grumbles, staring down at me.

"You," I say, "I want you."

"Tell me you want to stay," he says, teasing me with his tip again. My body is bucking, pulling toward him like a magnet, but my heart is stilling in my chest. "Tell. Me," he says, pumping in and out with each word. The achingly slow movements make me call out his name. I look into his eyes, and behind his desire, his desperation for a climax, is the same fear that's been camping out in me. I reach my hands up and let my fingers get lost in his hair. I pull him down to me, kissing him harder than I ever have, letting my tongue collide with his. I pull away, and push him back.

"I want to stay," I whisper. Because it's true. I don't want to go. I don't want to leave him. We can wait until tomorrow to discuss the fact that we don't always get what we want.

He kisses me again, just before thrusting into me one more time. The orgasm rushes through my body, the combination of my pure attraction to him and the emotions exploding inside of me. He falls on top of me, propping himself up on his elbows. I wrap my hands around his wrists, letting him pulse inside me for a few more moments.

When we gather ourselves, he leads me to the bathroom and turns on the shower. I let him wash my back and kiss my neck, and I do the same for him. We stand there, wrapped around each other, steaming water pounding against us for what feels like hours. When we're done, he hands me one of his shirts, and the scent of him wrapping around my body is almost enough to make me push for round three.

But I don't. Not tonight. Tonight, I just want to lie next to him, right up against him, feeling the breath move in and out of his body. Feeling the safeness, the certainty that his arms bring me—something I never felt before he came into my life. It's such an intense feeling of security with Jesse. It's not just that I feel physically safe with him. I mean, his sheer size and strength definitely help to ease some nerves. But it's also the fact that I can fall apart with him. I can lose control completely; I don't have to be the girl with the plan. For once, I have someone waiting for me to come back down to Earth, someone who will plan with me. Someone who doesn't mind catching all of my pieces and putting them back together. Someone who reminds me all that I'm capable of.

A few hours pass, and the exhaustion is finally starting

to hit me. My eyes are getting heavy, and I'm about to finally give in to sleep when I hear him whisper my name. I roll over so that I'm facing him, tucking my hand under my head.

"Did I wake you?" I ask, stroking the outline of his jaw with my finger. He shakes his head.

"I haven't slept yet," he says. He wraps his arms around me tighter, pulling me closer to his chest. "Pretend Tiger doesn't exist."

I pull my head back.

"Huh?"

"Just for a minute," he says. "Pretend Tiger doesn't exist. We know Millie and Caleb are safe. Okay?" His eyes are still closed as he talks. I humor him.

"Okay."

"What would you say to staying here, with me, for a few more months, and opening the inn back up?"

My heart begins to race in my chest. I pull back again, trying to keep my breathing from going haywire. But he feels me, and pulls me back into him.

"Shh. They're safe, remember? Caleb and Millie are safe. Tiger's gone. What would you say?"

I swallow, letting my finger twirl a piece of his hair.

"I'd say I'd love to," I whisper. "And that I know it will be a huge success, just like it used to be. Because of you."

His eyes open, moving back and forth between mine.

"Then stay," he whispers. I pull back again, this time further, causing his hands to break apart behind me.

"Jesse, we don't—"

"I know, I know. We still need to talk to Josie. But what if we *can* make this work? What if you could stay, all of you, and be safe?" He pulls himself up so that he's sitting now, and I do the same. He gets up and walks around the bed, then kneels down by my side, putting his hands on my knees. "If she can get custody, if we can stop him, would you stay? A few more months, just to give it a try?"

I lift my eyes to his, the pleading hope in his voice making me simultaneously melt and panic. I put my hands on his, then lift them to either side of his face. I blink back the tears that are prickling at my eyes.

"If we knew we were safe, I'd stay as long as you want me," I whisper.

A boyish smile crosses his face, and it all but tears me to shreds. He pops up, kissing me hard before climbing back in bed. He wraps himself around me again, nuzzling into the back of my neck. And as I clutch onto him, I stare blankly ahead, knowing the hours I actually sleep tonight will be few and far between.

27

JESSE

We wake up late the next morning, rightfully so, since we spent so long fucking and talking. I swear to God, I want to spend every night like that from here on out. Inside her, next to her, wrapped around her. But after I'm fully awake, the reality of the situation rests in my gut like a sack of bricks. I remember that the hypothetical question I asked her about staying with me was just that—hypothetical.

I threw myself out there last night. Asking someone to stay, giving someone the ability to crush me the way I was crushed when Mom and Dad died—it's not my MO. Not part of my persona. I'm the no-bullshit, no-strings-attached, quick-screw in the parking lot kind of guy. At least I was. Until this tornado of a brunette blew in here a few months ago.

Now I'm vulnerable again. It's fucking terrifying, but I need her, and my desperation to protect her and to make her happy...it's more than any fear I have left inside of me. It's stronger. I guess in some weird way, I never left Baycrest because I was waiting for something. And now I know that something was Lena.

She stirs in my arms, then rolls over to squint at the alarm clock on my nightstand.

"Shit," she whispers, her eyes closed again. She looks so cute in my big t-shirt, and I wish she never had to put pants back on.

"What?" I ask, leaning over to kiss her neck, her ear, her cheek. She smiles as she reaches a hand up, scratching my head.

"I gotta get up. I told Caleb I'd fish with him today," she says. I chuckle. "What?"

"Nothin.' It's just that it's not hard to tell you're from the city whenever you 'fish,'" I tell her. She smiles and playfully nudges me. "Sorry, but the way you handle the bait is just too good." I pinch my fingers together, imitating the dainty way she attempts to get the worm on the hook each time. She snorts and nudges me again, then she rolls over on top of me. I place my hands on her ass as she looks down on me.

"Yeah, well, I baited you pretty well I'd say," she teases, leaning down to kiss me. Her tongue trails my lips as she pulls away, and my body ignites. I moan.

"Yeah, you did," I say, smiling back and propping a hand behind my head as she hops out of bed to put her own clothes back on. I watch the way she bends over, memorizing every curve of her body. I whistle with satisfaction, and she rolls her eyes, smirking. "I want to take you out tonight."

She turns to me, eyebrow raised.

"Take me out? Where?"

"Some place nice," I tell her. "On the boat. Not that hooking up in the barn...and the bay...and the washroom…haven't been hot." She smiles. "But I'd like to take you on a real date."

She tugs her mane up into a bun on the top of her head, stray hairs falling out as she does. God, she's beautiful.

"Okay," she smiles. "Millie has the day shift today, but I can go when she gets back." I nod and smile.

"I'll be waiting."

She kisses me again, then disappears out of my bedroom door. I lean back against my headboard for a minute, soaking in the last twenty-four hours. This is going to work. It has to. I want her to see how amazing it would be here—it *will* be here. I know Josie will figure this out.

I clean up the yard some—mowing this property takes me a few hours on the ride-on, but it's my favorite chore. Mindless, breezy, the warm Baycrest sun on my bare back and shoulders. It's home. When Dad was alive, we'd do it together—well actually, when Mom *and* Dad were alive, we'd do it together. She loved getting on the tractor as much as he and I did.

When I finish the last row I pause to look back at the inn—freshly painted, shutters all straight and repainted a deep green, the trees in bloom. The steps are fixed, and the new porch furniture all points in the same direction. Coby's lounging in the shade of the house, now that the lawn is manicured and up to Scarlett Rowan standards. This place is alive again, and it's all thanks to Lena.

I have this urge, now, something I haven't had since they died. I want to open the doors, plaster a "vacancy" sign, post flyers, get the website rolling again. This place deserves to be seen, to be shared. Weddings in the backyard again, honeymooners, family vacationers, romantic getaways. Except, of course, for sneaky getaways, say by a married man and his mistress. I remember one time, mom checked them in and realized that it was an affair. She couldn't help herself but mail the "Thanks for Staying with Us" card to his home address, care of he and his wife.

I smile at the memory. Mom was so mischievous, it surprised people. My god, I miss my parents.

I hear laughing toward the house, and I watch as Lena chases Caleb around to the front porch. She catches him, laying him on the ground and tickling his belly as he giggles.

How odd it is. I grew up in this charmed little town, with more room to grow than one kid could ever need. So much love all around me, so much happiness. And here she is, with no real example of love, aside from what she's taught herself to feel for Millie and Caleb. Yet, she's teaching me how to feel it again. Picking *me* up. They stop when they see me, and Caleb begins to trot across the big old yard toward me.

"Whatcha doing, Jesse?" he asks, his cheeks red from playing in the sun. Lena follows close behind, shoving her hands into her jean short pockets. When she does, it lifts the hem of her tank top, and I can see the defined lines of her stomach muscles as she breathes in and out. I force my eyes to peel away.

"Just finished mowing the lawn," I tell him. He nods.

"I like your tractor," he says, scratching his little head and tracing the entire body of the mower with his eyes.

"You wanna ride it back to the shed with me?" I ask him, looking to Lena for approval. She smiles and nods.

"Yeah, yeah, yeah!" he says, jumping up and down.

"One quick ride, bud, then I gotta take you to your mama. She wants you to have dinner with her at Berta's," she says. I smile and nod. Then, it's our time.

I stick my arm out and let him climb on, pulling him up so he's sitting on the seat in front of me. I show him how to pull the choke, and switch it into gear. When the machine roars to life, he claps his hands excitedly, then grips onto the steering wheel.

"Hang on tight," I tell him, giving Lena a quick wink. She smiles back and bites her bottom lip, and Caleb and I pull away. I let him take the mower around a few unnecessary loops before we pull into the shed.

"Great driving, Caleb," I tell him, once we hop down off it. He smiles. As we're walking out of the garage, I freeze. I look down and realize that he's taken my hand. He doesn't think anything of it, the same as if it were his mom or Lena. But it's huge for me, and my heart swells into my throat. This kid trusts me.

They can't leave.

I swallow and give his hand a little squeeze, walking back toward the front of the house.

"I like living with you," Caleb says matter-of-factly, delivering another blow to my gut. I let out a shaky breath.

"I like it too," I tell him. He smiles up at me, then squeezes my hand tighter. Lena's sitting on the porch step and hops up when she sees us coming. I watch her eyes drop to our hands, then meet mine. Her head drops to the side slightly, and her eyes fill with emotion. She smiles at me as we make our way toward her.

"You ready, Mr. Driver?" she asks Caleb. He smiles and nods. "I'm gonna run him to the Shell, then I'll be back." I wink at her.

"Can't wait."

As soon as her car disappears from the driveway, I head to the barn to grab the cooler I packed. It has a few beers, and a chocolate pie for later. I drag it down the dock and load up the boat. I go back inside and change into a nicer button-up and some khaki shorts, then head back down to the boat. I'm lying on the back seat while the wake from a passing boat rocks me back and forth, when I hear her coming down the dock.

She's got on a little sundress again, some sandals, and her hair is pinned back, spiraling down her back. I sit up and smile.

"I wasn't sure if this was nice enough, for where we're going," she shrugs, looking down at her ensemble. I stand up and offer her my hand, helping her onto the boat.

"You look perfect."

She smiles and kisses my cheek, then settles down in one of the seats. I untie us and push off, then start the engine.

"So, where are we headed?" she asks. I smile and shrug as I pick up speed. It's like the Bay knows I'm trying to sell it. The sky is streaked with pink and orange, and the Bay is reflecting them back onto us. The air is warm but not clammy, and the water is weirdly calm. We ride for a while before we see the lights ahead.

"What's that?" she asks, leaning forward.

"Good old Nap Town," I say.

"Nap Town?"

"Annapolis," I smile. "It's where we're having dinner."

A few minutes later, I pull the boat into the public dock, cut the engine, and tie it off. Her eyes are gleaming, reflecting the lights of the bars and businesses, and I can't help but smile as she takes it all in. I step off onto the dock, then help her follow me, lifting her by her waist. I take her hand and start leading her down the picture-perfect streets of Annapolis.

"This is so cute," she says, looking up and down at all the shops and windows. Finally, we get to the spot I've been looking for, Blu's. I made a reservation for eight o'clock, and

Carson, the owner, never lets me down. He greets us at the door and shakes our hands, leading us to the back of the restaurant, and out onto the patio. He takes us to a table all set up in the back corner. I smile and shake his hand again.

"Thanks so much, Carson," I say. He smiles and claps my back.

"You got it, man. Let me know if you need anything while you're here. Lena, so nice to meet you," he says, before swinging back around and heading into the busy restaurant.

My parents used to give out coupons and flyers for Blu's. It's a quick drive or boat ride to Annapolis from Baycrest, and Mom and Dad did a lot of advertising for them, and vice versa. Carson's mom passed away from cancer a few years back, and his dad has advanced Alzheimer's. We're sort of brothers in arms in that we both have a huge, beautiful burden to carry on for our families.

"Do the Rowans just know everyone on this Bay?" she asks, settling into her chair. I smile.

"Only the good ones."

Carson's staff brings our food in record time, and we shovel it down hungrily—me more so than her. I'm anxious to get to the rest of the night. I pay our bill, leaving a generous tip since I know that Carson already comped half our meal, and we head back to the boat. We take off again, and she's leaned back against the seat with my jacket over top of her, breathing in the cooler night air.

I take a detour on the way home, steering us out toward the open water. Only a few other boats are in sight, and they're all strung up with bright lights. When I see Thomas Point Shoal Lighthouse, I cut the engine. I make my way toward her, grabbing the cooler and pulling out two beers on my way. I spread a blanket out across the bench seats at the back of the boat, and motion for her to come back. She does, we clank bottles, and throw back a swig.

"It's amazing out here," she says, and I smile as I pull her into me. I look around at the water, getting darker as it mimics the sky. My Bay is doing its job tonight. She leans over to set her beer down, then turns back to me, putting a hand on my face.

"Thank you for this," she says. "This is amazing." She pushes up to kiss me. Our lips part and she rests her forehead on mine. "Ugh. I don't ever want to leave this place."

My heart begins racing in my chest at the thought. I've been doing a good job at suppressing it.

"Josie's working on it," I tell her. I use my finger to tilt her chin up. "Because I don't want you to leave, either." Her eyes search mine, and she traces my lips with her thumb.

"Let's go back to pretending everything's taken care of," she whispers. I smile against her lips as she presses them onto me.

To my surprise, she lifts up her dress slightly so that she can straddle me. She squeezes her thighs against me as she runs her fingers through my hair, gently tugging it to tilt my head back. She kisses my neck and gently bites my earlobe, and immediately, the rest of my body springs to action...if you know what I mean.

She moans against my ear as she bites, and it sends a shock down my spine. My grip on her thighs tightens as I pull her closer.

She pulls away for a moment, and I clear my throat.

"Ms. Winter," I say, staring down at her lips, swollen from their conquest of my neck and ears. "You're getting me excited out on open waters."

She smiles, leaning down to take my bottom lip in her teeth.

"Then I guess you're just gonna have to fuck me on open waters."

My jaw drops as she leans back. She takes my hand, slowly dragging it up her thigh to her panties underneath. She reaches out and unbuttons my shorts, tugging them until she has the access she needs. Her hand strokes me a few times, getting me ready. She reaches her hand up, using a finger to pull her panties aside, then slowly, *painfully* slowly, she slides down on top of me, taking all of me in. She moans and throws her head back, and I swear I'm about to bust right this second. It's unbelievable how fast she can make me this way. And how when we're done, I want nothing more than to be with her again.

She begins to ride me, and I know neither of us are going to last long. With the cool breeze, the last of the sunlight, and the small danger of someone seeing, it's way too intense to make it last.

But we don't need it to. Because I know *we're* going to last. We have to.

She moves up and down a few more times, clenching around me until I can't take it. I worry I'm going to leave fingerprints on her ass from clutching it so hard, but judging by the way she's digging her nails into me, I think I'll have some marks of my own. Finally, as she rocks back and forth one more time, she pulls my head into her as she clutches on, letting my name escape her lips in the sexiest way it's ever been spoken.

"Yes, baby," I whisper into her hair, as she slowly comes down off of her high while I'm finishing, too. When she opens her eyes again, I smile and kiss her lips gently. Then her jawline, her neck, her cheekbone, her nose. She shimmies off of me, and I reach for a napkin for her. She collapses back onto the seat, curling up against me.

"Well," I say, letting out a long sigh. "That's the hottest fucking boat ride *I've* ever been on." Her face bursts into laughter and my heart swells.

"Me too, Captain," she says with a wink. A few moments of silence pass, then I feel her grip around me tighten. "What if Josie can't fix this?"

I'm not sure what to say. I don't know how to answer her. So I don't. I just pull her in close to me, praying to the high heavens that my smart-ass sister is figuring this out as we speak.

AFTER ANOTHER HOUR OR SO, the air is getting uncomfortably chilly, so we head back to the inn. When we dock, I help Lena off the boat and we stroll down the dock together, my arm draped over her shoulder. It's late, but as we make our way to the house, I notice the kitchen light is on.

"Huh," she says. "That's odd. Millie's usually in bed by now." I nod and follow her to the parlor door. We walk into the kitchen and Millie jumps at the sound of the door creaking. She's sitting at the kitchen table, one foot up on her chair. Tears are staining her face, and she's clutching something in her hand so hard that her knuckles are white. On the ground next to her, a shovel is leaning up against the table.

"Mill? What's going on?" Lena asks her, striding over to her and rubbing her shoulders. "What is that?"

Slowly, Lena reaches for the piece of paper that's been crunched to oblivion, and slides it out from Millie's fingers. She unfolds it, and her face goes pale. Slowly, Lena sinks down into the chair next to Millie as she hands it to me.

The note is scribbled on a napkin in chicken scratch.

Time's up. Tiger's coming for his boy.

My hand starts to shake.

"Is this from the brother?" I ask, my voice stern. She nods.

"He probably never left. Tiger's not dumb enough to trust us to stay once he knew that we realized we'd been found. He's probably been watching us this whole goddamn time, ready to follow us if we left." Millie's lip is quivering. The tears are streaming down her face, and she makes no attempt to stop them. I snatch my phone off the counter and storm out into the front yard.

"Jo?" I ask, the second she picks up. "Jo, listen. The brother is still here. He left a note on her car while she was at the Shell tonight. I think he's been watching us."

"You've got to be fucking kidding me," Josie says. "We're applying for custody and for the restraining order. If he's already there, we can ask for another protective order, but if no one's there to enforce it…"

I pause. I know Josie's mind is racing as fast as mine is.

"I am," I say.

"Jess, no. You don't know this guy or what he's capable of, or who he's got with him. There's no use in you getting hurt. What good would you be to them then?"

Fuck. Big sister wins again. I sigh, rubbing my temples with my thumb and pointer finger.

"There's got to be something, Jo. Please," I whisper. She sighs.

"I'm working on it, Jess. For now, hang tight. Maybe let the sheriff know what's going on so he can set up his own surveillance. And Jess?"

"Yeah?"

"Get dad's shotgun."

I sigh and tell her goodnight.

I make my way back into the house. Millie's sitting on the couch, and Lena has her arm draped around her.

"Josie's working it out," I tell them. "But for now, I'm going to stay in the house with you all. I'll drive you to work until we know this is sorted out." Millie nods, and Lena reaches for my hand, giving it a squeeze.

"Thank you," she says.

"When I was a kid, and we used to get those real bad thunderstorms out here, it's scared the shit outta Josie and me," I say. "And mom used to say, 'don't worry, the Bay will protect us.'"

They both look up at me, eyebrows knitted together.

"I think it was all bullshit, honestly," I laugh. "But she'd say that the Bay turned the inn into a fortress, protecting it from all the bad stuff. Of course, we realized years later she was full of it when the first bad hurricane hit." I smile, and thank God, so do they. "But anyways, whenever it would storm real bad, she'd bring us in here, deal a hand of gin rummy, and tell us to just ride out the storm."

I walk over to the desk in the corner of the living room and open the top drawer. I grab a pack of playing cards and walk over, sitting down on the floor on the other side of the coffee table from them. I deal a hand, and look up at them.

"Let's ride it out," I say.

28

LENA

I'm kneeling behind my sister on the bed in the room next to the one Caleb's sleeping in, tugging her long hair into a braid. When we were little, after our dad would finish his display of dominance over our mom, she, Millie and I would all take turns braiding each other's hair. It was a mind-numbing task that seemed to help us forget how ugly his so-called "love" could be. Millie's staring blankly ahead, and I know no amount of braids will keep her mind off the Bentley brothers tonight.

"We're gonna be okay, Mill," I tell her, knowing damn well that there's no way to be sure of that. At least for tonight, we have a big, hulking, handsome bodyguard. Although, the thought of him standing between me and harm makes me queasy, too. Millie doesn't say anything for a minute. As I fasten her hair, she turns to me.

"I think we need to leave tomorrow. Let Caleb get some sleep tonight, pack up tomorrow morning, and leave tomorrow night. Maybe while Jess is working the night shift," she says. Her voice is low and trembling, but she's holding strong to her words.

I swallow, staring at our reflections in the mirror. My hands drop to my waist.

"But, Josie..." I say, my voice trailing off as I desperately try to formulate a plan on the spot. Millie's eyes drop, and when she lifts them, they are full of tears.

"She's doing what she can," Millie says, "but we both know that there's no judge or stupid piece of paper that's going to stop him from getting what he wants." She turns to me, taking my hands in hers. "This kills me, because for the first time in our lives, you have something—*someone*—you actually want. And who's so, so good to you. So I can't ask you to come with us."

My eyes widen and I take my hands out from hers.

"What?" I ask. My brain is spinning. On one hand, I'm hurt, feeling like an outsider to the two people that mean the most to me. But on the other hand, it's an out. It's the approval I need to be with the guy who has turned me into the best version of myself—who I'm damn near falling in love with.

Actually, I think I already have. On the dock, on the bay —shit. Maybe the first damn time I laid eyes on him, his asshole front and all.

"I mean it, Lee," Millie says. There's something in her eyes that's not usually there—I think it's assertiveness. I like it, but then, it also means something—it means she doesn't need me to be assertive for her. It means she has found the strength she's never had before. And although I can't quite figure out what it means for me, it's a beautiful thing. "Look, Lee, I am in no way trying to push you away or sound ungrateful. Do you think I don't know how sad it is, that after all these years, after all this time, my little sister still takes care of me? You've halted your life for us so many times. I'm not asking you to do that again. I'm just asking you what your next steps are. Because for the first time ever, I need to know if they are going to match up with mine. I have to do what's right by Caleb. And if Tiger is still out there, I have to keep moving. I know running isn't the best option, but right now, it's the only one."

My heart is beating in my stomach and my throat. I try to swallow the lump that keeps rising, but it's forcing its way to the surface. And my sister knows. She knows me. She takes my hands again, then presses her palms to my cheeks.

"Little sister, you've been nothing short of an angel to me for our whole lives. I'm not built like you. I'm built like... like mom," she says, her eyes filling with shame. I squeeze her hand. "But I like to think that you've rubbed off on me a bit. I know how much you love us. I know what we mean to you. But Caleb, he's my life. And it's because of me and my life that you haven't really gotten to live yours. I don't want that to be the case this time. Not if you want something else. So tomorrow, Caleb and I are leaving. But if it's not your path to keep running, please, please don't come with us."

She kisses my forehead before sliding off the bed and walking down the hall back to our room. "Our" room, although, I haven't slept in it for days. Millie told Caleb that I was having a slumber party with Jesse because he was lonely in the barn. That seemed to be enough for him before his four-year-old mind moved on to asking about something else. I walk down the hall slowly, the tears falling from my face. How in the world am I supposed to make such an impossible decision?

I creep to the door of Caleb and Millie's room, opening it quickly to avoid the creaking sound it makes when opened too slowly. I stare at them for a moment, watching as their breath moves their chests in sync. I stare at Caleb, his angelic little face, like the perfect little cherub as he snores away, still clutching onto his little dinosaur that he hasn't put down since he got here. I think of everything I've been through with him. We've done a lot in his short four years, and I can't imagine missing a moment of his life going forward.

And my sister. My true life partner, the one who's been to Hell and back with me. The bags under her eyes are prominent, even in the minimal light of the moon. She's right. They have to go. The Rowan Inn is no longer a safe place for them.

I close the door quietly and creep down the hall to the big master suite where Jesse's staying. I open the door and close it behind me quickly. He's fast asleep, his shoulders moving up and down in the pale moonlight. I strip off my shirt and slink into the bed next to him, curling up against his warmth. I want to feel his skin on mine, let him keep me safe and warm. Just for tonight.

He doesn't wake up fully, but he turns so that he's spooning me. He pulls me into him, his arms wrapping around me as if it's instinctual. Because it is. Everything with us is instinct. That's why it's so damn hard to walk away.

But I know I have to.

I know I will.

Tomorrow.

I turn my head to stifle my cries against his pillow. My tears saturate it, but I don't dare to move. He can't know I'm going, because he'll try to stop me. And if he asks me to stay, I just might.

THE NEXT MORNING, I wake up with a knot in my stomach. I roll over to get a good look at him, but he's not there. I feel around the sheets as if he might appear. I hear a shriek of laughter coming from the backyard, and I trudge over to the window. Millie's perched on a chaise lounge, watching as Caleb and Jesse play.

Meanwhile, I'm standing here, my heart crumbling in my chest. I look at the smile on Caleb's face, and I know my heart won't be the only one that breaks tonight.

I make my way downstairs, grabbing two cups of coffee for Millie and me, and sit next to her. She turns to me slowly. I know what she's asking, no words necessary.

"I'm coming with you," I say, my eyes lifting to Jesse down on the lawn. "But I can't tell him." Millie nods, taking my hand.

"Are you sure, Lee?" I suck in a long breath and nod.

"Yes, I'm sure."

The day passes painfully slowly, but I do a fairly good job of not letting Jesse know that the clock is ticking. After dinner, he heads into the barn to get dressed for his night shift at the Shell, and I join him, watching with hungry eyes as he strips down to shower.

As he walks to the bathroom, he drops his boxers and raises an eyebrow at me.

"Care to join?" he asks, his lips tugging up into a smile. I smile and nod, putting my hands up in the air so he can take my shirt off.

As we climb into the hot shower, the water stings my skin. But his kisses to the back of my shoulders make me lose all my senses. I turn around so that we're facing each other, and take his lips with mine. I press against him hard, our wet, soapy bodies sliding against each other effortlessly. I feel him growing against my stomach, and slowly lift my legs so they're wrapped around his waist. He adjusts himself, leaning back, and entering me fast. He takes my breath away with every stroke. It's quiet for us, no moaning and groaning, just our bodies clinging to each other as we move. He pushes me up against the wall, his fist hitting the cool tile as he releases inside of me. But I'm not ready to release him. We stay like that for a moment, entwined in every way. He finally sets me down, kissing me again. He smiles as he pulls away, and the last piece of my heart officially breaks in two.

"I love you," he whispers, and my breath catches. I stare at him, blinking feverishly. The smile slowly fades from his lips. "Sorry. Was that too—"

"I love you," I whisper back, lunging toward him again. I wrap my arms around his neck and bury my head in the crook of it. He kisses the top of my head, my cheek, and then my lips.

As we get out and dry off, I pull my hair up off my neck, and he's smiling at me.

"What?" I ask. He shakes his head.

"Nothin.' I just already can't wait to see you tonight. I've never had anyone that made me wanna rush home."

Crack. All of me. Cracking into two, turning to dust and floating away.

I walk him down to his truck and kiss him goodbye one more time. He pulls away with a huge smile on his face, and I wonder what's better: knowing the heartbreak is coming, or being blind-sided. Does it hurt less, one way or the other? Is it more deadly if you can't see it coming?

ONCE JESSE LEAVES, it feels like the night is moving a mile a minute. Millie is packing bags and consoling a crying Caleb.

"I don't wanna go," he says. "Please Mommy. Please can

we stay with Jesse?"

I watch my sister hide her own tears as she packs her life back into two suitcases. I'm moving a lot slower as I pack my own.

"Aunt Lee, can you stay here and I'll stay with you? Please?" he asks me, tugging on my hand. I kneel down to pick him up and cradle him like a baby.

"Cay, we gotta go buddy. It's not safe here right now," I tell him, kissing his forehead.

"But Jesse's here. He will keep us safe, I know it!" Caleb says. I swallow. Because that's exactly what Jesse would say if he were here.

We've packed everything we came with, and have all our things at the door. We look around, putting anything back into place that wasn't here before. I walk to the kitchen table, leaving the note I wrote to Jesse in the center. It says I'm sorry for leaving without saying goodbye. That I'm sorry I can't choose him. That I'm grateful to him for changing my life. That I know I'll never love someone else like this. Ever.

I leave some water for Coby, then turn around and get one last look at the only place that's ever felt like home. Then we walk out the front door and load up my little car, with no idea where we're off to next. I peel off down the dirt road to the bridge, and the inn is growing smaller and smaller in the distance behind us. I turn onto the main road and look around Baycrest, a place that means more to me in the few months that I've been here than Boston ever could.

We pull off into the diner, knowing our ride will be much more pleasant if we fill Caleb's belly. I poke at my salad, but I can't fathom eating right now. Caleb finishes up his milkshake, and we get back into the car.

I stop at a red light as Millie fumbles with a map, and I

freeze when I hear the music coming from the open windows of the Shell, just a block away. I know he's there behind the bar, pouring drinks and smiling, thinking he's coming home to me tonight. I suddenly realize my jaw has started to shake. I feel Millie's hand on mine.

"Do you want to stay?" she whispers. I look to her, the light in front of me turning green. I shake my head.

"No. But I can't leave without saying goodbye to him. I just can't," I say. She nods.

"Then let's go say goodbye."

We pull into the Shell's parking lot, and my legs are wobbly as I stand. I kneel down to the car window.

"I'll be back," I say. Millie nods.

I head inside, smiling politely and waving to all the locals I've come to know and adore. Even to Amber. Berta's behind the bar, pouring drinks and shouting orders, until she lays eyes on me. She wipes her hands on her apron and comes out from behind the bar.

"What are you...what are you doing here?"

"I came to see Jesse," I say.

"Some man came in here just a few minutes ago, while Jess was out back unloading a shipment. Asking where the inn was. We told him we'd never heard of it, and he took off. Jess came back in and we told him, and he took off back to the inn."

My eyebrows raise, and I can feel the blood swirling in my head.

"What did the man...what did he look like?" I ask.

"Tall, skinny, blackish hair. Weird, hazely kinda eyes," Berta says. My eyes grow wide, and then hers do, too. "Oh, Jesus. That was him, wasn't it?"

My heart is pounding in my chest as I back away slowly from the bar.

Tiger Bentley is in Baycrest.

I turn to run out the door, but I stop. I can't bring Millie and Caleb back there. I turn back to Berta, and she's dangling her keys in my face.

"Please, watch them," I say. She nods, following me out the front door. She heads to my car as I run to her truck, speeding away without putting my seatbelt on.

As I fly down the Baycrest's main road, blowing through stop signs and stop lights, I have no idea what the *fuck* I'm going to do when I see Tiger Bentley. But none of that matters if he gets to Jesse first.

When I get to the inn, everything is eerily quiet. I slam the truck into park and hop out before it even stops rocking. There's a black rental car parked haphazardly in the center of the driveway, Jesse's truck butt-up against it. The house is dark, with no lights on, no sound coming from anywhere. I tiptoe across the grass to the side of the house, sliding across it as I make my way around the back. And that's when I see him.

Tiger Fucking Bentley. He's stumbling on the lawn of the Rowan Inn, barely able to stand straight. But he's got a gun pointed right at the love of my life. My heart is beating so loud, I can't hear myself think.

Girl with the plan. Always.

Except for right now, when the fucking plan needs to be how to stay alive.

Jesse's got his back to the water, and he's slowly stepping closer and closer to it. He's holding his hands up, trying to talk Tiger down. Tiger's grunting and spitting and stepping closer and closer to him.

Jesse sees me, and his eyes grow wide. His breathing steadies, and I know he's trying to tell me with his eyes to run. But he knows there's no way in hell that's happening.

I step closer, and my foot crunches on the gravel. Tiger whips around, and I duck back into the shadow of the house. Suddenly, Jesse starts yelling and hollering, trying to get Tiger's attention back on him.

I watch as he continues backing up toward the water.

What is he doing?

Then I remember his mother's words.

The Bay will protect you.

If he thought we were still in the house, he was trying to lead Tiger away from it. If he could get him into the water, he could disorient him.

"I know you fucked her," Tiger growls.

"Calm down, Tiger. I haven't touched her," Jesse says.

"You did. My fucking kid probably calls you 'Dad,'" Tiger says, with a sadistic laugh. I'm looking around for something—anything—I can use as a weapon. I remember the shovel that Millie had brought inside for protection, but there's no fast way to get to it right now.

"Where are they?" Tiger asks. "Where the fuck are they?"

Jesse's voice stays low and calm.

"I don't know," he says. "They were gone when I got here."

"Fucking liar!" Tiger shouts, his gun waving in the air, the moonlight bouncing off of it. Suddenly, he lowers it so it's aimed right at Jesse. His arm is shaky, but it's pointed right at him. Jesse's eyes find mine, and in that instant, he closes them like he's saying a prayer. In the same instant, Tiger's gun goes off, and it feels like I've been shot. I watch as Jesse falls backward, but I can't focus. My vision blurs, and before I realize it, I'm charging Tiger. I jump on his back, pulling my arm tightly across his neck, squeezing with all the force in my body. He's spinning, punching, kicking, doing all he can to get me off of him. I see him turn the gun toward me, and suddenly, I don't care. I'm still clawing away, gouging at his eyes, desperately finding the strength to get the gun. Somehow, he loosens my grip and throws me on the ground. But as I look up at him, standing over me, gun pointed down, I see a figure behind us.

It's my sister.

And she's got the goddamn shovel.

She runs at him, slamming it against his head once. He stumbles, turning toward her. *Bam.* She hits him again.

"What the—" he mumbles, and then *bam.* He drops the gun, and drops to his knees. She kicks the gun across the lawn, arches back, and slams the shovel into the back of his head one more time.

"Fuck you, Tiger Bentley!" she cries out, tears streaming down her face. "Fuck. You!"

I turn, running toward Jesse, the Bay lapping up against him. He's clutching onto his shoulder, and the water around him is murky with his blood. I drag him out of the water, with Millie grabbing onto his legs to help.

I kneel down to him.

"Jess?" I ask. "Can you hear me?"

But he doesn't answer, and I feel my heart sinking into the water.

"Jess? Open your eyes, please, baby," I whisper into his hair. I'm pressing my hand against the bullet wound, hoping the pressure helps someway, somehow.

As we lift him up, the sky above begins to turn purple and the air fills with sirens. Police come from every angle, and I turn to my sister.

"I told Berta to call them," Millie says.

Cops and EMTs surround us, and I slowly back away as they do their jobs.

29

LENA

I'm standing at the kitchen sink, idly washing a pot that I've been scrubbing for the longest time, gazing out the window. My eyes are heavy, and the weight of not sleeping is finally catching up to me. These last few nights haven't felt real, and I wonder how many nights I can stay awake before my body actually crashes.

I'm startled by the timer on the washing machine, and it snaps me out of my dishwashing trance. I dry my hands and slowly walk across the kitchen to the basement steps. I open the washing machine and mindlessly begin tossing clothes into the dryer, until I realize I'm holding his shirt—the one he was shot in—in my hand. No matter how much treatment I've tried, it's still stained. My hands begin to shake as I stare down at it. I lean against the dryer, clutching the wet shirt to my chest.

Because of me, and the drama I brought here to Baycrest, this shirt is stained with blood. It's been almost two weeks, but I can't shake the clarity of that night, as much as I wish I could. I can't escape the image of his body flailing as he fell into the water. And I can't shake the image of Tiger's bloody, beaten face after my sister had her way with the shovel. I can't forget what it looked like, watching the EMTs work on Jesse. I can't forget anything about the fear in Josie's voice when I called her to say that her brother had been shot.

I toss the shirt into the dryer, then make my way back upstairs. When I get to the top of the steps, I hear someone in the kitchen.

"Berta?" I ask, my voice lifeless and sleepy.

"Hey, kid," she says, turning around from putting some groceries away in the cupboard. She leans back against the counter. "How ya holdin' up?"

Each time someone's asked me that, I've wanted to burst into tears. I've done a pretty good job of keeping it together, only letting myself really cry at night. Especially when Caleb's around. He can't see me like this.

I take a deep breath and let a single tear roll down my cheek. The timer on the oven goes off, and a smile actually crosses my lips.

"Well, he could be dead," I say, "so overall, I'm doing alright." I walk toward the oven to turn off the timer and reset it for a few hours later. I nod toward it. "Reminder to take his medicines." Berta nods and follows me into the living room.

We've set it up like a hospital room, which Jesse absolutely can't stand. They delivered a hospital bed, and we even have a medcart set up next to him. There's a bedpan he refuses to use, and we have the recliner pushed up real close, in case he needs a change of scenery.

I hand him a glass and his antibiotics to prevent any infections. Then I pull out the creams they gave us at the hospital and get ready to change his bandage. When I pull it back, he hisses. Caleb pops up at his bedside. He's fascinated with the injury. He leans onto the bed, his hands holding up his head.

"Does it hurt, Jesse?" he asks. Jesse forces a smile.

"It's not all that bad," he answers. Caleb doesn't know what happened to Jesse. We told him he hurt himself outside by the dock. Not a full lie, not a full truth. Someday, we will tell him. And he'll be so, so angry. But not yet. He deserves to be a kid for now.

I stare down at the bullet hole in Jesse's chest, just next to his shoulder. Each time I've done this, I just go through the motions as though he's not the love of my life. Like I didn't almost lose him. If I don't stay stoic, I know I won't be able to take care of him.

As I'm finishing, he stares up at me, squeezing my other hand.

"Hey," he says. My eyes flick up to him. "I'm fine." I smile and shake my head.

It's about the twentieth time he's had to remind me that he's okay, because he knows that I'm petrified. Still. That the gunshot still rings in my ears.

Josie comes in just as I'm wrapping him back up, making a gagging noise as I tug the bandage back. She can't stand the sight of it, so she hasn't been much help in the nursing department.

"How ya feelin'?" she asks as she plops down on the couch next to us. He shrugs.

"Like someone shot me," he says. She laughs and rolls her eyes.

"And how are *you* doing, Lee?" she asks me. Now I roll *my* eyes.

"I'm not the one who got shot," I say. "Why does

everyone keep asking me that?"

My sister snorts as she walks into the room.

"Maybe because none of us have ever seen a panic attack like the one you had. You hyperventilated. Do you not remember?"

I shrug. I actually don't. I don't remember anything about what I was doing. Only him. Only what he looked like. Only wondering if he was going to make it. He tugs on my hand and holds his arm out. I smile and carefully, masterfully crawl into the hospital bed next to him, like I've done every day for the last two weeks.

"So, you kinda like me, huh?" he says. I smile and nuzzle up against him. Another timer goes off in the kitchen, and I know the lasagna I made for dinner is ready. I hop up, but he tugs me back, kissing the side of my head.

"You need to relax," he says. "You're doing too much. I need to get out of this damn bed."

I roll my eyes.

"It's been two weeks. You'll get there," I tell him, then scoot out of the bed.

"Caleb, Jo, why don't you two go help Lena in the kitchen?" he asks. Josie raises an eyebrow as Jesse turns to Millie. "I gotta talk to Millie."

Josie still has a perplexed look on her face, one that I'm sure probably matches my own, but takes Caleb's hand and follows me into the kitchen.

That night, we all sit around the hospital bed like we've been doing for two weeks, eating off of T.V. trays, talking, laughing, smiling at the fact that Jesse's still here, and that Tiger is gone.

The cops picked him up that night, arrested him, and he's being held without bail. I know it will be tough to keep him behind bars permanently because of his dad's money, but luckily, my sister has a great lawyer. Josiane Rowan, Esq., is no one to mess with.

After dinner, Berta leaves, and Josie, Millie, and Caleb head upstairs. I make sure Jesse is caught up with his medications, help him out of bed so he can use the bathroom, and get him all settled. Then I carefully slide into the tiny bed next to him, where we'd both prefer that I sleep every single night.

The next morning, while I'm standing over the kitchen counter again, making breakfast, Millie comes in behind me. She leans up against the counter, plucking a strawberry off the plate in front of me.

"Wanna go to town today?" she asks. I stop cutting and look up at her.

"What?" I ask like it's a completely unfathomable idea. I haven't left the house—or Jesse—since the shooting.

"I need to get a few things, and I wanted to see if you wanted to come. Josie's going to be here."

I think about it for a minute. I could use the fresh air, a change of scenery from the same three rooms I've been confining myself to for the last fourteen or fifteen days.

"Okay," I say reluctantly as I bring the platter to the living room and let everyone dig in.

After we eat, Millie stands up, collecting dishes and taking everything to the kitchen.

"Alright," she says, "Lena and I are headed to town. Josie, you're sure you're okay keeping an eye on Caleb?"

Josie smiles and throws an arm around Caleb who's looking up at her, almost as lovingly as he looks and me or Millie. I smile.

"Yep, we're good."

I kiss the top of Caleb's head, then lean down to kiss Jesse.

"I'll be back really soon," I say. "But call me if you need me before then okay?"

He rolls his eyes.

"Go," he says. I nod and follow my sister out the door.

We get to town, and Millie stops at one of the few boutiques in Baycrest. We're weaving in and out of the aisles, spinning the displays around.

"So, what exactly do you need?" I ask. She chuckles and shakes her head. "What?"

"Lee, he's okay," she says. "He's going to be fine."

I nod and swallow. So many people have told me this over the last few weeks. So many people. My sister, Josie, Berta, his doctors, Jesse himself. I need to try to believe it.

"So," I say, clearing my throat as I pick up a straw hat from one of the counters, "what did Jesse want to talk to you about?"

Millie pauses, then reaches in and pulls something out of her purse. She hands it to me, and I see that it's a check. It's a check to Millie from Jesse for ten thousand dollars. Ten. Thousand. Dollars.

"What the hell?" I ask. Millie smiles, tears sparkling in her eyes.

"He asked me what I wanted most, and I told him to start over. To start my own life. Get Caleb into a good school. Move on from all the bullshit that is Tiger Bentley."

I stare at her, blinking every few seconds.

"Josie talked to me last night, and there's an open position for an assistant at her law firm in D.C. She already talked to the hiring manager, and they are pretty confident they can hire me. It doesn't pay a whole lot, but it would be enough to get me back on my feet. And this," she says, holding up the check, "would cover a nice pre-school for Caleb for an entire year until he starts kindergarten. I was going to ride back with Josie next week and look for an apartment."

I'm still staring at her, taking in all that she's saying.

"Mill, that's...that's amazing," I say, breathily. She smiles and squeezes my hand. "But I...I can't leave him. Not yet. I—"

"I know, Lee. I'd never ask you to do that. But Caleb and I, we're gonna be okay now," she says with a smile, the tears rolling down her cheeks.

We ride back to the inn silently, so many thoughts racing through my head. I've been with Caleb his whole life, and I've never been without my sister. And after Jesse is healed, what then? Do I go to D.C.? Stay here at the inn?

We pull into the driveway and I rush up the porch steps. The house is weirdly quiet, and all I want to do is get to Jesse. Loving him is the one thing in my life that makes sense all of the time.

But when I walk into the living room, the hospital bed is empty.

Panic rages through my body as I circle through all the rooms, calling out everyone's names. Not in the kitchen, not in the bathroom, not in the parlor.

But when I walk to the window, I see him.

He's standing by the water, dressed in khaki shorts and a button-down shirt. His sandy hair is blowing in the wind, and though we're a good distance away, I know his bay-colored eyes are gleaming like sea glass. I suck in a deep breath as I open the back door. Josie sits at the back of the patio, a big smile on her face.

Caleb runs to me, taking my hand.

"Come on, Aunt Lee. Come down to Jesse," he says, his voice riddled with excitement. My sister comes from the side of the house, stepping onto the patio. There's a trail of flower petals leading from the patio down to where Jesse stands. I swallow.

"Oh yeah," Millie whispers, "he also asked for my permission."

I swallow again.

No fucking way.

"Your permission for what?"

"To give you the chance to live your own life, now that you've given us ours back," she says, her voice cracking as more tears stream down her face. Josie appears next to her, looping an arm around her shoulders. "Go get him."

I swallow one more time, my eyes following the trail of flowers down to where he stands. When I finally make it to the end, I stare up at him.

"You shouldn't be out of bed yet," I whisper. He smiles, taking my hands in his. "What is all this?"

He smiles, looking down at our intertwined fingers. Then he takes a breath.

"I spent a long time thinking people were disappointed in me. Thinking I was a disappointment. And you changed all that for me. You brought me back from the dead after I lost two of the most important people in my life. You saved my inn. You saved me. So now, Lena Winter..."

His voice trails off, and he slowly, wobbly, gets down on one knee. My breath hitches in my throat. Oh, my God. No way. No fucking way. I stare down at him, and he smiles back.

"I'm not asking you to marry me," he says. I stare at him, puzzled. "Not yet. I'm just asking you to stay." He reaches into his pocket and pulls out a key—a key to the inn. I laugh as the tears stream down my face. I take the key and squeeze it in my hand. Our sisters are cry-laughing from the patio, and Caleb is jumping up and down. I look down at the beautiful man before me, my whole body shaking.

I pull him to his feet, and jump on him as carefully as possible, leaving a long kiss on his lips.

"Always," I whisper. "This is home."

EPILOGUE

Beverly clears her throat.

"Mrs. Rowan, can you, uh, tell me about your husband?"

Just then, a rusty pickup truck rumbles down the gravel driveway, and I can't help but smile.

He hops out of his truck, using his hand to wipe off a bit of dirt from the front bumper. He walks around to the front, and then freezes the moment his eyes meet mine. We've been doing this for over thirty years now, and it still takes my breath away.

"Evening, Mrs. Rowan," he says, taking the porch steps-two-by-two. He kneels down to kiss my lips, and I'm twenty-four again, breathing him in and never wanting to exhale.

"Evening, Jess," I say. I look at Beverly. "He's been referring to me as 'Mrs. Rowan' since the day we got married." She smiles.

"That's just the sweetest thing," she says, jotting down a note in her book.

"Jess, this is Beverly," I say. He sticks his hand out to greet her.

"Well, lemme get out of your hair. Where's that boy of ours, anyway?" Jesse asks me. I nod toward the barn.

"In his bachelor pad. Where else?" I ask with a smile. Jesse smiles back. We know what used to go down in that big ol' barn. And I'd rather not think of it now that my son stays there. *Our* son.

"Well, I'll leave you two to it," Jesse says, kneeling down for one more kiss. "See ya later?"

I nod and smile.

"Always," I say.

ACKNOWLEDGMENTS

This book has been on my brain for a few years now, and I'm so happy to finally have it out on paper! My home state of Maryland is special to me. I absolutely loved growing up here, and I try to paint the beauty that is Maryland in all of my books that take place here. If you've never been to MD, or visited the Bay, think about it!

I'd like to thank my fellow authors who are constantly letting me vent, bounce ideas off of them, and reminding me why I do this in the first place! Indie authors are some of the most resilient people I have ever met, and I am so thankful to be a part of such an uplifting community.

D-Ma, thanks for sharing your stories, your love, and your son. Your strength is astounding.

To all of my second pairs of eyes—THANK YOU!

Mr. & Mrs. A, thank you for letting me drag you out to those docks and take a million and one pictures. I am so lucky to have such good-looking, model-esque friends!

Little, thanks for telling me, every single time, that this one was better than the last.

Hubs, you the bomb. Teamwork makes the dreamwork.

ABOUT THE AUTHOR

Taylor Danae Colbert is a romance and women's fiction author. When she's not chasing her kids or hanging with her husband, she's probably under her favorite blanket, either reading a book, or writing one. Taylor lives in Maryland, where she was born and raised. For more information, visit www.taylordanaecolbert.com.

Follow Taylor on Instagram and Twitter, @taydanaewrites, and on Facebook, Author Taylor Danae Colbert, for information on upcoming books!

Are you a blogger, or a reader who wants in on some secret stuff? Join **TDC's VIPs** - Taylor's street team on Facebook for exclusive information on her next books, early cover reveals, giveaways, and more!

OTHER BOOKS BY TAYLOR:

IT GOES WITHOUT SAYING
BUMPS ALONG THE WAY
OFF THE RECORD

NOTE FROM THE AUTHOR

Dear Reader,

I can't tell you what it means that you've decided, out of all of the books in all the world, to read mine. If you enjoyed reading it as much as I enjoyed writing it, please consider leaving an Amazon or GoodReads review (or both!). Reviews are crucial to a book's success, and I can't thank you enough for leaving one (or a few!)!

Thank you for taking the time to read ROWAN REVIVED.

Always,
    TDC
    www.taylordanaecolbert.com
    @taydanaewrites

CPSIA information can be obtained
at www.ICGtesting.com
Printed in the USA
LVHW031354141019
634125LV00007B/2743/P